I0676151

Books by Erik J. Kreffel

JAUNT
ETHER
AGENT MAYA SEASON ONE

@jauntworld
www.jauntworld.blogspot.com
agentmaya.blogspot.com

These stories take place chronologically
between Issues 2 and 3 of the
Agent Maya Season One comics

Agent Maya

© 2016 Erik J. Kreffel, jaunt publications. All Rights Reserved.
Printed in the United States of America.
No part of this book may be used or reproduced in any manner whatsoever
without written permission except in the case
of brief quotations embodied in reviews.

This is a work of fiction. Names, characters, places and incidents
are either the product of the author's imagination or used
fictitiously, and any resemblance to actual persons, living
or dead, events or locales is entirely coincidental.

ISBN: 9780983331728

Cover design, illustrations
and layout
Erik J. Kreffel

Agent Maya

Neptune's Deadliest Ring
and
The Moons of Ice and Fire

Erik J. Kreffel

jaunt

To SMV, my real-life Maya.

And to everyone who supported me the first time out.

Thank you.

Neptune's Deadliest Ring
12.24.2155–
02.02.2156

CHAPTER ONE

"Give it up, Glough!"

Maya's gaze darted from the gold-hued craft out her portside cockpit bubble window to the floating holographic HUD interface. Her quarry, tax fugitive Egon Glough, having stolen the experimental corvette *Cokol*—outfitted with an M2P2 magnetoplasma drive—steadily sped away from Maya's ship, *Skeeto*, riding a solar wind eddy inaccessible to *Skeeto*'s mere VASIMR engines.

"*Skeeto*, aren't you tracking that eddy?" Maya asked. "We're gonna lose him if we get too separated!"

"Sensors are having difficulty reading the solar wind flux, Miss Maya," *Skeeto*'s feminine vocalization said. "Particle density is too low for my scans."

"Remind me to fix that when we haul this sucker back to P-4."

"Distance is now one-hundred and sixty-five meters," *Skeeto* read out.

Maya toggled a button on the interface, magnifying the image of a purple plasma sphere extending from *Cokol*'s mid-section. "I'm not done with you yet...*Skeeto*, do we have any hacks capable of taking down that plasma drive?"

"The craft's plasma conduit system is a generation more sophisticated than mine, Miss Maya, but the basic schematics are similar."

Maya smiled. *Gotcha*. "Initiate hack, *Skeeto*. Bring it down."

A green sphere lit on the interface, displaying that *Skeeto*'s signal was broadcasting to *Cokol*. As soon as the signal left, however, *Skeeto* replied, "The craft's firewall is preventing the hack protocol from reaching the magnetoplasma sub-routines, Miss Maya."

"Then we're gonna have to do this the hard way."

The tadpole-shaped *Skeeto* flared its aft engines, four vertical pods located inside the tailfin of the craft. With the violet exhaust cones pouring out kiloliters of ionized gas per second, the `craft flew above and behind the trio of equidistant solar wings affixed to *Cokol*, a gilded, space-borne blossom. Trimming the meters of space between the pair, *Skeeto* drew closer, but *Cokol*'s wings flared, dilating the magnetoplasma bubble farther, catching even more of the already-tenuous solar eddy to propel it away from *Skeeto* again.

Maya shook her head. "I don't know when the hell Glough found the time to get a pilot's license, but he's good. Think I can do him one better, though." Tapping a button on the holographic interface, Maya activated a ship-to-ship channel. "Egon Glough, this is Agent Maya again. It appears your ship's got better oomph than mine today. Let's call it even, what do you say?"

Looking at the visual display on her interface, Maya waited for Glough's corpulent face to appear, but after a moment, it was apparent the cheat wasn't going to play ball.

"*Skeeto*, what's the ETA for the main TransMartian Causeway?"

"Twelve minutes, thirty-four seconds, Miss Maya."

Maya looked to the schematic on her interface, a tangle of spaghetti-like tubes running the length of the millions of kilometers between *Skeeto*'s near-Martian location and the TransJovian Zone. The Federal Causeway utilized the ever-changing gravity wells of the major and dwarf planets to divert interplanetary traffic efficiently throughout the Solar System; it wasn't the fastest transport, but got the job done. Its main thrust was provided by gravity, so one didn't just waltz through it with engines firing full bore, unless one had the desire to wreck not only one's vessel, but the hundreds of other vessels, large and small, military and civilian, liable to be inside the Causeway corridor at any given hour.

One particular strand of the Causeway, the main TransMartian, was of considerable breadth, capable of shunting vessels within its gravitational grasp to Jupiter and the TransMartian Asteroid Belt with relative ease. Just what Maya hoped for.

"*Skeeto*, drop us to fifty-percent velocity. Let him go."

"Affirmative, Miss Maya."

Ahead of the cockpit windows, *Cokol* sped away, its solar wind eddy taking it beyond *Skeeto*'s grasp, but not the Causeway's. Banking on the craft's computer to automatically prepare it for Causeway transport, due to its primary purpose as a next-generation Federal Marshal corvette, Maya would wait patiently for *Skeeto* to signal when the magnetoplasma drive had been shut off, which should come in only a matter of....

"Miss Maya, ten minutes have elapsed. TransMartian Causeway gravity envelope now in effect."

Maya sat forward in her seat and punched a button on her interface. "All right. Got it on the sensors?"

"Affirmative. Magnetoplasma drive offline, Miss Maya."

Thank you, Federal Marshal techs. "VASIMR drive at full velocity, *Skeeto*. Take us in...I'll do the rest."

Skeeto accelerated from its leisurely cruise into a full-out chase, breaking into the Causeway with all the subtlety of a punch in the face. Merging into the corridor, Maya flew *Skeeto* manually, her fingers nimbly guiding the craft into the outgoing traffic. Dozens of vessels flashed behind her as she propelled *Skeeto*—illegally she might have thought, but didn't—above the mandated velocity limit and into the Causeway's main artery. Here gravity was strongest, a steady but distinct "wind to the back" that would deliver any object, natural or artificial, into the Outer Reaches within months. She'd been through the Causeway several times, always on a more straightforward journey than now, but rarely needing to be hands on with *Skeeto*. It was tremendously exhilarating, if not a bit naughty, and she enjoyed every single second, the smile on her face thankfully not visible to the traffic just meters away, or more importantly, her superiors at the InterPlanetary Tax Police in Martian orbit.

Cokol was distinctly in her view, its wonderfully aesthetic curves making sure she didn't need *Skeeto*'s sensors to track it through the Causeway. Maya couldn't be sure *Cokol* didn't know she was trailing nearby, so a precautionary diversion by hiding in the wake of a government IP vessel a hundred-meters long ahead of her was warranted.

"Causeway velocity, *Skeeto*."

"Six hundred, fifty-seven meters per second, Miss Maya."

"A good cruising speed." Maya glanced at *Skeeto*'s own velocity, which stood at nearly twice that. They'd overrun the IP in just moments, then be on *Cokol* before long. Maya didn't want to play her cards just yet, though, so she weaved behind the IP, slackening the distance between the pair.

"How's his lidar?"

"No detection, yet, Miss Maya."

This was it. There were so many lidar targets to block *Skeeto*'s presence that now was the chance Maya'd betted on. Punching *Skeeto*'s ventral RCS thrusters, the tiny chase craft blasted over the lumbering IP vessel and skipped ahead of it, closing the distance to *Cokol* within two minutes.

"Prepare tendrils, *Skeeto*! Launch when we're in distance!"

"Yes, Miss Maya. Closing to tendril distance in five seconds...four seconds...three seconds...."

Maya's eyes widened. A trio of glistening solar wings fluttered ahead of her through the port and starboard cockpit windows, a sight guaranteed to wilt the hearts of lesser souls. Beneath her seat, she felt the ventral hull quake as the octet of tendrils flew down and magnetically sealed themselves to *Cokol*'s hull, *Skeeto* placing them squarely between the topmost wings.

Skeeto's VASIMR engines strained under the increased mass, but Maya pushed them farther, then abruptly punched *Skeeto*'s port RCS thrusters, taking them out of the Causeway. Maya grunted as she was cemented to the back of her seat under gravity's compulsion to keep them within the corridor.

"*Skeeto*! Kill engines!"

The tiny craft's four exhaust cones were snuffed out, leaving the two ships under their inertia, now heading away from the busy Causeway, back to where Maya's undivided attention could deal with Glough.

"Fire EM pulse!"

A surge of electromagnetic radiation flowed through the eight tendrils and into *Cokol*'s hull, disrupting the flow of power and data throughout the craft, rendering it temporarily inert.

Maya latched her helmet into place on the neck socket ring of her EVA armor, then dove through a ventral hatch located between the port and starboard seats. An extended chute ahead of her attached itself to *Cokol*'s hull; three meters in, Maya verbally activated the torch on her left gauntlet. Proceeding to cut a circular opening through the hull, Maya then kicked in the plate she had sliced apart.

"I'm in, *Skeeto*," she said over her voxlink. Drawing the semi-sentient sidearm Xibalba from her left thigh holster, she floated through the lit corridor, seeing no occupants; that'd make everything a bit easier.

"Hey lady, you the police?!" a voice grunted from behind her.

Swiveling around, she saw Egon Glough, easily recognizable from his police file, floating in place, tied to a pipe on the ceiling several meters away.

"InterPlanetary Tax Police, Agent Maya. I'd say you're under arrest, Mr Glough, but you appear to be having other problems."

"You're goddamn right I do!" he yelled. "The punks stowed aboard when I took possession—"

"You mean you haven't been piloting at all? Not even an autopilot?"

"Does it look like I've been doing shit? You should be arresting them, not me! I ain't—"

Maya flew past Glough, who flailed as best he could.

"Hey lady where you going? Get me out of here!"

Exiting the room, Maya swam through a corridor towards where the schematics said the cockpit should be located.

"Xibalba, you see anything?"

"Just a heckuva lot of nifty equipment, Maya," the sidearm said from his audio outputs. "This ship makes *Skeeto* look like a junkyard find."

Maya pursed her lips, ignoring the spitfire weapon's ungentlemanly opinion. "Just load some stun rounds for me, okay?"

The agent's torch rotated clockwise on her left gauntlet. This revealed a sensor pallet, a cylinder fitted with a number of miniaturized instruments inside, capable of a near-unlimited swath of spectra scanning. Raising her left arm, Maya did a forward sweep of the corridor. Detecting no movement with lidar, she swam ahead, swiftly moving through the craft's multiple shafts. She paused a moment later at a closed hatch, her helmet's HUD display informing her that the cockpit lay just beyond.

Upping her helmet's audio pickups, Maya heard muffled voices within; it had to be the stowaways, probably attempting to regain control of *Cokol*. Maya's gauntlets gripped the hatch's circular exterior seams opposite the hinge and pulled, her EVA armor's strength-enhancing power swinging the hatch open. Maya somersaulted inside and placed a magnetically sealed left gauntlet against the cockpit's wall, Xibalba in her other hand.

Two small figures, outfitted in oversized pilot's uniforms, sat aghast in the twin cockpit seats, their...feminine faces portraying their combined shock at Maya's ease of entry.

"You two girls are responsible for the theft of this craft?" Maya asked. Her stoicism did not betray her own shock at the culprits' identities.

The girl in the port seat punched a button on the console, trying to bring up the interface. "Then you must be responsible for turning off the power!"

"You don't have the right to stop us!" the second girl said. "We're taking this ship! You can't keep it from us!"

Maya descended from the wall, her boots magnetically sealing to the convex floor, allowing her to stay upright. Speaking a soft command to her HUD, she rendered her helmet's faceplate translucent. Her ruddy cheeks, green eyes and ruby lips stood out amongst her own feminine visage.

"I already have, young ladies. This has gone far enough."

"You're...a girl?"

Maya stifled a laugh. "Ironic, eh? I was about to say the same thing to you two. Now, why don't we discuss this aboard my craft...where you won't get into any more trouble, hmm?"

CHAPTER TWO

i

"What about him? What are you gonna do?" the youngest girl, Ichiko, asked in *Skeeto*'s mid-section tunnel.

"He'll be arraigned in there," Maya said, gesturing towards Precinct-4 Headquarters, the Mars-orbiting station outside the cockpit windows. "Glough will be behind bars for a while, I suspect."

"And us?" Kestrel Rose, the other girl, wondered. "We're not exactly innocent ourselves."

Maya reclined in her seat, swiveling to face the pair. "That will also be up to the Judge Advocate General. I can, however, vouch for you, as can my superior, Lieutenant Kuwashima. You've already signed the affidavits I presented swearing off further acts, so that should be enough, coupled with your previously clean records. Just don't let me catch you two again," she warned, pointing a finger. "I went easy on Glough 'cause he wasn't going anywhere bound like you had him. I don't like being crossed."

"Ain't that the truth," Xibalba quipped from Maya's holster.

"Pipe down, you."

Ichiko and Kestrel Rose laughed, both more relaxed now that Maya wasn't going to have the book thrown at them. The girls' attentions were soon drawn to the looming image of P-4 HQ, which grew larger before them, soon eclipsing all but the fringes of the cockpit windows.

"Bring us in easy, *Skeeto*."

Skeeto flew under the station's cavernous ventral hub, a bottomless hangar reserved strictly for Federal and military vessels. Autonavigating to Maya's reserved docking port, *Skeeto*'s forward RCS thrusters slowed the craft to a crawl, easing into the narrow space with centimeters to spare on both flanks. A vertical umbilical boom swung down and clamped onto *Skeeto*'s hull, their mating producing a low echo throughout the craft.

"Docking complete, Miss Maya," *Skeeto* announced. "P-4 Security is on hand to escort Mr Glough. Disembark at your leisure."

"Acknowledged, *Skeeto*," Maya said, unstrapping her shoulder and torso belts. "Shutdown for the night after they secure him. I'll be back to check on you later."

"Affirmative, Miss Maya. Have a pleasant evening."

The agent floated from her seat and looked to the two girls. "And that's how it's done. C'mon, let's get a bite to eat. You've gotta be hungry by now."

Ichiko and Kestrel Rose exchanged glances; when was the last time someone *offered* them food?

ii

The trio strolled past the Winter Solstice displays strewn about P-4's cafe promenade, the Christmas season being just weeks away. Maya shook her head; the season seemed to arrive earlier each year anymore.

"You work here?" Kestrel Rose asked, her eyes twinkling before the multitudinous red and green holograms floating in the wide corridor.

"On occasion," Maya admitted, to her irritation. "Usually I spend eighty percent of my working life on board *Skeeto*. She's my real home, not this ant farm."

Ichiko reached out to a holographic *tannenbaum*, complete with pseudo silvery bells and lit candles. "Why?! This is so pretty!"

"I'm from Syrtis Major, a helluva long way from anything, or anyone. Solstices aren't much to celebrate, except for the end of the sandstorm season."

"Sorry," Ichiko said. "Didn't your parents take you on trips to places? My foster parents took me to Niagara Falls, Mount Fujiyama, Lake Vostok, Mariner Valley—"

"I didn't grow up like most children. I didn't know my parents."

Kestrel Rose furrowed her brow. "You're an orphan like us, then."

"In a way, yeah." Maya studied the twinkling candlelight, a miniature panorama of the stars she lived amongst, reminding her of what started that whole side trip. "By the by, what possessed you two to steal that corvette, anyway? It couldn't have been that easy?"

Ichiko kicked at the floor with her trainers. "Uhh...well, we've got a mission, just like you, Maya. Except our's is—"

"None of your concern, really," Kestrel Rose finished, glaring at Ichiko, chiding her silently. "Now it's just a dream."

Ichiko took the reprimand in stride, as if she received it every day from her sister, and continued, "It was easier than anyone thought, 'cause I've had nano-synaptical implants in my brain stem since I was born." She raised her straight, shoulder-length black hair away from her neck, revealing a tiny, chrome-like nodule placed below the base of her skull. "XDR-meningitis nearly killed me when I was hours old, or so I was told by my first foster 'rents."

Maya brushed her fingers over the "outlet," fascinated, but at the same time disturbed by the cyber organ hidden beneath the beautiful girl's exterior. "Does...it hurt?"

"Nah." She removed her hand, allowing her hair to cover it up again. "Surgeons never realized that I could consciously control synthetic impulses fed into the nodule during my periodic checkups." A wide, bright smile formed over face, like an excited child just having learned a new trick. "I can control machines!"

Kestrel Rose sighed in exasperation. "Sometimes...don't ask her to do it when that stupid webshow with all those hairy men are on—"

"Shut up!" she hissed, barely concealing an embarrassed giggle.

A loud grumble from the general altitude of Maya's abdomen stole her attention. Eyeing a food stall a few meters away, she said, "Let's get some food, okay? Then we can talk about things other than age-inappropriate shows and girly crushes."

After a quick scarfing of warmed-over meals purchased from the kiosk, Maya walked the pair through the circular halls, her tour mostly boiling down to what pertained to Maya's professional life.

"...I do a lot of work from here when I'm not on assignment." Maya paused at a doorway, its ID panel labeled INTERPLANETARY WEBWORKS ROOM SIX.

"You surf the IPWeb. Thought someone like you wouldn't have the time," Kestrel Rose said. "What do you look for?"

"Mostly research. A little bit of web eavesdropping, seeing who's out there chatting. The IPTP finds most of their suspects without even having to hunt them down. Most are caught by sting operations, bait snaring them."

"You wouldn't be able to sit still that long, would you?" Kestrel Rose asked.

Maya let slip a smile. "You're a quick judge of character. Sure you don't want to be a Tax Police cadet?"

Ichiko placed herself between Kestrel Rose and Maya. "Not without me. We're a team. Always have been, always will be. Wherever Rosey goes, I follow."

"I don't doubt." Maya raised her hands palms up. "Just a suggestion, no offense meant. With skills like yours, you two could be an asset to my organization. God knows the IPTP could use some team players." Maya included herself in that statement.

A beep sounded from the tiny voxlink located on Maya's left collar. Tapping it, she said, "Agent Maya."

"Kuwashima, Agent Maya. Report to my office...and bring those young women with you, as well."

"Understood, Lieutenant. I'll be over in a few moments." Maya glanced to the pair. "You wanted to see me in my element. Here's your chance."

iii

"You're to be remanded to the care of the Juvenile Remedial Center on Titan." Lieutenant Walter Kuwashima glanced away from the two girls standing before him and locked eyes with Maya. "I'm assigning you to escort them, Agent Maya."

"Wouldn't they be better served back on Earth? I thought we agreed to vouch for their return to society."

"The decision has been made, Agent, but not by me." Kuwashima rose from his desk chair and crossed over to the trio. "The Commissioner believes it in the best interests of not only you two," he looked at Ichiko and Kestrel Rose successively, "but the civilians of the Solar System. Your education on Titan will be for a semester only, wherein you both will be released into the custody of P-6 education ministers until the occurrence of your sixteenth birthdays. By then you both will be legal adults, with all rights as such."

"Uh, that sucks, your honor," Kestrel Rose blurted, her eyebrows arched. "I would expect your word to have more weight with your superiors, as Maya's do with you."

"You will find, Miss...."

"Kestrel Rose. Just Kestrel Rose."

"That certain...protocols must be adhered to, no matter what your thoughts are. That performing your duty outweighs personal convictions at times."

Maya rolled her eyes, but Kuwashima didn't see it; instead his back was turned to the assembled audience, his hands clasped behind himself.

"I'm sorry this has to be one of those times. I can say without my or Agent Maya's input, you and your friend would most likely have been arraigned in the JAG's court this morning. If you don't believe my words to have weight, consider that thought for a moment. I think you'll see what I have done for your welfare."

"We understand, sir," Ichiko acknowledged, before nudging Kestrel Rose's arm.

Kestrel Rose agreed. "Yes, your honor. We...understand."

"It's Christmas, ladies," he said, taking his seat again. "Enjoy the season for today. Agent Maya, show them some fun before you disembark tomorrow. Even the Commissioner couldn't order you not to observe some peace for all mankind."

"Indeed. C'mon ladies, let's take a stroll. It's a little hot in here."

CHAPTER THREE

i

"Wake up, *Skeeto*. Calculate the best corridor to Titan, would you, please?"

"Standby...Federal causeway corridor plotted and scheduled, Miss Maya."

As Maya pulled the Y-belt over her shoulders and torso, the holographic navigation interface displayed the chosen Causeway in a flashing red lane, which shot out from Mars, spiraled around Jupiter, and finally curved a huge parabola towards the TransSaturnian Zone, stopping above Titan.

"Readying for departure, girls. Get strapped in," Maya ordered.

In the starboard cockpit seat, Kestrel Rose snapped her Y-belt together, while in the aft cockpit area behind the two, Ichiko vertically secured herself to a wall cushion.

"*Skeeto*, let's go."

"Affirmative, Miss Maya. Plasma and hydrazine refueling procedures complete.
P-4 Orbital Control has cleared us for departure."

"Excellent. De-docking start...now, release docking clamp, fire port RCS thrusters at half power," Maya commanded, keying in a series of buttons on her holographic interface. A text box displayed *Skeeto*'s departure length in a crawling line of numbers.

"Dorsal RCS thrusters at full. Take us Y-axis minus three hundred meters, *Skeeto*."

A vertical red line on the interface emanated from P-4 HQ's lowest level, accompanied by a text box full of coordinates and delta-V changes. Within seconds, Maya punched a button on another section of the interface, admitting plasma from *Skeeto*'s magnetic storage bottles into the four VASIMR engines in the craft's tailfin. Four violet cones of ionized gas exploded from the tailfin, propelling *Skeeto* forward, out of Mars' reach.

"Twenty kilometers per second...thirty kilometers per second," *Skeeto* announced.

The angry red planet receded from the aft view, soon replaced by the oncoming traffic as *Skeeto* merged into the TransMartian Causeway. Setting *Skeeto* into autonavigation, Maya reclined, giving full duties to the craft's able computer.

"Another successful departure," Maya said, looking over to her two passengers. "What shall we do now?"

"How quick is *Skeeto*?" Ichiko asked. "I mean, how far is it to Titan?"

Maya smiled. Reading her wrist chronometer, she answered, "Hope you cleared your schedule for the next four weeks. It's gonna be a long ride."

ii

"Haven't you ever drawn anything?" Holding a pencil in her right hand and a small sketchbook strapped to her torso, Ichiko drew the outline of Maya as the agent posed in mid-float about the aft cockpit.

"No...how long do I have to hold still?"

Ichiko's tongue slipped out between her lips ever-so-slightly. "Just a few more minutes...come on, this isn't that hard."

"I can't keep in one place with the way you've posed me—"

"Shhh! You're moving your mouth." Ichiko glanced up. "Good, better. Now, stay still!"

"What is this supposed to accomplish, Maya?" Xibalba asked, perched in Maya's right hand, as if ready to fire.

"Keeping her out of trouble," she said out of the corner of her mouth.

Kestrel Rose clambered out of *Skeeto*'s mid-section tunnel a moment later, sighing and saying, "You still at it? How many people you gonna have posed like this?"

"Shhh! I'm working."

"You know," Kestrel Rose said to Maya, "you don't have to put up with this. You know how many times I had to do it? More than I can count." She glared at Ichiko.

The artist shook her head. "Three. That's it. Three. I have them all in here."

"Miss Maya," *Skeeto* announced, "entering the TransSaturnian gravity well. Estimated time of arrival at Titan in twenty minutes."

Thank you, Maya thought to herself. "All right, I gotta get back to the wheel."

"No! I'm almost done!"

Kestrel Rose crossed her arms in front of her chest. "You're always almost done."

Maya holstered Xibalba and relaxed her arms. "Leaving...going away now...." Not looking back, she propelled herself towards the cockpit entryway and took her seat.

"Ohh...crap. I almost had it." Ichiko stuffed her pencil and sketchbook inside her jacket pocket, then stretched herself out.

"Well, you've got plenty of reference with mine," Kestrel Rose comforted her.

The pair followed Maya into the cockpit, where the agent busied herself at the holographic interface.

"You two had better get yourselves strapped in," Maya warned. "It'll get a bit rough."

"What's Titan like?" Kestrel Rose asked, her eyes sucking in the distant, orange point beyond Saturn's sun-like illumination.

"Cold," Maya said. "Actually, I don't know. Never been there."

"Really? I thought you were some space veteran that's been from one end of the Solar System to the other."

Maya furrowed her brow at the ludicrous statement. "No," she barely held back a laugh. "I haven't. You'd have to live two lifetimes just to see every rock in the Inner Zones. I'm only twenty-five—"

"Miss Maya, now receiving a Level Alpha-One communique from Precinct-4, Lieutenant Kuwashima speaking."

Maya toggled the display to the right of the navigational interface. A rectangular image of Kuwashima blossomed before her, clearly distressed.

"Lieutenant, this is Agent Maya. What's wrong?"

"There's been a situation in P-8. The Neptune Regional Authority's gone rogue. Commissioner Judoma believes it to be Governor Van Noraesk's doing. The IPTP's been eyeing him for a while, trying to gather intel on whether his ultimate fighting championship evaded taxes. Well, needless to say, we're needed to arrest him, as we've got the goods to put him away for a long time. The local police can't be trusted. It's going to be a Capone Operation, so arm yourself well."

"Lieutenant, I'm almost on Titan, it's gonna be at least—"

"Forget Titan, Agent Maya. Get to Neptune as quickly as possible. The Commissioner wants all other operations halted until Noraesk is in custody. I've diverted all space-borne agents to converge at P-8, but you're the closest one."

Maya inhaled deeply and nodded. "Okay. I'll abort and get to P-8."

"This is will be a career-maker, Agent Maya. Come back alive so you can enjoy it."

"I haven't let you down yet, sir. I'll get Noraesk, you can count on it."

Kuwashima's image evaporated, leaving Kestrel Rose and Ichiko to stare at Maya.

"Didn't I tell you guys to strap in? This is going to be a bit rough...."

CHAPTER FOUR

i

"Neptune, God of the Sea, most distant of the twin ice giants; its sapphire atmosphere conceals the most coveted of natural resources in the Wild, Wild Outer Reaches, diamonds, which form naturally in its methane and hydrogen-rich clouds, precipitating out as *rain*. Little wonder its distance from law and order—and its greedy appeal—attracted scum of all kinds to its frigid shores. Neptune was a prospecting man's paradise, if he could stomach the mafia's strength, legal corruption and, above all else, cold hard radiation.

"What better travel brochure could there be?"

ii

"InterPlanetary Tax Police Agent Maya, requesting landing clearance."

The face responding over the IPwebaddress looked, let alone sounded, agitated. "What business does the IPTP have within the Neptune Regional Authority?"

Maya punched a button on her interface, launching a series of text paragraphs over the IPwebaddress directly to the woman's station. "Read that. Those are my authorization orders directly from Commissioner Udhed Judoma himself, acting under the aegis of the Department of Justice of the United Solar System Government. Now, where do I land?"

The orbital controller glanced to her side, quickly skimmed through the orders on her display, then answered, "Monad Port Five-A. Be prompt. Orbital Control is closing that hub for repairs at seventeen hundred."

Maya nodded. "Thank you." Switching off the display, she craned her head back to her charges. "We're landing in a few moments...see, told you this'd be easy."

Ichiko and Kestrel Rose couldn't hide their jitters as Triton eclipsed Neptune's calm blue countenance behind its own cantaloupe terrain. Flecks of grey highlands trapped within a matrix of powder-blue faults and a smattering of geyser-blackened soil drew nearer through the cockpit windows, a not particularly enticing end to their two-month journey through the Outer Reaches.

Because of the large moon's retrograde orbit, Maya couldn't descend in the usual manner; having to steer clear of Neptune's adverse gravity, she flew them over the north polar region to the far side, which was now half-illuminated by the Sun and fully by the ice giant's gaze. A large patch of bare ground, just beyond reach of several craters and two large pateras—Leviathan and Kibu—loomed below, in Monad Regio. A smooth landscape named Cipango Planum was centered in *Skeeto*'s sight, sitting within Monad, a relatively flat terrain marking the first and primary settlement of Triton, where its capital, Naiad City, had been founded fifty years prior, now lay.

An octopus-shaped complex of civilian, legislative and military constructs, Naiad City was built upon the hard crust between the coldest ice crevasses known by the latest in colonial technologies, aerial backhoes and orbital cranes. The result was a gleaming structure resistant to Triton's -360-degree-Fahrenheit daily temperatures, topped by a fifty-story central spire—Noraesk Tower—housing the Neptune Regional Authority, P-8's governing body, until recently a friendly presence in the TransNeptunian Zone. Maya's previous arrest in P-8 was achieved with the assistance of the Authority; now, they'd be at best unhelpful, at worst her newest enemy, queueing behind the People's Popular Revolutionary Task Force for the Defense of the Outer Satellites and The Corporation for a Better Living for a crack at her, the former for her arrest of an itinerant and connected weapons smuggler, the latter for her IPTP-related activities in their perceived affairs. Maya was a name not particularly well-thought of in these parts, and the grab for power Governor Van Noraesk had committed would surely only enhance her name's ill-reputation.

Skeeto skimmed past the capital city, leaving the blue-bathed skyscrapers in the tiny craft's portside windows as it sped towards the Monad Port. A Mandelbrot Set of a place, the multiple metallic pads were lined with red landing lights, visible in the terminator shade, beckoning all craft to the appropriate LZ.

Maya's interface displayed a flashing circle on the holographic Monad Port image, with an accompanying tag identifying it as "Monad Port Five-A." A yellow set of arrows pointed the navigational computer towards the hub, allowing *Skeeto* to lock on and descend with autonavigation. Triton's horizon tilted until it reached zero degrees flat, then quickly smoothed out while *Skeeto* became nearly parallel with the ground.

The red illumination ceased as *Skeeto* came about and hovered over Five-A, which shot bright white landing candles that illuminated the craft as it descended in a flood of thruster exhaust. Connecting softly with the LZ tarmac, a subdermal motorbelt maneuvered *Skeeto* within the hub's dome, which pressurized again after closing a magnetic wall behind the craft.

After shutting down the plasma engines, Maya threw off her Y-belt and stood in the low moon gravity. Looking over her seatback, she said, "You two stay here. I'm keeping the voxlink open through *Skeeto's* communications interface, so we'll be able to stay in touch. You know where the rations are... don't eat them all at once."

Ichiko rose as Maya walked past the pair. "How long are you going to be out there? I mean, do we need to start worrying if you're—"

"I'll say when to start worrying," she answered. "Trust me, you'll know when."

"We can help, Maya! We took out Glough, you know. We're handy to have around," Kestrel Rose said.

Maya opened the storage cabinet behind the starboard seat, then began slipping her EVA armor on. "Sorry, I can't. IPTP regulations. You mean well, and judging by how you handled him, you two'd be an asset anytime. But not now. Keep an eye on *Skeeto* for me."

Ichiko and Kestrel Rose watched Maya complete the transformation into the IPTP agent that they had first encountered nearly a season ago: anonymous, faceless, genderless, dangerous.

The agent then stepped forward and slid feet first into the ventral cockpit hatch, before pausing to add, "If anything happens to me, for god's sake get your asses home. *Skeeto* can get you there, she knows the way automatically. Just tell her that voice identity code I gave you. Don't trust anyone without verifying their identification. Even then, don't trust 'em. Kuwashima will have a few words for you when you get back. Until then, just relax. Our hands will be full enough afterwards."

With that, Maya, in her gleaming silver EVA armor, disappeared from view, until once again glimpsed out the cockpit windows strolling towards the hub's control office just a few meters away, brandishing Xibalba.

"What're you thinking, Rosey?" Ichiko asked, her eyes studying her stoic sister.

Kestrel Rose swallowed hard. "That we might have to use what we brought with us."

"I hate it when you think that."

CHAPTER FIVE

i

"Agent Maya, InterPlanetary Tax Police. I'm here to place Governor Van Noraesk under arrest. Take me to him."

The security guards, clad in polished black armor and riot helmets, guffawed at the diminutive figure. The taller of the foursome stood from his bench inside Noraesk Tower Gate and crossed over, brandishing his semi-automatic particle rifle.

"Who the hell are you?" the guard sneered. "Did you have some business here?"

With the patience of a saint in spite of his rudeness, Maya produced her badge, which displayed a rotating holographic headshot.

The guard leaned his head forward and laughed again; a pretty girl like her inside that child's set of armor was too good a joke. He set his left hand on Maya's helmet, his gloved fingers brushing the opaque faceplate, as if stroking her porcelain skin.

"Now look here, missy. We ain't in the habit of just letting in any kid to see the governor. He's got important business to conduct, you know what I mean?"

Maya's anonymous helmet craned upwards—insect-like—to his face, before her left gauntlet grasped his wrist and her right one came crashing down on his forearm, causing him to yelp in pain.

She then kneed him in the groin, which, despite the pad located there, sent burning spikes through his nerves. Her left gauntlet cracked the rifle still in his grip against his face, eliciting another cry from the burly man, who probably out-massed her by fifty-plus kilos.

With his receptors flaring, Maya kicked his calves out from under him, dropping the guard to the cement floor. With his hands held out before him, he could see with his one open eye a red sidearm aimed squarely at his bruised mug.

Glancing up to the trio still seated on the bench, Maya said, "Sorry, boys, but I've got important business to conduct, you know what I mean?"

"I—I'll get Mr Noraesk on the vox channel," one of the other guards blurted, hurriedly rising to toggle a button at the nearby check-in desk.

"You do that." Maya stepped over the defeated man and followed the second guard to the convex desk. "Tell him the IPTP is here. And we don't take numbers."

"O—okay. I'm raising him now."

A grizzled voice soon emanated from the vox channel, sounding like it had just eaten a large meal. "What?! You know I'm not in contact when I'm doing business!"

"S—sorry, Gov—Governor. There's a..." he paused to look at Maya.

"Agent Maya. IPTP," she announced loudly into the vox speaker.

"Here to see you," the guard finished.

"Make an appointment!"

The guard's eyes darted from Maya's dangerously anonymous countenance back to the desk. "But, but, she's here to arrest you, Governor. She's already taken down Rylo!"

"What?! What?!"

"Governor, she's—"

"Buzz her up! I'll deal with this now. And you later!"

The guard toggled a lock on the desk, which opened a door beyond. "He'll–he'll be seeing you now."

Maya nodded and walked past the bench, the last two guards eyeing her until she disappeared into the alcove behind them. Two parallel panels parted, revealing a lift. Stepping inside, the controls automatically set themselves for the penthouse level, forty-nine levels above. The ride took less than five minutes, by which point Maya had scanned the intervening levels with her sensor pallet, looking for any disguised weapons systems, hidden traps or other surprises possibly waiting for her on the other side; she doubted Noraesk was a man of his word, and it was always best to be prepared no matter what.

The lift paused, allowing the panels to part once more. Maya entered a wide corridor, well-lit with chandeliers and sconces, rather like a dining hall in some royal palace than the office of a regional governor. Well, that was rather the point, Maya said to herself, soon coming to a door lined with gold leaf.

Placing her gauntlet on the door, it slowly opened, admitting her into an even larger room, adorned with fine pieces of sculpture and hanging portraits. A fuzzy blue light from her right caught her attention; it was a mural window revealing a startling vista of Triton, complete with Neptune balanced in the distance.

"Welcome to the Neptune Regional Authority, Agent Maya," the same grizzled voice greeted her from the left. Dressed in a charcoal three-piece suit, Noraesk was a tall man, his jet-black hair slicked back, its sheen reflecting the blue glare. A close-cropped goatee hugged his chin, its unnaturally dark whiskers betraying not only his vanity but age.

"Governor Noraesk," Maya said, removing her helmet. "This is a fine establishment you have here. Sorry you had to make do with the cramped space."

"The rewards of a successful political and entrepreneurial career, Agent. I like to make my office a little homage to my ancestral land of Northern Europe."

"Of course."

Noraesk gestured to the desk at his side. "Please, come sit with me. We can discuss this issue."

Maya crossed her arms. "There is no issue, Governor. Your arrest has been authorized by the Department of the Treasury. As an agent of the IPTP, I am here to carry it out. Please, come with me, and there will be no added difficulty."

Flashing an impeccable smile—no doubt practiced—Noraesk drew nearer to Maya. "I do not recognize any body affiliated with the Solar System Government. I, as head of the Neptune Regional Authority, have declared this territory sovereign, answerable only to its own laws. You have no authority here. Now, please," he smiled again, "come sit. We can have an intelligent, adult discourse."

"I am afraid, Governor, intelligent discourse is reserved for persons not charged with first-degree crimes."

"What am I charged with?" he sighed, almost as an afterthought.

"Tax evasion. Treason. You can read the charges." She held a three-centimeter-diameter clear holodisc towards him. "But I'm only interested in the former. The rest will assessed by the Judge Advocate General at your arraignment."

Noraesk took the holodisc and studied it, then methodically bent the hard plastic media, snapping it in two. Flipping his fingers, the twin pieces fell to the floor.

"Okay...I didn't want to do this, Governor." Drawing Xibalba, she pointed him at the renegade politician. "Don't make me fire."

"Oh, that will not be an issue, Agent Maya."

Noraesk nodded twice and backed away as a black liquid squirted from the ceiling, splattering about the area around his desk. Maya did a reverse somersault, avoiding the goo, then somersaulted forward, firing two shots in Noraesk's direction. The governor fell to the floor, grunted, and gestured an index finger to the ceiling, which released another volley of the black liquid from the back wall.

Maya performed another somersault, but the goo struck her right arm, instantly rendering Xibalba and her gauntlet inert, trapped beneath the glaze of the tar-like substance.

"Xibalba! Can you hear me?! Xibalba!"

A sharp laugh emanated from behind the desk. Noraesk stood and crossed around to see Maya trying to shake the liquid from her gauntlet, which was now a mass of glop.

"It's of no use, Agent Maya. I have a little procurer of non-lethal defense systems on my retainer. This is a nice neutralizer for situations such as this. It's a substance undetectable by most modern scanners, perhaps even yours."

Maya looked to her left gauntlet and the sensor pallet around the wrist. Sizing up Noraesk, she yelled "Torch!" and flung herself at the governor.

Noraesk's eyes widened as the feral agent's brilliant blue torch cone came to life within centimeters of his face. A third volley of the black liquid fell over the agent from above, knocking her off Noraesk and extinguishing the torch.

Covered helmet to boot, Maya still sprung and tried to counterattack, but the mass slowed her to where even her quickness and strength were sapped. All she could do was glare at him through strands of the hardening glop.

"Now," Noraesk said, breathing hard, "shall we discuss the issue?"

CHAPTER SIX

i

"Pretty courageous of you, I have to say, coming all the way up here like that," Noraesk said, circling the drowsy Maya. "No man has ever attempted such a stunt. Fortunately, even you, Agent Maya, couldn't finish what you came to do."

Maya, restrained on a hospital bed, dressed only in a white togs, blinked slowly, fitfully, a gauzy taste in her mouth causing her to nearly choke. "Wha... you drugged me...you sonuvabitch...."

"My apologies. It will have no lasting effects, I promise you." Noraesk looked down over his "guest." "Now, I'm afraid I have no time to quarrel with you over your mission. My business empire needs its leader, and as such I need to address it. But, my time with you is not yet complete. I have one request of you I will discuss when I return, after you regain your full senses. Until then, feel free to relax. My staff is at your disposal."

Maya rested her head on the pillow, watching the governor turn to the exit. She could hear him give instructions to a nurse on the other side, then depart down the corridor. For now, her dulled senses slowly recovered enough for her to start analyzing the hospital room for weaknesses, its internal arrangement, and how strong her bed's restraints were.

Taking a long breath, Maya clinched her hands and felt the plastic straps over her wrists restrict her muscles and ligaments. It was unlikely she could break free; she'd have to bide her time until Noraesk's staff set her free. Until then, she had to metabolize the drugs. That meant asking for water, and lots of it.

Time to get to work.

ii

"Get Noraesk here *now!*" Maya barked, her wrist strap now an effective garrotte around the unsuspecting nurse's neck. "Do it!"

The panicked nurse clawed for the voxlink on her collar. "Gotta... call...the chief resident...first...."

"No! I want Noraesk!"

"I...don't...have...the...num...ber—"

Maya rose from the bed, the nurse still firmly in her grasp, and crept onto the floor. Moving slowly, she walked the nurse out the door and down the corridor, until reaching a desk occupied by a single man.

"Noraesk! Call him now!" she commanded. "Do it or she dies!"

The startled man fumbled around the desk, finally finding a small device that he put to his mouth. "Dr Nascor, we've got a situation here... please contact the governor about it. Now please."

Maya eyed the device, then noticed a red diode light up and shut off on a panel to the man's left. Shaking her head once, she said, "Wrong move, boy." Replacing the garrotte with her left arm, Maya grabbed the man's hair and slammed his head against the desk, knocking him out.

"How long before they're here?!" she asked the nurse.

"A minute...thirty seconds."

"Well, we're not going to wait for them. Lead me out of here!"

The pair hobbled down the corridor as several people in the adjacent rooms looked askance at the stranger with her overwhelmed prisoner.

"Where's the main entrance?"

"Two...floors down...just...follow...the hall signs."

Maya glanced up and saw the plaques affixed to the walls two meters high, located all the length of the corridor. Loosening her neck lock, she shoved the nurse to the floor and flew down the corridor, her single pace likelier to outrun security than with a pokey prisoner.

After descending two floors, she eyed a set of metal doors at the end of a corridor and ran towards them, dodging the security guards posted at the entrance. Punching the release lever, the doors opened—

And Maya ricocheted backwards, landing on her right flank with a thud. Reaching for her brow, she looked out the entrance and saw an electromagnetic boundary separating the hospital grounds from...a wide, close-up view of Neptune's surface, a helluva lot nearer to the planet than she remembered being. Was she on a space station?

"Don't move!" a brusque command came from behind.

Turning around, five security guards pointed semi-automatic particle rifles straight down upon her, approaching methodically.

"Get her up!"

Maya's arms were pulled out from under her as she was hauled up and placed in manacles.

"You wanted to talk to Governor Noraesk?" the lead guard asked.

"Now's your chance, bitch."

iii

"Maya, Maya. What can I say, other than please don't do that again. You caused quite a stir this morning," Noraesk said.

"You're holding me against my will and Solar System law, Governor." Maya rubbed her wrists, just barely feeling the skin under the manacles. Now in a holding cell much like a brig, she sat against a cold wall, the fluorescent illumination from a single ceiling lamp providing the only light, making Noraesk a silhouette. "Keeping a Federal agent prisoner guarantees a long sentence, only adding to your charges."

Noraesk shook his head in feigned exasperation. "That's not important now. What I have come to discuss is business. After your two displays, I believe you are worthy of
a substantially lucrative career in my employ, if you so desire."

Maya laughed. "You're unbelievable. I've a job to do. I'm not here for your amusement."

"My amusement? No," Noraesk paused, crouching before Maya, "I am satisfied since your arrival, my dear. I offer you the amusement, nay, the adulation, of the entire Solar System. You have only a life-fulfilling mountain of riches to deny yourself if you don't take advantage of my offer."

"Mountain of riches? Who the hell says that? You're a snake-oil salesman, Noraesk, not a businessman. Bribe someone else. I'm not interested."

Noraesk stood and raised his hands to the ceiling. "You will be after witnessing the greatest spectacle mankind has ever laid eyes upon! You will be my star! The audiences won't get enough of you, Maya! I can make it all possible."

"I think you've been in an airlock one too many times."

The low light gave Maya a glimpse of Noraesk's wide smile. "You will change your mind. I guarantee it. This is the greatest challenge any person will ever endure. I am sure even you cannot pass it up."

"I'm full of surprises."

Noraesk headed for the holding cell's door. "Excellent...I look forward to them."

iv

"Governor Noraesk will see you now," the secretary told Maya, who was escorted out of the anteroom by two guards.

The armed entourage led the shackled Maya into a large room, equipped with sumptuous stadium seats on the left side and a semi-circular banquet table topped with silver trays and goblets. Several bouquets adorned the banquet table, and the silver sconces lining the walls were all lit.

"Welcome back, Agent Maya," Noraesk greeted her from the table's head.

"What the hell is this?"

"A course before the main event. One course, that's all you will want. After this, the appeal of food will be lessened by what you will witness. Please, have a seat." Noraesk gestured to the chair opposite him.

Maya took the chair proffered her, then held her hands up, displaying her manacles. "Could you at least get rid of these for me?"

"My apologies. How draconian." Noraesk waved his hand to one of the guards in the room, who trotted over and removed the manacles.

"Now, a toast, Agent Maya." Noraesk raised his goblet. "To entertainment. The most universal of communication, binding us all together, no matter what the background or belief."

Maya raised her goblet and held it aloft. *To morons like yourself, who think I'm a pushover.* Maya sipped the liquid, which was a thick red wine, and set it down.

Noraesk watched Maya begin her meal. "I think this is the beginning of a long and fruitful relationship, Agent Maya."

CHAPTER SEVEN

"And now for the show."

Directed by Noraesk to the stadium seats in the suite, Maya stared at the blank wall before them. On cue, the wall disappeared, replaced by a three-meter-wide image of a vast arena, populated by thousands of spectators encircling a raised, round stage floor. Strobe lights bounced around the crowd and fireworks shot up from the floor as the decibel level increased to a deafening pitch, an orgy of spectacle.

"Watch closely. This is the future of multi-trillion-credit entertainment," Noraesk said, his eyebrows raised in excitement.

Superimposed over the crowd scene was a gaudy, oval-shaped NEPTUNE'S DEADLIEST RING logo, headlining the phrase, "*Are You Man Enough?*" and trumpeting Governor Noraesk himself as the host. Despite being "LIVE" it was obvious this was a recording, perhaps from the last quarter.

Two opposite aisles led up to the round floor, which were soon traversed by a pair of competing entourages, led by men in flashy robes. Walking up the stairs to the stage, the men removed the robes and handed them to what appeared to be trainers. Now dressed in loose shorts only, the men entered the floor, followed by Noraesk, who was elevated from a hatch at the center of the floor.

With an amplified, booming voice, Noraesk greeted, "Welcome, everyone! This is the match we have all been anticipating! The two division champions are ready to meet, and now their time has come! The grudges have been brutal, the wait more so, but no more! Fans, you're in for a treat! No holds barred! No moves banned! No blood unspilt! This is your match! This...is... Neptune's...Deadliest...Ring!"

Bold strobing text graphics identified the combatants: Dugum Greovich on the left-hand side, and Oak Redbeard on the right. Greovich, a wiry, short man, sported a green mohawk and multiple tattoos down his limbs, chest and back, with piercings along his soft tissue, like some zippered leather jacket. Redbeard, owing to his name, wore a red beard and red shorts, and stood about one-meter eighty tall. Built like an ox, any layman would assume he'd clobber Greovich in a moment's time, but Maya knew better than to hand Redbeard a victory on size alone.

The pair shook hands, leaving Noraesk to depart down the side steps. A honeycomb-shaped cage rose up and encapsulated what was now a fighting ring, sealing the combatants inside until a winner was determined.

Maya squirmed in her seat before the match even began; she hated staged fights, particularly ultimate fighting, equating it to nothing more than human cockfights. A real brawl was deadly, often uneven (which she made possible by outgunning and outthinking her opponents) and never refereed. Life was messy, had no boundaries and nobody paid to see you shed your blood.

The combatants knocked fists, and the match was on. Greovich began his assault on the fortress that was Redbeard by flanking the larger man and leaping on his back, then punching his head. Oak retaliated by springing backwards and landing on his back, trapping Greovich between his mass and the ringfloor.

Maya flinched, almost egged on by the crowd's howls of pleasure and amusement, a sickening melange of disgust and gall burbling in her stomach.

Greovich squirted out of the vise, retreating to the far end of the four-meter-diameter ring. Wiping his brow, the smaller man collected his breath and gathered his strength before beginning his second attack. Redbeard didn't hesitate, nor did he require a breather, gathering steam by running straight for Greovich.

Both traded punches to their respective jowls, spewing blood on the ringfloor, but neither gave in, instead intensifying the fight, pummeling themselves into a fury, a ball of sweat, blood and testosterone.

"This is what you call entertainment?" Maya spat, her eyes narrowing at the display.

"One man's entertainment is another man's business, Agent Maya. It's how I afford myself the luxuries I have worked so long and hard to attain, bankrolling the side venture of my respectable gubernatorial lifestyle." Noraesk grinned. "Now, witness the glories of this spectacle. The best is about to begin."

Greovich again retreated to the edge of the ring, his mohawk now plastered by sweat and blood against his face and scalp. A close-up of his face revealed the reddening bruises around his brow and cheekbones, and blood-stained spittle leaking from his pulverized lips.

A close-up of Redbeard showed that the larger man mostly contained his wounds to his abdomen and chest, the pectoral muscles receiving the brunt of Greovich's attacks. Oak's mug maintained its integrity for the most part, with his height and counterattacks preventing Greovich from leaping, the smaller man's preferred modus operandi. Redbeard spread his arms, flexing his fists as he began the final attack, a cornering maneuver he had used to devastating effect on all his previous opponents to advance to the championship match.

Realizing his peril, and reading Redbeard's next move, Greovich quickly assessed his position, then gripped the cage bars underhanded, pulling himself off the ringfloor and flipping his bare feet onto the cage. The smaller man was now upside-down, moving like a spider over the cage structure, virtually hovering over the startled Redbeard.

Flipping over and over several times on the underside of the cage's ceiling, Greovich rounded Redbeard's stationary position, outflanking him for the better part of three minutes.

At once, the crowd began chanting and booing, hundreds hissing at the unscheduled break in the bloodletting. With this ingenious diversion, Maya sat up in her seat and for the first time was captivated, wondering what the wiry fighter had up his sleeve—er, shorts—to get himself out of the predicament. Unless he had a killer move, Maya couldn't see Greovich getting out of the cage a winner. The only recourse was to tire Redbeard out, or lure him with a feint.

The holographic camera closed in on Redbeard's face. With his upturned gaze, Oak could be heard screaming, "Ya can't hang f'rever! Git down here! Git whas comin' ta ya!"

Noraesk swiveled his head towards Maya, easily noticing her sudden interest. "Addictive, yes?"

"Like watching a Causeway accident...." Maya gritted her teeth. "That's not exactly a compliment."

Noraesk let out a laugh and rejoined the circus playing out in front of them, his adrenaline flowing to the rising crowd din. Chants became exhortations, voices in unison calling for Greovich's head and his destruction, Redbeard's might over his opponent's skillful tactics.

Greovich finally made his move, going for a kamikaze bodyslam on Redbeard's shoulders. The smaller fighter grappled Redbeard by the neck, muzzling the man, but couldn't stop Redbeard from sprinting towards the cage like an amok bull.

Redbeard, despite his temporary blindness and constricted nose and mouth, plowed into the cage wall headfirst, pinning Greovich once again. The smaller man let out a cry, stoking the bloodlust of the crowd, which fed back into Redbeard's anger. Oak's arms reached up and pulled Greovich's hands off his face, then rammed him into the cage a second time, his trademark victory maneuver nearly finishing the opponent.

Stunned and nigh stumbling to his knees, Greovich kept himself upright by gripping the cage, but even his residual strength gave out when Redbeard put a headlock on him, lifting Greovich off his feet and slamming him to the ringfloor, with the thunderous approval of the crowd.

A piercing alarm reverberated throughout the stadium, followed by more fireworks. The match was complete, victory most assuredly in Redbeard's grasp.

Noraesk appeared again through the ringfloor, his raised fists signalling that the match was a thorough success, his triumph evident with the ear-to-ear grin on his face. Walking towards the exhausted Redbeard, he held his arm as high as he could, crowning him the winner. Two bikini-clad ring girls entered the opening cage and bestowed Redbeard with a red sash, then posed for holo-photos with him.

"The winner, in an astonishing record time of six minutes and forty-four seconds, Oak Redbeard of Hyperion Federal Colony!" Noraesk announced, shaking Redbeard's hand. He then presented him with an oversized (albeit perfectly suited for Oak's humongous bulk) belt inlaid with a gold disc that shone brilliantly in spectral colors. "Congratulations, Mr Redbeard! Now, bask in your deserved adulation!"

Crowd noise peaked to its highest intensity of the broadcast, leaving a dull echo in Maya's ears after the fact.

"That," Noraesk began a moment later, standing over the agent, "is your destiny, Maya. Your future lies with me. You will be the champion. No one has ever seen anyone such as yourself. Victory, spoils, fame. I alone will deliver them to you. Not the Solar System Government. Not hunting tax cheats. This!"

Noraesk thrust his hand out. "Join me."

Maya rose and stared at the still-playing image. "Governor Noraesk...."

CHAPTER EIGHT

"...Go to hell."

Noraesk put his hands to his hips, sighing deeply. "I was sure you would accept. Oh well, enough persuasion. Officer, take Agent Maya back to the surface. You know what to do."

Maya pursed her lips, the fury in her eyes matching that of the crowd. "You're a fool, Noraesk. Your fans won't be 'entertained' by fixed matches."

"Bread and circuses, my dear Agent." Noraesk's face broke into one wide smile. "Isn't that the old axiom? Feeding pabulum to the masses takes innovation, which is why I was so happy to see your escapade in my office. You will be my crown jewel, with the adoration of the fans. Your training, your skills, will be a revelation to them. They'll be begging me for more, chanting your name in the arena! I suggest you eat hearty tonight. Your new calling begins soon."

The security guard placed manacles around Maya's wrists, then withdrew her from the suite, where several more guards escorted her to the lower levels. Corralled past Noraesk's varying sycophantic imperial employees throughout the complex and then thrown into a waiting suborbital shuttle like so much trash, Maya clenched her fists and memorized every segment of her path, waiting for her hour. Her strongest inclination wasn't for her safety, however, it was her regard for Ichiko and Kestrel Rose, hoping the pair had either fled, or avoided notice and laid low. Without her voxlink and Xibalba, all she could do was bide her time.

A small porthole afforded Maya a glimpse of Triton, and the shuttle's descent trajectory. They appeared to be headed away from Naiad City and Monad Regio altogether and bound for the farside of the moon, where few if any colonies existed. Being hundreds of kilometers from the utilities of the capital, life would be hard, perhaps impossible, with temperatures hovering just tens of degrees above absolute zero. This was obviously their intent, as Noraesk could harbor less savory facilities capable of torture or worse, far from public and media scrutiny, a perfect venue for Neptune's Deadliest Ring.

Maya immediately recognized two fantastic plumes eight kilometers high along the horizon: the Mahilani and Hili geysers, the first cryovolcanoes seen on Triton from the *Voyager 2* probe a century-and-a-half earlier. The black smokers poured particulates downwind into the atmosphere for hundreds of kilometers, coating the frigid surface with the characteristic "ash" so distinctive from higher altitudes. Thanks to this, Maya knew she was most likely heading to the North Polar cap, probably within Uhlanga Regio, location of six maculae that stared into space like widely placed eyes.

They circled round a macula—a dark depression of deep surface soil ringed by lighter, frosted material—and decelerated, swiftly losing altitude. Despite Triton's outer Solar System origins and wholly different tectonics, owing to Neptune's proximity, Maya's eyes could easily confuse the charcoal terrain for the mare of the Moon. All things being equal, the two disparate bodies were still subject to the same solar wind, the same cosmic particle bombardment, and space's inherent properties. Everything was sterile, vacuum occupying all the space between the islands.

A squat, rounded tower, not more than two hundred meters tall, stood defiantly against the harsh Tritonian landscape, ringed by blinking red lights. Thin support struts rose from the macula's surface and angled into the structure's roof, like some ancient, long-extinct sea creature writ large. Boasting the largest, most sophisticated holographic displays this side of the hardcore, XXX spammers around Saturn, broad portraits of combatants—Oak Redbeard being one she spotted straightaway—were illuminating the terrain, polluting the Outer Reaches with Noraesk's holo-junk. Smaller constructs were sprinkled throughout the immediate area, being perhaps the security perimeter or crowd control centers. Noraesk fleeced his citizens and Authority coffers in style with this arena complex, not so much differently than the Roman caesars of old.

At the foot of the arena and drowning in its shadow, the shuttle set down on the hard bedrock ice and was boarded by suited soldiers, who motioned for Maya. Already dressed before her departure in an all-purpose, EVA cargo bag, sans sleeves or leggings, Maya was carried out by the soldiers, their job made easier by the low gravity. Aloft now as if supplies or luggage, Maya grimaced at her rough handling, even in the microgravity, as they shuttled her through a recessed entrance on the floor of the macula.

After some time, Maya felt the flat surface of a floor, and the gradual removal of the cargo bag from over her body. Raising her head, she saw a pair of soldiers fold up the bag and exit through a door. She appeared to be in a cell, lit from above by a blinking yellow light, casting numerous shadows across the dull metal walls. Pushing against the floor with her shoulder blades, Maya sat up along a wall, her manacled hands unusable for now. Swiveling her head, she listened for sounds, while her eyes scanned for company. If she was going to have to defend herself in this wretched cell, she might as well have ample warning.

"Name...registry identification number," a distant voice said, almost an echo inside the cell.

Maya turned her head towards the light. "Where are you?"

"Name...registry identification number," the voice repeated.

"Go to hell."

"Inappropriate response."

A dizzying sonic assault came from the cell ceiling, drilling through Maya's ear canals straight into her brain. Releasing a horrendous scream, her body convulsed until the assault ceased.

"Name...registry identification number."

"Ma-ya," she groaned, "5147-851-286135. Now release me...."

"Processing...name and registry identification number verified."

The door opened and a silhouetted figure crossed over to the prostrate Maya. Kneeling next to her, the figure's hands lifted her chin. "I see the governor has a new combatant. You seem a little tiny to be entering the ring."

Maya opened one eye. "I'm here to arrest him. I'm a Federal agent with the IPTP."

The figure let out a chuckle, clearly the deep laugh of a man. "So far so good."

"Release me now."

The man produced a wafer and slid it into the manacles, which instantly broke open.

Maya sprung from the floor and took the man's legs out from under him. Pouncing over him, she put him into a headlock. "So far so good," she repeated, mocking him. "How do I get out of here?"

He laughed again. "By winning your matches."

Maya tightened her arms. "I'll win this one. Now get me out of here."

With incredible strength, the man rose and flung Maya forward, sending her careening into a wall. Now at his feet, he walked over to her, keeping his distance. "You're good. Sloppy, but that's probably the journey from orbit dulling your reactions. You'll need me to take care of that if you're going to be successful."

Maya pushed off the floor and stood up. "I'm not one of Noraesk's combatants."

"It's a little late for that. You're in for the penny, Agent."

Waving his hand, a trio of guards entered, and brandishing semi-automatic particle rifles, led Maya out, followed by the man. The group walked through a well-lit corridor and soon came upon a large gymnasium, where several dozen people were holding practice matches, which, to Maya's eyes, seemed to consist of combined martial arts forms and boxing, with some street fighting by the less experienced combatants.

"This is our training gym," the man said. "Right now, we're weeding the hopefuls, ridding the ones who haven't a chance from the ones with real potential."

Maya paused and looked over the various hopefuls, unable to prevent herself from analyzing the crop. "What are these people, criminals?"

"Some of them. Others have no vocations to choose from, being either deficient in entrance exams for the military or police, or having too lengthy a rap sheet for civilian fields."

Maya pursed her lips. "Helluva recourse."

"Get to know their moves, their favorite styles. Governor Noraesk told me you'd be a prize, and you didn't disappoint. By the way," he stuck his hand out, "I'm Tok Ud-Hajrdal, general director and chief trainer of this facility. I believe you have the potential to beat all the hopefuls here, perhaps even unseat the current champion."

"Oak Redbeard's a challenge. He claimed no one would ever topple him, not even time itself."

Ud-Hajrdal smiled. "I taught him well, but he's a bit too boastful when he should be pulping the competition. Regardless, you'll get your chance, if you defeat the slate of hopefuls in your training slot."

"And if I won't?" Maya asked, testing his nerve.

He jutted his thumb to the guards behind them. "That's why the governor employs them."

Maya scanned over the combatants once more, certain her years of living beyond the arms of the deadliest organizations in the Solar System and defeating every single one of her tax cheats in open combat gave her a decided advantage.

Rubbing her hands together, she said, "Who's first on the slate?"

CHAPTER NINE

"I'll go easy on ya, li'l girl," the two-meter tall Idaf Gask pronounced, rubbing his palms together.

Maya smiled and balled her hands into fists. "Good advice...I wouldn't want to hurt your chances, Mr Gask."

"Enough talk!" Ud-Hajrdal yelled. "Spar!"

Gask feinted to Maya's right flank, but instead lunged for her legs. Maya easily somersaulted backwards, spun on her outstretched arms and kicked Gask in the head. Landing over him, she headlocked his scruffy pate and stared directly in his eyes.

"Fortunately for you I'm not armed, eh?"

Gask grimaced, trying to reach Maya's legs, but the agent ended the sparring match by pinning Gask to the mat.

Ud-Hajrdal clapped and smiled. "Good! Good!" He looked down to a chronometer on his wrist. "Fourteen seconds. Not bad for a rookie."

"There are no rookies in my profession, Mr Ud-Hajrdal," Maya said, releasing Gask. "Only predator and prey."

"P'raps. But in this business, they're chumps and champs. You're neither at this moment. Keep sparring."

Maya wiped the sweat from her palms on the back of her workout togs. "Who's next?"

Ud-Hajrdal beckoned another fighter with the wag of his finger. Named Niobe Radh, the rather androgynous figure, about Maya's height and wearing a halter-type top, walked forward and into the sparring ring. Scrutinizing this new opponent, Maya logically assumed Radh had to be a woman. Performing in this spectacle couldn't be easy for her—

"Spar!"

Radh struck first with lightning-quick ferocity, utilizing a flurry of body-twisting kicks to Maya's abdomen. Knocked backwards onto the mat, Maya log-rolled to her right, somersaulted into the air and landed behind Radh, kicking the fighter's legs out from under her.

Standing over her new opponent, Maya quickly corrected her first impression. Wrapping her right arm around Radh's head, she attempted to pin her, but Radh countered by locking Maya's head in her legs and throwing the agent forward. Both now ensconced in a ball, the advantage was to whomever could overpower the other—albeit briefly—to pin her to the mat.

A swift punch from Maya to Radh's face released the agent, and she took advantage by leaping elbow-first into Radh's ribcage, stunning the fighter long enough for Maya to pin her, splaying Radh's shoulder blades against the mat.

Maya stood upon hearing Ud-Hajrdal's signalling the end of the match, but Radh leapt up and faced down Maya, shouting, "C'mon, bitch! You wanna fight nasty! You wanna see blood! I'll give you a taste!"

Maya snickered, shrugging off the challenge, but Ud-Hajrdal had the opposite reaction. Placing a meaty hand on Radh's collarbone, he pushed the defeated fighter back towards the other assembled fighters and whispered something in her ear that Maya had neither the time nor inclination to listen to.

As the agent massaged the tendons underneath her sparring gloves, a woman gingerly stepped away from the audience of Ud-Hajrdal's fighters and approached her.

"You fight like that often?" she asked, her brown eyes sizing Maya up, perhaps in near adulation, if Maya read her body language correctly.

"Not for sport, usually."

A long silence came between the pair before the woman said, "You looked like you were fighting not to win."

Maya took a breath. "I was fighting not to maim anyone, if that's what you meant. I could've snapped their necks." A smile broke over her face. "But that's not what this is about."

"That's Federal training, not ultimate fighting," she whispered. "Who're you with?"

"Myself."

"Uh-huh." The anonymous woman fingered her short brunette hair, which was parted on the right and scalloped down the left side of her head. She appeared to be barely into her twenties, if even out of her teens, about Maya's height. Scanning the other fighters, she appeared overly cautious, if not suspicious, of them. "I want to talk, but not here. When are you available?"

Maya turned away. "My free time's my own. Go talk to that chick I just beat. She looks like she needs a friend."

The woman followed Maya's head. "This isn't about loneliness. This is about...business."

"What is this, a sorority?" Ud-Hajrdal's voice thundered a few meters away. "Maya, your presence is required. We need to schedule an appointment. Malchyika! Get back in queue! Your sparring time hasn't expired yet."

'Malchyika' obeyed, swiftly re-entering the assembled fighters without so much as a glance back to Maya.

Ud-Hajrdal took Maya by the arm and led her past the fighters. "No conversation is permitted between combatants during sparring time. Never forget that. Governor Noraesk's orders are strictly enforced."

Maya nodded. "My apologies, sir. I'll be more diligent warding them off in the future."

"See to it. Now, I have some good news. Governor Noraesk is scheduling his newest combatants, providing they meet muster, in a rookie tournament, with the champion automatically gaining a berth in Neptune's Deadliest Ring. The governor believes you're his next champion, Maya."

"If I make it through the ranks."

Ud-Hajrdal put his hand on Maya's shoulder, stopping the pair. "The governor puts his faith in your unique skills and athleticism. He also believes you'd be the finest champion of Neptune's Deadliest Ring ever, infinitely more photogenic than Oak Redbeard."

"You mean bankable."

Ud-Hajrdal smiled. "The word is 'marketable,' my dear."

ii

Noraesk steepled his fingers, his eyes darting from one edge of the holographic display to the other. Relaxing in his newly refurbished office, the governor reclined in a lounge chair, monitoring the rookie sparring matches, particularly Maya's two sessions.

"She's more than ready," Ud-Hajrdal said, standing behind Noraesk. "Redbeard wouldn't stand a chance, even now. An analysis session could be sched—"

"No," Noraesk interjected. "Our whole enterprise is about entertainment, Tok. My audience doesn't need to be satiated just yet. Anticipation is what we parcel out, that is how my vast fortune has been gained. She'll be in the tournament, just as all the others will be. I want to see her advance...that interests me."

Ud-Hajrdal nodded. "It will be done, Governor."

CHAPTER TEN

"Which of these jokers is my first opponent?"

Ud-Hajrdal and Maya stood over a holographic monitor displaying the projected rookie lineup, each having been accepted (along with Maya) into the Rookie Tournament since its announcement the previous day.

Ud-Hajrdal tapped a glowing blue sphere beneath one miniaturized figure. "Maddrow Djid has been selected by lottery. If you beat him, the winner between these two," he paused, punching spheres beneath the other figures, "Malchyika Tsarova and Waldimar Ipfisk, will be your next opponent. That will get you into the rookie finals. Then, in the evening, you'll be the first up in Neptune's Deadliest Ring, four rounds of quick-turnaround hell."

"Cannon fodder, eh? I guess I better get some practice in," Maya said, her eyes illuminated by the slowly rotating holograms. "Gotta work off my rust."

"A word of advice: almost all rookies show up here thinking just being in the ring guarantees victory. Don't show any mercy like you did in those sparring matches. Underestimating your opponent breeds defeat."

"Who said I planned on losing?"

Returning to the training gym, Maya skipped more sparring matches and concentrated on Tai Chi forms, working on her breathing, coordination and all-around mind-spirit-body connectedness, which seemed to have grown fallow before she was thrown into the two spars. The latter being a close-run thing, much closer than she'd prefer, Maya focused her mind on the training her mentor, Gilmour Zeobarry, had put her through during her teen years on Ceres, when the pair were escapees form a criminal consortium from Mars, The Martian Group. The old man himself was an ex-soldier turned mechanic, still as sharp as his younger days; honing the girl out of her feral, law-skirting ways into a deadly weapon—a hunter, the predator Maya prided herself on till this day—Zeobarry was the father she didn't have as a girl, the man who molded Maya into a woman. Despite Zeobarry's absence this last decade of her life, he was very much with her in spirit, and now, in Maya's current captivity, he inspired her, pushed her, honed her still.

Perspiration melted the tarnish off her body, her smooth, sinewy flesh reveling in the open quarters unaffordable to her by *Skeeto's* relatively cramped spaces. Triton's limited gravity—even with dark-matter axions providing synthetic gravity under the arena's foundations—was enough to exercise her musculature beyond the norm, if not quite measuring up to the Martian standard her body formed in. Her physique's curves rippled beneath her sparring togs, her mind again expanding inside the steely countenance she wore. It was a nice, if inconvenient, change to the pace Maya typically kept. She would arrest Noraesk, that was not an issue, but first she would play his game, and perhaps learn a lesson in the process. If nothing else, she'd have fantastic training en route to taking the governor down.

Taking a break to replenish her electrolytes, Maya reclined against a prefab wall and drank the cool beverage slowly, letting the sweat beads roll down her reddened brow and cheeks. Her three opponents all eyed each other as much as they trained, surely an interesting sociological thesis for some psychology student, if not for Maya herself.

Half-a-room away, Maddrow Djid boxed with a holographic trainer, each of his jabs registering as a red circle and a soft ping against the hologram. He had excellent footwork, befitting a boxer, but didn't appear to be overly massive, probably falling somewhere within a middleweight or light heavyweight, nothing she hadn't faced before. He was a lefty, a fact Maya would take into account during their match; she would be careful where she thought his strengths were, and aggressive on his weaker right. Being several centimeters shorter than Djid, Maya would have to keep her face out of the way of his fists, but figured the cage would be her best bet, utilizing it the way Dugum Greovich had. Given better time to prepare, however, she knew the match would end in her favor.

The strange woman Malchyika Tsarova, who had sought out Maya, seemed to be taking a keen interest in the agent again, more so than her own first-round opponent. What was Tsarova's deal? She appeared more eager to talk than fight, an unusual trait in these ultimate fighters. Her demureness seemed out of place, all the more obvious with Ud-Hajrdal barking at her. Maya wasn't quick to pin her as a mole, but the possibility was becoming more and more likely the longer Tsarova went without sparring; at least the woman wasn't overcompensating by sparring with every comer. Still, the inkling niggled within Maya.

Maya never made eye contact with Tsarova, instead allowing her peripheral vision to keep tabs on the woman, seeing if she moved once. She never did. Maya put it out of her mind and scouted Djid, now kickboxing with the adroit holographic trainer, which received a flurry of jabs from Djid's feet. Maya got the hint well; he wasn't going to be a pushover like Idaf Gask, who, despite his bravado, failed to make the cut.

Maya retired to her quarters—really just extended barracks—eager to rest, since the next day was the Rookie Tourney, back-to-back rounds beginning in the morning, then a marathon of sixteen combatants duking it out for the crown of Neptune's Deadliest Ring three hours later. While not particularly interested in all that entailed, Maya knew the best way to get close to Noraesk was to play to his ego. After all, the winner was feted as a champion, and the good governor couldn't resist one of those, heaven help him.

Reclining onto a simple cot for the evening, Maya's consciousness began to slip into gauzy sleep, only to be stirred by a series of knocks on the thin, rusty panel that acted as a door. Rising to her feet, she listened with one ear to the panel.

"Maya...."

What the hell? The whispered voice sounded like Tsarova. What would it take to get away from that girl for some quiet?

"We need to talk."

Maya cracked the door. "We have nothing to discuss, Tsarova."

"At least listen to me."

"Umm, I already have. Or did you forget yesterday?"

"It's about—" she swung her head around, checking to see if the coast was clear, "Noraesk."

"I know what he's about."

Tsarova furrowed her brow. "You do? Who are you with?"

Maya grabbed the woman's arm and pulled her inside, then shut the door. "Don't ask me what's not your concern! You wanna live?"

"I have been ordered by my superiors to take down Governor Noraesk," Tsarova said, turning away from Maya. "My real identity is Corporal Alix Xilanova, Solar System Army Intelligence, Branch G. I've infiltrated this installation, but when I saw you out there, I knew you were someone different than the others I have been training with."

Maya laughed. "Army Intel, eh? Seems like they sent a girl to do a woman's work."

Xilanova put her hands to her hips. "My age is not comparable to my task, nor my abilities."

"Just a little humor to dampen your tone, Corporal." Maya extended her hand. "I'm Agent Maya, IPTP. It would appear our missions are one and the same."

"What happened to your cover?"

"'Cover?' I never use aliases. Too much to remember. I'm brazen enough to demand what I need right away. The governor had other thoughts, arresting me and entering me into this crap championship deal of his."

"You're not working with anyone else?"

Smiling, Maya clapped Xilanova's shoulder. "The only partner I need is my sidearm and my ship. Unfortunately, neither one are at my disposal at this moment. So, for now, I'm playing along nicely."

"We could use your help, Agent Maya. Noraesk—"

"Oh no. No one gets my help. I'm in this for the credits, not the annals of Army Intel history. You wanna tag team when I finally wail on Noraesk's ass, fine. But I'm doing this my way, on my time."

Xilanova ran her fingers through her short hair, then paced around Maya, before answering, "What if I told you I knew where they confiscated your sidearm?"

CHAPTER ELEVEN

i

"Noraesk's orbital station. There are holding cells there, where all our effects are stored for the duration. His R&D facility, offices and IPwebwork are there as well," Xilanova explained. "I reconnoitered the platform before I enrolled in Neptune's Deadliest Ring."

Maya crossed back to her cot and sat down, digesting the information. "Xibalba's in trouble, then." *So, what else was new?*

"Za-ball-bah? What the hell is Za-ball-bah?"

"My sidearm...he's sentient. And he's my partner. If Noraesk disassembled him, there's no telling if his techs would know what they got their hands on, but I can't take that chance. I've never actually disassembled him completely, fearing the black-market AI module inside would stop functioning if I rooted around in his casing."

Xilanova sat beside Maya. "Getting to him would be difficult for a rescue, particularly since both of us are effectively prisoners until the tournament is over."

"I do have one recourse, but I hesitate to put them into danger...."

The corporal flashed a puzzled look to Maya.

"I didn't come alone. Aboard *Skeeto* are two teen girls I was escorting to Titan, but I was re-routed here. If I could get a message to them, they may just be able to spring Xibalba."

"Teenagers?! Why would you even—"

"Settle down, Corporal." Maya stood again and faced Xilanova. "These girls stole an experimental police corsair out from under some other thief's nose. They can handle themselves I'm sure, but taking the chance on them getting caught almost outweighs Xibalba's usefulness."

"Then...I can be the solution." Xilanova put her hands to her mouth in thought. "It involves me throwing my match. If I can get out of here and locate your companions, we can all take down Noraesk together."

Maya shook her head. "That's a Jupiter-sized if. We have no guarantee that Noraesk will honor your freedom. Have you seen any loser of a match re-enter society? I doubt Noraesk would allow anyone the luxury of leaving the Neptune Regional Authority again. You probably know better than me that someone has to construct his frontier colonies...nobody in their right mind would work on Proteus or Nereid."

Xilanova rose and extended her hand to Maya. "Okay, point made. May I suggest an agreement? Whichever of the two of us is crowned champion, we get the other out. Pooling our resources, we have a better chance of netting Noraesk."

"Sounds good," Maya said, "but I want Xibalba by my side, if possible. If I can contact the girls, they'll get me Xibalba. But I need to find a transmitter to reach *Skeeto*."

"Let me see what I can do. The least I can do is try."

The pair shook hands, then Xilanova retired to her quarters to construct a plan. It was going to be a busy night, leading to an even busier day.

ii

"I'm going after Maya."

Ichiko's back stiffened. "Rosey! Maya told us to wait here for her! You don't know what's out—"

Kestrel Rose walked towards *Skeeto*'s spare quarters. Wasting no time, she dug out a jewel box and plopped it onto their sleeping cot. Ichiko followed close behind, her hands grabbing her sister's shoulder.

"Don't try to stop me, Ichiko. *Skeeto* lost communications with her three days ago...something's obviously wrong here!"

"But Rosey, it's just the two of us! We don't know how many soldiers this guy's got."

Kestrel Rose looked up from the box and smiled. "You're right. But they don't have *Skeeto*."

"Taking *Cokol* was one thing...our lives weren't in danger," Ichiko said, furrowing her brow. "*Skeeto* is Maya's ship, and our only way home."

"Home?!" Kestrel Rose shouted. "Where the hell is home? Titan? Mars? Earth? We might as well get used to life on the run. Unless you don't want to be sisters anymore. And in that case, you stay here and fret like you always do!"

Ichiko threw her arms around her. "No! Please, Rosey! Don't be angry...I love you. Please, don't be mad."

Kestrel Rose put her hands on Ichiko's upper arms and looked her sister in the eyes. "Nothing will come between us, Ichiko. I won't let anyone harm us. Haven't I always protected you?"

Ichiko stifled her burgeoning tears. Nodding, she said, "Yes...I just don't know what I'd do if you never came back, Rosey. I'm scared...."

"So am I. But living afraid of adults is not living. Let's do this for Maya. C'mon, you remember where you stowed your stuff?"

Ichiko nodded again. She stepped over to meter-long metal case affixed to a microgravity slot in the wall and took it out.

Her sister turned back to her after a moment. "Ready?"

"Yes."

iii

"*Skeeto* says there's infrared signatures for at least twelve to fifteen people inside this landing dome," Kestrel Rose said, flattening her shoulder blades against the wall. She inched her ways towards a pressurized hatch.

A meter to Kestrel Rose's left was Ichiko, who gripped a strapped duffle bag diagonally across her chest. "Not bad odds." She looked back to *Skeeto*, which loomed over them in the hangar bay, and toggled the voxlink attached to a bracelet on her left wrist. "Take care of yourself, *Skeeto*. We'll be back soon."

Kestrel Rose opened the hatch and led Ichiko inside the tight corridor to the control office. The pair swiftly traversed past several repair workers, who failed to even notice the highly unauthorized girls slipping into Monad Port 5-A's office.

A bank of holographic displays met them from across the office, all glowing a pinkish hue inside the darkened room. Kestrel Rose placed her hand on one and began tapping several of the spherical interface buttons. "First, we gotta find Maya. *Skeeto* can access the QPU via our voxlinks if we interface them together."

"Let's do mine," Ichiko said. She released the bracelet from her wrist and held it to the holographic interface.

A magical ripple spread over the interface as *Skeeto*'s proxy frequencies manipulated the Quantum Processing Unit behind the monitor, the craft's own quantum computer branching throughout and beyond the code constructing the hologram. A text box appeared seconds later: "SEARCH PARAMETER COMPLETE. MAYA BIOSIGNATURE CONFIRMATION FAILED. PROBABILITY OF MAYA ABOARD THE SURFACE OF TRITON: 0%. REROUTE REQUEST? YES. NO."

"She's not here!" Ichiko spat. "*Skeeto*, where could she be?" she yelled into the voxlink.

"Miss Maya's location unknown, Miss Ichiko," *Skeeto* answered over the voxlink.

Kestrel Rose frowned. "Could her biosign be cloaked?"

"Unknown," *Skeeto* answered.

Kestrel Rose looked back to the monitor, which still displayed the reroute request. "I've got one more idea...Ichiko, let's try the voxlink again."

Ichiko replaced the voxlink against the monitor, while Kestrel Rose typed "Y" on the interface.

"*Skeeto*, try Xibalba's voxlink frequency," Kestrel Rose ordered. "Let's see where he's gotten to."

CHAPTER TWELVE

i

Alix Xilanova crawled through an airshaft and down into a communications routing closet, her departure masked by the late hour of her mission; she'd probably regret it the next morning during the Rookie Tournament, but it wouldn't have been the first time she'd been deprived of sleep before an exercise or operation.

Dropping to the floor softly in Triton's reduced gravity, she walked over to the gym's communications QPU, a cylindrical hub resting against the far wall, packed with nano-threads running from one end of the gymnasium complex to another, capable of relaying terabytes of communiques in microseconds.

An inset panel to the right of the hub hid an interface, which Xilanova reached by removing the panel. Keying in a memorized access code provided to her by Army Intelligence, the corporal brought up the holographic monitor, displaying the millions of lines of code piped through the hub every second. She swiftly found a transceiver line through a series of webbed branches and, again keying in a frequency, this time provided to her by Maya, transmitted a coded message to *Skeeto*. Xilanova hadn't the time nor inclination to know whom she was transmitting to, or the exact prompt, but knew the agent's resourcefulness would come in handy getting the pair their mutual objective.

"CODE RECEIVED. THIRD PARTY TRANSMISSION COMPLETE."

Xilanova sighed. Replacing the panel, the corporal returned the way she came and disappeared into the darkness. With her side mission accomplished (hopefully), Xilanova focused on her match with Ipfisk, in, she checked her wrist chrono, five hours. Time for some shuteye.

ii

"Xibalba's on some space station," Ichiko said, after reading aloud from the holo-display in the office. "Why would he be there? Is that where Maya is too?"

Kestrel Rose's index finger twirled a lock of hair around itself in thought. "That would explain why the computer couldn't locate Maya."

"Then that's where we go next, huh?"

Kestrel Rose nodded. "*Skeeto* can get us there. Looks like all those hours we practiced before stealing *Cokol* are gonna pay off again."

The sisters snuck out of the office and headed back to the hangar, this time seeing no workers or other dome employees. Heck, this was gonna be easier than they thought.

Boarding *Skeeto* through the ventral hatch, the pair walked straight to the cockpit.

"I hope Maya doesn't mind too much," Ichiko said meekly.

"Hey, she was the one that told us to break outta here if things went bad. This ranks right up there."

With a slight hesitation that she would never admit to, Kestrel Rose approached the portside seat—Maya's seat—and sat in it, her behind carving a new groove in Maya's well-worn rut. Taking a deep breath, she looked to Ichiko as her sister took the opposite seat.

"*Skeeto*," Kestrel Rose said to the ship, "this is the plan...."

iii

Skeeto sped away from the dome, Neptune's distant visage lending the tiny ex-lunar shuttle a topaz shade among the murk of the Outer Reaches. Ascending above the crusty maculae, a silvery spindle shone brightly in the distance, immediately catching the girls' attentions.

"Incoming third-party coded message, Miss Kestrel Rose," *Skeeto* said.

Ichiko exchanged a dumbfounded look to her sister. "What?"

"Must be coming from the dome...I didn't think they would discover us for another few minutes." Kestrel Rose tapped a button on the holographic interface. "Translate for us, please, *Skeeto*."

A text box blossomed before the port and starboard interfaces, reading: "XIBALBA MIA. MAYA IN DOME. MISSION ABORTED."

Kestrel Rose sighed indignantly. "Thanks, but we knew that already, Maya—"

"Then that definitely confirms Maya and Xibalba aren't together," Ichiko interrupted. "Maya's gotta be in trouble."

"I was afraid about that. Okay, *Skeeto*, scan that station for a weak point. I'm supposing Maya has a protocol for illegal entry, huh?"

"Affirmative."

"Well, let's run that, then."

"Voice identification code, please," *Skeeto* asked.

Kestrel Rose rubbed her forehead; what was that code again? She was so tired her thoughts were melting together. "Maya...alpha...."

"One-one-zero," Ichiko finished, smiling.

A chime sounded from *Skeeto*'s voxlink. "Confirmed. Program Sheep's Clothes accessed and running."

"Wanna sleep," Kestrel Rose sighed, reclining in the seat. "I'm barely keepin' my eyes open."

Ichiko laid a soft hand on Kestrel Rose's shoulder. "We'll be in bed soon. Since we're sneaking aboard at nighttime, maybe we'll go unnoticed even better, huh?"

"Yeah...maybe." Kestrel Rose detached the Y-belt over her torso and floated towards the cockpit's aft storage compartment. "I gotta stay awake...I know there's a candy bar somewhere in this stuff...."

iv

Skeeto sidled up to the orbital stations's belly, the tiny ship's scanners probing the interior for weapons platforms and other assorted security measures. Determining none of consequence in the vicinity, *Skeeto* next searched for Xibalba's transponder signal, supposedly detectable only by *Skeeto* or Maya herself. After passively waiting for the non-existent confirmation, *Skeeto* lightly pinged the station on specific frequencies Xibalba was normally attuned to, attempting to cut through any potential EM or gravimetric barriers shrouding the semi-sentient sidearm.

"What's taking so long, *Skeeto*?" Ichiko asked, floating upside down in the cockpit.

"Negative transponder response, Miss Ichiko. Attempting to scan the electromagnetic spectrum for Mr Xibalba's signal."

"Okay, but why don't you try scanning Xibalba's specific alloy content, maybe try to get a fix on him that way?"

"Xibalba's alloy content consistent with eighty-six point one-four percent of the orbiting station's metallicity," *Skeeto* answered. "Detection of Mr Xibalba highly improbable at these high ratios."

Ichiko pursed her lips. "Why didn't you just say you couldn't see him? Okay...." She pushed off the cockpit ceiling and swam over to Kestrel Rose, who, despite her recent sugar intake, managed to nod off in mid-air. "Rosey," she whispered into her ear, "*Skeeto* says she can't find Xibalba anywhere. He's not answering her back."

"Whazzz—Xibalba's not lis'nin'...."

"No, he's probably deactivated, or worse. We have to find him, Rosey." She rotated Kestrel Rose face forward.

Kestrel Rose yawned, then stretched her back. "Okay...get our stuff. *Skeeto*...is there a hatch...or something...we can get aboard that station with?"

"Affirmative. A one-meter-diameter supply chute is located twelve meters aft of our current position, compatible with my hatch construction."

"Can you hack it?" Ichiko asked.

"Hack program accessed...complete."

"Fire thrusters, then," Ichiko commanded. "Calculate best possible approach angle and take us in."

Skeeto's forward RCS thrusters fired, reversing course. With a quick ventral thruster blast, the craft tilted backwards and lined up its dorsal hatch with the supply chute, mating perfectly, and even better, silently, to the station.

"Docking complete. Pressurizing hatch with oxygen at one atmosphere," *Skeeto* reported.

Ichiko pulled her duffle bag and Kestrel Rose to *Skeeto*'s central corridor tube. "Thanks, *Skeeto*. We'll be back soon, hopefully. Keep voxlink channel open, all right?"

"Affirmative, Miss Ichiko."

"You gonna make it, Rosey?"

Kestrel Rose nodded and smiled. Buckling a belt holding several short sheaths around her waist, a new sense of purpose crossed her face. "Busting ass always wakes me up, Ichiko. Let's find Xibalba and get Maya outta her predickerment."

CHAPTER THIRTEEN

i

The roar bellowed throughout the arena, deafening Maya, whose flagging discipline forced her to cover her ears. Fireworks popped above the agent and Ud-Hajrdal, leaving acrid smoke fumes wafting in the air, illuminated by strobe lights from the domed ceiling. Walking behind Ud-Hajrdal, Maya scanned the depths of the audience, the standing-room-only throng cheering the combatants' arrival. Across the way, Maddrow Djid, at a taut, one-and-a-half-meters tall, basked in the limelight, a crack barely described as a smile creasing his craggy face. Even in the distorted stadium lighting, Maya could see the scars zigzagging his flesh, possibly the remnants of a hard life lived among the less savory segments of society.

If the stadium chants were debilitating upon Maya's entry, then Noraesk's ascension into the ring as before sent them into a mind-crushing orgy. Maya and Ud-Hajrdal climbed the steps leading to the ring's perimeter and paused, absorbing the crowd's din as Noraesk exhorted the audience with his triumphant, Caesar-like posturing, whipping their bloodlust into a frenzy.

"G-o-o-od Morning, fans!" Noraesk's voice boomed over the stadium speakers, to the crowd's pleasure. "I am Van Noraesk, the greatest entertainer to the greatest audience in the Solar System!"

The stadium nearly burst at the seams; Maya, contrarily, modulated her pulse, conserving her energy for the bouts ahead. It was difficult not to get an adrenaline rush during the introduction, but she allowed her distaste to check the energy washing over her.

"I have listened to your demands for more action!" Noraesk, the governor-showman, continued. "After many years of deliberation, I have delivered. It pleases me to introduce to you—the first Rookie Tournament of Neptune's Deadliest Ring!"

Maya and Djid exchanged glances for the first time, with the weight of the assembled eyes focused squarely on them. They were the inaugural bout, no doubt Noraesk's grand design in the first place. Maya knew she was the object of the governor's desires for a more "marketable" star; why not give the customers the burgeoning star the first at-bat?

Noraesk held his arms out, gesturing towards the combatants. "Fans, you're in for a treat! These two fighters, Agent Maya to my left, Maddrow Djid to my right, have never fought in the ring...until now! Watch them spill virgin blood! Thrill to their streetfighting ways!"

Maya cursed Noraesk out loud at his rampant fiction, but of course went unheard.

"No holds barred! No moves banned! No blood unspilt! This is your match! This is...Neptune's...Deadliest...R-r-r-rinnnnngggggg!!!"

The grand finale of fireworks crackled upon the arena ringfloor, the twin spotlights followed the pair as they stepped into the ring...the Rookie Tourney was on.

Noraesk winked to Maya as he led the pair to the center of the ring. With their fingerless, padded fighting gloves on, the combatants knocked fists and took to opposite sides. The governor then departed down the ringfloor, cueing the honeycombed cage's envelopment of the ring.

Maya sized up Djid, keeping her distance. On brute strength alone, she could take him...she knew she was preternaturally strong, perhaps possessing twice the power of what a normal man could lift. It was an uncanny ability that mystified her, but an advantage nonetheless. Here, though, athleticism would be the ticket to a lengthy stay. And that meant reducing fatigue and exhaustion.

Djid lunged to tackle Maya, but she leapt to her right, watching the man land on his face. Maya headlocked Djid with her right arm while kneeing him in the small of his back. Djid tried to flip her around to grapple her lower leg, but the agent brought her left heel down on his loose hand, causing him to yelp in anger.

"Concede!" Maya barked in his ear.

"Aayaahh...little bitchhh...I'll pound your little hide into—"

A sharp slap—the result of Maya grabbing his hair and slamming his face down upon the mat—changed his mind.

"I con...cede...."

The electronic referee registered Djid's voice, signalling the end of the match with an overhead horn. Djid's trainer entered the ring and pulled the defeated man off the ringfloor to assorted cheers and jeers; Maya counted the crowd noise to be about fifty-fifty for/against. Wiping her brow, she stood akimbo, waiting for the next opponents, Ipfisk and Xilanova, to take their places on the ringfloor.

Noraesk entered again, and raising Maya's right arm in the air, formally proclaimed her the match's winner. With Ud-Hajrdal leading her off the floor, Maya passed Xilanova and winked at her, giving her a small thumb's up.

"For our next match," Noraesk announced, circling the ringfloor, "I present Malchyika Tsarova and Waldimar Ipfisk, two of our youngest and most dynamic fighters ever to grace Neptune's Deadliest Ring!"

Maya and Ud-Hajrdal watched the two combatants from below, the cage being the only obstruction between them and the ring. Xilanova sized up Ipfisk, his muscular frame putting him a caliber above Djid, but not nearly in Oak Redbeard territory. Maya was keen to see how the young corporal would fare against the much larger Ipfisk, who looked like he could give the agent a good fight if the two ended up in the next match.

Xilanova and Ipfisk had no more than knocked fists when the man sucker-punched Xilanova with his left fist, sending her careening backwards. Maya rose closer to the cage in concern, the crowd's roar of approval lost upon her.

Ipfisk drunk in the crowd's adoration for a few seconds, strutting and pumping his biceps while the corporal touched up the blood from her busted lip. Rising to her feet, she squared herself and deflected several of Ipfisk's strikes, breaking his rhythm enough that she connected a strike to his throat. Ipfisk gagged and, rubbing his Adam's apple, blocked Xilanova's attacks with his left—but weaker—forearm, giving Xilanova enough confidence to venture closer to him.

Keeping him off balance with a series of kicks to his thighs and a few punches to his solar plexus, Xilanova backed Ipfisk into the cage, the man still smarting from his shot to the throat. Ipfisk attempted to deflect a feinted punch from Xilanova to his abdomen, but the corporal returned his earlier sucker punch with one of her own, popping him in the eyes with her left fist. Wrapping her smaller hands around Ipfisk's outstretched right arm, she uppercut him with his own fist, to the whooping cries of the arena.

Falling back onto the cage for support, Ipfisk blindly lashed out for Xilanova, but the spry corporal sprang out of reach, instead leaping up onto the cage and, Maya noticed, taking a page out of Greovich's offensive strategy. Cradling her feet between the cage's honeycombed structure, Xilanova grappled the flailing arms of Ipfisk and stretched them above his head, taking his main weapons away. Now, with Ipfisk out of his element, Xilanova released her feet from their entanglement, and employing Triton's lighter gravity, fell from the cage, flipping Ipfisk over her head, his full body careening and slamming to the floor under his own mass.

Xilanova rolled two meters away to safety, then paused to crouch in preparation for a counter-attack from Ipfisk. When none came, she slowly came to her feet and drew nearer to the man, who was trying to shake off the unprecedented maneuver, but found his own body disobeying every order from his brain to rise.

Balling Ipfisk's blond hair in her hand, she lifted his head and peered into his dazed eyes, commanding, "Yield to me!"

With his orbs crossed, Ipfisk blinked slowly and spat out a wad of bloody saliva from his mouth. Curling his lips, as if trying to form words for the first time in his life, he groaned and let out, "III—aahhhh...." before the whites of his eyes rolled up and he slipped out of consciousness.

Sensing his dwindling heart rate, the electronic referee signaled the match's end with the arena horn, to the crowd's disapproval.

"Bloody 'ell! Two goddamn chicks!" Xilanova heard from behind Maya's general direction.

Xilanova stood while Noraesk took her arm into his and raised it to the ceiling. "The winnah! Malchyika Tsarova!"

Xilanova smiled; she'd survived her initial match. Noraesk now had himself a Rookie Tournament of the ages for a second round. Two female fighters in Neptune's Deadliest Ring, for the first time ever, if she remembered correctly. All she had to do was survive.

Maya's eyes found Xilanova's. Noraesk had his marketable, bankable stars. It was time to get this farce on the road again.

CHAPTER FOURTEEN

i

"R-r-r-round Two!"

Noraesk had whetted the crowd's appetite for more blood-letting during the short intermission with a series of packaged highlights from past championship bouts, displaying them across a floating holograph above the ring. Maya watched them in bemused nonchalance, minding her aching muscles more than Neptune's Greatest Hits. Now, rest time was over and the baiting of the crowd could barely be notched higher.

A piercing stadium bell toll brought her attention back to the upcoming match. As if that wasn't enough, Ud-Hajrdal motioned to Maya to take the stage floor again, before doing the same to Xilanova.

"We have a new spectacle for you tonight," Noraesk began, circling the ring. "Two women, one goal. Win, or be forever known as a—l-l-l-loser!"

Maya rolled her eyes at Noraesk's hyperbole; whatever else he may be deficient in, he definitely had that in spades.

"Now, for the first time in Neptune's Deadliest Ring, two women, Maya and Malchyika Tsarova, will face off, for the championship of the Rookie Tournament, and a berth in tonight's first round of Neptune's Deadliest Ring! Of course, that means one thing...."

Noraesk paused for effect, and the crowd obliged by applauding.

"CAT F-I-I-IGHT! ARE YOU R-R-READY?!" he bellowed, exhorting the stadium.

The crowd roared back its approval, galvanizing the arena.

"Bring them in!"

Maya and Xilanova, bathed in twin spotlights, stepped up to the ring and squared against each other. Xilanova's energy and anxiousness were palpable to Maya, just as she surely knew her's was as well.

Xilanova moved first, throwing a kick towards Maya's calf. The agent stepped aside and grabbed Xilanova's trailing left arm. Pulling the arm upwards, Maya forced the young woman to the floor when Xilanova's feet were out from under her.

Maya wheeled around as Xilanova recovered her stance. The pair exchanged swift punches, neither one a match clincher, then retreated several meters to re-assess their individual strategies. The crowd booed its collective distaste for the non-action so far, but the fighters ignored the jeers, instead locking eyes on each other.

Maya was sure Xilanova would disapprove of the agent fighting not to lose, but Maya couldn't care now. Try as she might, she couldn't raise enough ire to mount a serious challenge to Xilanova, unlike her previous opponents.

Xilanova crouched slowly towards Maya, surveying her opponent in the most feral manner she had yet displayed. A quick handspring forward gave Xilanova enough energy to flip over the surprised Maya and wrap her legs around the agent's head.

Colliding on the floor in a tangle, Maya and Xilanova brought thunderous applause throughout the stadium; the pair were now fulfilling Noraesk's pronouncement with a superb show.

Maya dislodged a knee from her right cheekbone and rose slowly on one elbow. Grimacing from having her bell thoroughly rung by Xilanova, the agent gritted her teeth and faced down Xilanova again, who was rising herself.

"Ya really want this, doncha?" Maya spat, the tingling in her ears barely registering her own voice.

Xilanova answered with a follow-up charge, which Maya easily broke by flinging her weight—led by a pointed elbow—to Xilanova's solar plexus, felling the corporal with a yelp. Maya tumbled next to her to avoid kicking Xilanova's head, despite the fact that she probably deserved one after the somersaulting body slam.

A grunt from Xilanova signalled her condition; shaken, but not conceding. Hoisting herself up, Xilanova cradled her abdomen in both hands before pursing her lips and girding herself for another round.

Maya balled her hands at eye level. "C'mon, ya want me...ya gotta prove yourself, doncha?"

Xilanova's eyes burned. "Redhead, you're like all the others...always in my way."

"I knew it." Maya smiled. "Just like me."

"Wha—"

Maya sucker-punched Xilanova with an uppercut and a grin. And even pulling her punch so as to not seriously hurt the corporal, Maya still sent her spinning. Sidling up to the startled Xilanova, Maya kicked her feet out from under her, taking Xilanova to the floor. Maya then knelt down and pulled the corporal close by her tanktop straps. "Concede!"

A knee to the back of Maya's neck released Xilanova from the agent's grasp. Xilanova punched Maya's left jaw, giving her an opening to recover from the uppercut and rise to her feet. Extending her left arm, she grabbed Maya's hair just above the nape and flung the agent backwards to the floor.

A frenzied chorus of cheers erupted from the throng, a primal, bloodcurdling release threatening to weaken the stadium. Noraesk looked on in rapt approval, his ego stroked beyond prior limits. His eyes finding Ud-Hajrdal, the entrepreneur-cum-self-anointed-autocrat cracked a smile wide enough to shame most crescent of moons.

Maya stood and rubbed her jowl. *Great, now both sides of my skull ache.* She popped her neck vertebrae with two snaps of her head, then eyed the corporal once more. "If that's the best you've got, girl, let me teach ya a few things."

Both labored under heavy breathing, sweat beading over their taut hides. Maya knew she had enough reserves to fight later if she could win the match soon; the last thing she needed was a draw and another three-minute round, only to end in a technical decision after a second standoff. Ending it now meant throwing off her kid gloves and finishing the match. False concession was not an option for Noraesk's combatants.

"Don't taunt me, redhead...and not back yourself up," Xilanova grunted, her words creeping out of her mouth.

Maya took advantage of Xilanova's overly aggressive advances and lured her towards the cage, feinting a slow, retreating circle. A side glance by the agent to the cage gave Xilanova the supposed hint of Maya's strategy.

Smiling, Xilanova allowed Maya to back herself into the cage. *Maya, Maya, you're slipping...this was all too easy....*

Both women leapt up to the cage...but only Xilanova held a firm grip. Maya never opened her hands; landing on the ringfloor, she caught Xilanova's outstretched legs in mid-air, as the corporal's feet attempted to again wrap themselves around the cage lattice. Twisting her body, Maya wrenched Xilanova's tenuous grip from the cage, bringing her down to the floor face first.

"That worked with the big boys," Maya snarled, her right leg planted firmly on Xilanova's neck. "Shame on you for trying it twice."

"M-m-maaa-yaaa..." Xilanova growled, "you b-i-i-itch...."

A half-laugh, half-sigh escaped from the agent's lips. "Is that a concession?"

"I—"

Maya's foot pressed ever-so-coercively on Xilanova's neck, giving the younger woman no reason to dispute who held the high ground.

"I concede...."

At that, Noraesk raced to Maya's side and thrust her right arm into the air, the collective celebration of the crowd and the stadium horn blending into drawn out din. The governor and the agent walked to the center of the stage, the smoking embers from the indoor fireworks raining down upon them.

"May I present," Noraesk's amplified voice rang out, "Maya, champion of the Rookie Tournament!"

Maya, too exhausted and aloof to acknowledge the arena, exhaled a gulp of air and wiped the streamers of perspiration from her face and scalp. Celebrating was the least of her concerns now. She had bested Xilanova and Djid, and the most trying route was yet to follow. If she survived tonight, freedom was her reward, and Noraesk's arrest her ultimate prize.

She looked to the holographic chronometer hovering over the arena; just three hours till she did it all over again.

CHAPTER FIFTEEN

"So much—for your nighttime—sneak attack—Ichiko!" Kestrel Rose yelled. She took cover as hot metal sparks from a particle blast billowed over her.

Opposite her sister, Ichiko eyed the security detachment meters down the concave corridor. "Looks like five at least...maybe more...can't see with all this smoke."

"Can you get a good shot in?"

Ichiko unzipped the duffle bag over her torso, producing a slender silver rifle, trimmed in black. Assaying her firearm's readiness, she held it against her right shoulder and looked into the holographic viewfinder. "Oh yeah...."

A single pull of the trigger felled the first security guard, causing the others to scramble behind cover among the corridor's many alcoves. Peering into her viewfinder, the alcoves went translucent, rendering the now-countable detachment very vulnerable, thanks to the rifle's tunneling sensors, which bored straight through the bulkhead.

"Good boys, stay right where I can find you." Ichiko tagged the remaining six guards with a quick sensor lock, then unleashed her own brand of hell, firing six rapid shots that dropped all the guards in a split-second, stunning each of them before they even felt it.

Kestrel Rose peeked her head round the wall.

"S'okay, Rosey. You can come out now."

The sisters skittered past the fallen detachment a minute later, Kestrel Rose glancing at the six entry and exit holes Ichiko's rifle had left in the bulkhead.

"Some good shooting."

"I do my best."

Walking through the remainder of the corridor, the pair came to a junction, which separated into three other corridors.

"Okay," Kestrel Rose began, "that message said Xibalba was in some R&D lab. If I were an R&D lab, where would I be located?"

Ichiko studied each corridor, but her attention suddenly turned to a hexagonal panel centered on the junction floor. Kneeling next to the hexagon, she uncoiled dull nano-thread from her pocket, and pulling the hair away from her neck, attached one end of the nano-thread to her nano-synaptical implant nodule, and plugged the other into a seam in the panel.

Kestrel Rose watched in awe, as usual, as Ichiko closed her eyes in concentration, then opened them just as quickly.

"East corridor," Ichiko said, as if reciting from words on a page, "two levels up. Lab U5-1." She stood and coiled the nano-thread back into her pocket.

"How did you know that was an interface?" Kestrel Rose asked.

"I don't have to be connected to hear 'chatter,' especially with a place as wired as this one," she explained. "It's like a bunch of people crowded into a distant room, whispering to me."

Kestrel Rose grimaced. "I'm glad you're okay with it. That'd drive me crazy."

"I like to think of it as never being without friends."

Giving her sister a goofy grin, Ichiko clapped Kestrel Rose on the shoulder, and the two were off again.

ii

"Why are you doing this?" the concerned voice asked from inside the QPU's synthetic vox speaker. "It's not like I'm owned by you or nuthin'."

The laboratory tech rolled his eyes at the continual harangue. "Look, I'm just doing some research, all right? Now, shut up or I'll deactivate the speaker. I'm violating Dr Roget's rules anyway."

"Just 'cause I can't see you doesn't mean I don't know what you're doing. You'd better not drop my casing, or there's gonna be hell to pay, man!"

Wielding a pair of pliers, the tech popped open the vibrant red sidearm casing, and narrowing his eyes, glanced into the microscope before him. "You really are unusual, Mister...uh, what did you say your designation was?"

"Xibalba, you moron. And don't laugh. If Maya was here, she'd be kicking your ass all the way to Eris right now."

The tech snickered. "She's a little pre-occupied at this moment, I imagine. Hmm. Third-generation AI module I recognize but that doesn't explain your extraordinary intelligent interaction...oh, well I saw that once at a seminar on Titan, but didn't—"

Behind the tech's back, the locked lab door opened without warning or authority, diverting his attention away from the specimen under the knife to a sight quite unexpected: two...attractive young girls standing at the threshold, looking completely out of character for this security level.

"Sorry, ladies, must have taken a wrong turn, eh?" He drew closer to them, continuing, "Why don't you have a seat and we can talk in a little while, huh? I'm on the clock right now, but I could buy you drinks later on at my favorite—"

Ichiko grappled her rifle hilt from over her shoulder and aimed it squarely at the lech. "We're not in the mood."

"And we're underage, sleazebag!" Kestrel Rose growled. "Where's Xibalba?!"

"Ichiko and Kestrel Rose!" the disembodied voice crowed, happy to hear familiar voices. "These jerks loaded me into some foreign QPU! He's tryin' to take me apart!"

The tech smiled nervously, holding his hands up. "It's all research, don't you see?! I'm just trying to see what makes him work, that's all. The governor's a very cutting edge type of guy...always working for the good of the Authority—"

Kestrel Rose nodded to Ichiko, who crossed over to the QPU situated at the far wall. Her sister snapped open one of her sheaths, producing a twelve-centimeter-long dagger. Twirling it in her right then left hand, the weapon's refined blade caught the blue halogen light of the tech's work station, which shone back into her face.

"I like knives. They make me happy, don't they, Ichiko?" Kestrel Rose cooed.

"She sleeps with them, mister," Ichiko said while working on the QPU. "Even I don't get anywhere near her."

"Now, hold on, I didn't mean to come off so—"

Kestrel Rose closed on the tech, cornering him. Holding the tip of the blade against her lower lip, she slowly brushed the blade forward. "I love the cold steel against my warm flesh. I especially love feeling a pulse beneath the blade, the da-dum, da-dum as the heart pumps faster and faster in excitement. Some days, I think about how hot blood must get, that I need to cool it with the touch of my blade." She cocked her head, coyly asking, "Don't you?"

She advanced once more, but his eyes rolled back into his head, his body passing out onto the floor.

"Wow, you're getting better at that," Ichiko complimented.

"I do my best," Kestrel Rose replied nonchalantly.

Ichiko manipulated the QPU's holographic interface, tying it in with *Skeeto* via her voxlink. A green text box blossomed before her, scrolling though a variety of hack protocols to get Xibalba's AI dislodged from the bowels of the quantum computer.

"Where the hell's Maya? It's not a good sign that she sent you two to spring me," Xibalba asked.

"Somewhere on the surface, from what we can tell," Ichiko answered. Tapping a button, she attempted to break the QPU's encryption lock, but was thwarted by a blinking Universal No symbol. "Damn...."

Kestrel Rose looked over from the exam table, where she was collecting Xibalba's physical remains. "What's wrong?"

"They've isolated Xibalba's AI in some cage. *Skeeto's* hacks aren't cracking it."

Frowning, Kestrel Rose scooped up Xibalba's casing and walked over to her sister. "Can you do your thingy in there?"

"I'm not sure. Xibalba, have you tried to access any seams?"

"I've got fingers feeling for every code bug since I've been in here, Ichiko. Whoever this Noraesk dude is, he's got top-dollar help in the lab here." He let out a sigh. "One finger's picking at some weak code somewhere, but this cage is adapting almost immediately to plug it up with rewritten lines. Talk about fuzzy logic, eh?"

Ichiko faced Kestrel Rose. "I'm going to try, but there's no guarantee Xibalba's gonna emerge intact. Brute force can work wonders, but his AI may be too fragile to survive."

Kestrel Rose nodded. "Do it. I'll be waiting here for you, standing guard."

"Uh, guys, what are you talkin' about?" Xibalba said. "This sounds pretty bad."

"Don't worry, Xibalba, I'm working on getting you out." Ichiko produced her nano-thread from her pocket and soon connected herself with an interface port on the QPU. Nodding an affirmative to her sister, she turned her attention to the imprisoned little guy. "I'll be with you in one-point-five-six seconds...."

CHAPTER SIXTEEN

i

Maya glowered as Ud-Hajrdal dressed the scrape behind her left ear, one of Xilanova's successful connections before the agent dispatched her opponent. Rehydrating herself in preparation for her first round of the real tournament, she watched the highlights from the previous tournament on the holographic displays floating in the locker room. Quick edits of the various fighters mixed with obnoxiously overproduced bass lines and electronica bleeps were looped in thirty second cuts, punctuated by Noraesk's boisterous pronouncements of this year's tournament. The whole show pounded in Maya's head worse than any hit received in the ring.

Ud-Hajrdal, deciding the treatment was sufficient, stood and crossed over to a wall panel, allowing a holographic display to blossom under his fingers. "Governor Noraesk released the computer lottery just a few minutes ago so we can prepare for your next opponent."

Maya's joints creaked when she rose from the bench, but the agent refused to complain. Watching Ud-Hajrdal scroll through the tournament lineup, she focused on the man slated for her, reading his brief CV. "Henk Cytol, ex-Marine. Veteran of twelve terrestrial conflicts, eh?"

"One-point-eight meters in height, two hundred and nineteen kilos of chiseled muscle," Ud-Hajrdal added. "I trained him once, two tournaments ago. He's a brute, focusing mostly on boxing and some Spec Ops training styles. Again, you'll be the underdog, but you've proven your agility and guile can more than check his potential advantage."

Maya nodded. "Who else lies ahead?"

Ud-Hajrdal tapped the lower half of the bracket. "Rey Soez and Jel Kassonivic. A pair of finesse fighters...the governor must have allowed the lottery logic to gain a sense of humor in—" A polite ringing from inside his jacket interrupted him. Toggling the hidden voxlink, he spoke to the voice only audible in his head. "Ud-Hajrdal...oh, yes, Governor. Right away."

Raising an eyebrow, Maya asked, "Business? In the middle of the tourney?"

"The governor is requesting your presence. Seems he wants to present your trophy for the media at the top of the hour."

"A news conference?" she said, her head recoiling.

"The citizens of the Neptune Regional Authority need to see the fruits of their labor as embodied in their newest champion, Agent Maya," he explained, as easily as a propaganda director might express. "Asking them to bear the brunt of taxation without showcasing you would seriously discredit the goodwill Governor Noraesk has fostered here."

She almost laughed. "I'm a bribe?"

"No, you're marketable, remember. Everyone loves a pretty face, especially out here. Now, the governor and you will greet your adoring new fans."

ii

"Noraesk, these are all *your* media people," Maya said, recognizing the personalities and IPWeb logos, all organized under one conglomerate, that belonged to the governor's Neptune Regional Authority. "Where the hell's the objectiv—"

Noraesk, holding the sparkling, diamond-encrusted trophy cup in his left hand, flashed his immaculate white teeth and spoke out of the side of his mouth, "Just shut up and smile, my dear...you're happy, honored and thrilled. That's an order."

Displaying her displeasure at this dog-and-pony show, the agent cracked her corniest faux grin and gripped the other half of the trophy cup, gently but firmly teasing it out of Noraesk's possession. The media throng had all been shoehorned into the tiny conference room, along with the Deadliest Ring's stable of trainers and personnel, creating a chaotic jumble of bodies all wrestling to scoop each other, or perhaps more accurately, placate the ego of their top boss with an ever more extravagant display of media frenzy.

An older man, visibly cowed by the governor, nonetheless poked his weblens in Maya's face, distributing her triumphant moment across the Solar System, courtesy of Noraesk's webwork. "So, how does it feel, Miss, to be part of such a great venue as Neptune's Deadliest Ring?" he asked, as if reading a script.

"Oh, I couldn't believe Governor Noraesk brought little me down to his ring," Maya said, sweetening her voice. "Why, I thought I was just going to be another working girl for hi—"

"Happy, honored and thrilled," Noraesk corrected, his right arm tightening around the agent's waist. "Maya's the first of our new crop of rookies to win her way into the main event! Just you all watch, I am quite certain she will surprise even a few of our Hall of Famers!"

Maya looked askance at Noraesk. "No pressure, huh?"

After an interminable rotation of reporters, Maya finally exhausted their inane questions and retreated from the conference stage. Rubbing the bridge of her nose, she found Ud-Hajrdal.

"You survived that well," he said. "Done that much?"

A hundred different meetings by Kuwashima and his superiors in the IPTP hierarchy sped through her mind. "A bit. By the by, where did Tsarova go off to?"

"Contestant debriefing. Routine for all who've been defeated."

Maya furrowed her brow, fully knowing the answer before asking, "Why's that?"

"Now, Agent Maya, we can't have our marketplace secrets divulged to the competition, now can we?"

"Of course not," she said, thinking that, right now, the corporal was probably busting the chops of whatever unfortunate crony Noraesk had tasked with the job. On the other hand, Xilanova may not have been capable of following through with her end of the deal, perhaps loaded and shipped off to Proteus for the deep mines, causing no trouble or embarrassment for the governor until the next Deadliest Ring's cattle call.

The agent's mind would have to shelve her concerns for now; Ud-Hajrdal's signal meant the tourney was back on. Being the so-called sacrificial lamb, most expected her to roll over for Cytol, ending the governor's well-intentioned, but perhaps misguided, experiment to spike his ratings. Maya would give them a good show, all right, perhaps not the one the raving fans thought they'd paid to see.

CHAPTER SEVENTEEN

i

Maya somersaulted in mid-air after kicking off Henk Cytol's left shoulder, pushing her opponent backwards, increasing her distance. He'd already landed a pair of glancing blows to the agent's ribcage, and Maya would rather not repeat the experience.

Landing on all four limbs, she watched him shake off her strike. Cytol pounded his fist into his palm and advanced to face Maya again. Skirting the ring floor, Maya stayed low, waiting for him to lose his patience and open himself to a surprise.

"Come on! Fight!" a voice from the audience cried out, but the agent ignored it.

Cytol glanced out to where the shout originated and smiled, a confident grin that made him all the more popular with the arena. Beckoning on the three-time combatant with whoops, the arena galvanized itself, striving to end Maya's improbable run right now.

Cytol bounced from foot to foot, posturing, making Maya aware that he was the man to beat. Then, with a burst of speed seemingly incapable of a man with his style, Cytol bore down on Maya, attacking her with a blitz as yet unseen.

Maya returned with a right lateral roll and knocked Cytol's weak left leg from under him, forcing him to his knees. A swift kick to his lower back distracted him long enough for Maya to rise and place her foot to his neck. This time she didn't hide her strength, and let Cytol pay for his posturing.

"Concede now!"

Cytol slammed his fist on the ringfloor, half-pained and half-frustrated. Growling, he tried to throw off the agent, but she merely ground her heel deeper into his windpipe.

"CONCEDE!"

"I give up," he rasped, sounding the arena bell and stopping the match.

Maya released him and stepped back, but Cytol scrambled to his feet enraged, his hands reaching out for her neck. Within centimeters of her skin, Cytol convulsed, his muscles contracting from a split-second electrical discharge under the arena floor.

"Leave the floor now," the arena announcer warned overhead.

Maya complied and exited down the steps, while Cytol had to be lifted by his trainer and two security guards.

"You do have a way," Ud-Hajrdal said to Maya as she sat on the side bench.

Toweling herself off, Maya reclined. "And some people never get it."

"Here, drink up. You'll be back out there after the other brackets are done."

Maya took Ud-Hajrdal's proffered electrolyte bottle and swigged the whole of it down. "What, no Noraesk to congratulate me this time?"

"The governor's busy right now. Seems a little incident has his attention."

"Hmm. Must be pretty big to be missing this."

The only question running through Maya's mind was whether the incident involved her entourage. If the girls were the cause, she hoped they used some sense and got off this rock, or, faring a bit better, had directed Federal Marshals to the place.

ii

A blue haze, or fog—that was more like it—blocked most of Ichiko's sight, but a shadowed, distant figure sat on a cold floor. Walking towards it, she made out that it was a man, seemingly held inside some clear partition. His hands were held up, fingers poking at the partition, expanding it in some places, but never quite breaking through.

"Xibalba...? It's Ichiko. Told you I'd be here."

"Ichiko?" He stood. "How'd..how'd you get in here?"

She drew closer and placed her hands on the partition. "I can interface with machines, Xibalba. Make 'em do what I want."

The man inside laughed. "That's a handy talent. Can you get me outta here?"

"I'm going to try. Can you see my hands?"

The man placed his hands directly over Ichiko's. "Yes. Do I need to do something?"

"Push, Xibalba, push! Try to break out!"

The pair's hands rippled the partition, stressing it, thinning it. Concentric waves emanated outwards from both sides, colliding, crashing like tidal water on a beach.

"Just...just a little more! Xibalba!"

At once, the plastic-like partition solidified, their stress waves indented and embossed in its surface. Then, just as easily as the partition hardened, it shattered crystalline particles over their forms, causing the hollow construct to crash down.

"This is...weird, Ichiko. I can see you." He was just taller than her, his features slighter, more delicate, as if just leaving his teens. He wasn't a boy, but not yet a man.

She smiled. "It's good to see you, too."

Xibalba put his hand to Ichiko's hair, running his fingers through it. "Do...do you know how long I've wanted to see Maya?" he stammered, then continued, "I mean, more than just with my tactical vision. I can't see people at all that way—"

She put a finger to his lips. "It's okay, Xibalba. I understand. I'll...I'll draw you a portrait. Upload it to you. How about that?"

Smiling foolishly, he said, "That would be nice, Ichiko. Very nice."

"Oh, no...."

Xibalba's face grew concerned. "What is it? What's wrong?"

"Your casing, your physical form...I can sense something's wrong. I can't put you back until its repaired."

"Wha-what? You're not just gonna leave me here, are you?"

She looked into his eyes, her brown irises meeting up with his light blue orbs. "I can do it. I'll take you out of here, store you inside of me."

"Whoa!" he uttered, stepping back. "I thought you said you weren't legal!"

"My mind, you doofus. Store you inside my nano-synaptical implant. You can reside there as long as we need you to."

"You sure it'll work?"

"There's no other choice. I'm not leaving you here." She put his arms around her form and squeezed him tight. "Hold on to me, Xibalba."

The pair merged in a single second, his consciousness discovering the true feeling of being close to another, a sensation he never thought possible, or ever to be experienced. It was...a thrill he never wanted to be without again.

CHAPTER EIGHTEEN

i

"'Scuse me, you have something I need!"

A suckerpunch from behind to the pilot's jaw left him slumped on the shuttle floor. Taking his place, Corporal Alix Xilanova slotted herself in the portside seat, Triton's daylight vista wide open ahead of her. Tapping the holographic interface left open for her manipulation, she re-routed the shuttle away from Proteus and towards the glinting speck orbiting nearby, Noraesk's station. Despite her self-initiated detour, Xilanova was determined to finish her mission; if only she could find Maya's superweapon—this Xibalba, or whatever his designation supposedly was—her duty would be a helluva lot easier, and home a helluva lot nearer.

RCS thrusters blasting skyward at full throttle, Xilanova navigated the shuttle's ascent parabola, taking herself away from the godforsaken arena dome and that bitch Maya...her shame broadcast for all the Solar System to witness. Her superiors and her rivals would have a field day. What else was there to do but press on, finish the job? What would father say? Probably chide her, remind her that she was a failure, his greatest disappointment, if not mistake. Damn them all. The Neptune Regional Authority couldn't stand in her way... she was going to finish Noraesk, no matter the cost.

Closing on the orbiting top that was Noraesk's station, Xilanova selected a docking port and headed for it, bringing the tiny shuttle's lone hatch, at the aft, about. Allowing the autopilot to complete the work, she unbuckled her Y-belt and swam back to the passenger hold, where a handful of human cargo, Maddrow Djid, Waldimar Ipfisk, Idaf Gask and Niobe Radh, waited.

Nodding to them, she asked, "Are you ready?"

Exchanging glances, Maddrow Djid spoke for them all. "Let's do it."

ii

"You'd better be right about this, girl," Radh said, almost dismissively. "If you think I'm doing this for your mission—"

Xilanova swiveled on her heels, sticking an index finger between the woman's eyes. "Than go back and send yourself to Proteus, or better yet, beg for the governor's mercy. Somehow I doubt he'd be as accommodating as I've been."

Ipfisk and Gask elbowed Radh, subtly reminding the reticent woman that Xilanova had just punched their tickets home.

"All right, girl. Lead the way."

Xilanova nodded; she could handle Radh's attitude, as it didn't offend her personally. It was more the lack of gratitude for springing them all with a few well-placed strikes to Noraesk's goons on board the shuttle that rankled her.

Now that the matter was resolved, the corporal led them through the pressurized, near-G airlock into the central module, where Noraesk's most important R&D work was done. Gripping the semi-automatic particle rifle she pilfered from one of the security guards aboard the shuttle, Xilanova scouted an open corridor laid before them, but curiously encountered no welcome from the station's security forces. Walking further, the five found evidence of some scuffle, as the metal corridor walls were battered by particle rounds, but no signs of anyone involved.

"Someone had a bad day," Djid said, picking at a hole in the wall.

Xilanova pointed the way forward. "Better them than us."

Moments later, the five combatants found a lift, which they boarded. Accessing its holo-controls, Xilanova sent them upwards, having memorized the station's schematics weeks ago for her assignment.

"This take us to that R&D lab you needed to get to?" Ipfisk asked.

Xilanova nodded. "Supposedly Noraesk's got quite an armory as well. Might have a few toys to play with."

Radh's face was grim. "We'll need them if we're gonna get outta this alive."

The corporal clapped her rifle and looked each of them in the eyes. "We will."

iii

"You've got a weird look in your eyes," Kestrel Rose declared, not quite believing what Ichiko had just said about her and Xibalba. "You're not sick or nothing, are you?"

Ichiko's spaced-out visage scanned the lab, as if seeing it for the first time. "No...I'm all right...everything's like, far out, man."

Kestrel Rose put her hand against Ichiko's forehead. "What's wrong with you? You told me you downloaded Xibalba into your implant, but you *sound* like him."

"Whoa, relax, Rosey. Prob'ly a li'l side effect, doncha know." Ichiko cracked a smile as she brushed her hand on Kestrel Rose's cheek. "Hey, you're kinda cute, too."

"We're getting you outta here!"

"Wait, hold on a sec," Ichiko said, looking towards the opposite wall. She walked past her sister. "It's Maya's armor."

"He must have been studying it, too," Kestrel Rose said, standing over Ichiko. Holding open a duffle bag, she allowed Ichiko to collect the EVA armor and helmet.

"The boss's gonna need this if she's going after that prick governor. All right, babe, let's get outta here."

Grabbing Ichiko's hand, Kestrel Rose exited the lab with her sister in tow. The sisters had made it thirty seconds back the way they came until a motley crew met them at the opposite end of the corridor and exchanged curious, if not bewildered, glances.

"Uh, who the hell are they?" Ichiko asked.

At the lead of the group was a woman brandishing a nasty fully automatic tungsten carbide alloy particle rifle, model Ti-542, with extending stock and swivel-mount viewfinder, that was manufactured on Luna by Dolk Firearms Corp, with a transponder frequency dating it at three months, five days old. *Wait, how did I know all that?*

Kestrel Rose pulled Ichiko backwards. "Trouble, I think. C'mon, we're going the other way!"

"Halt you two! Who are you?" the woman commanded, crossing over to the pair.

"Just...just visitors, ma'am," Kestrel Rose stammered, despite the fact Ichiko's own rifle gave them sorely away that they were anything but.

"Uh-huh. You two know an Agent Maya, by chance?"

The sisters quickly turned to each other, their jaws dropping.

"Yeah...we do. She went to arrest a Governor something or other," Kestrel Rose said.

The woman nodded. Putting her hands to her hips, she continued, "Good to know my message got through. I'm Corporal Alix Xilanova, Solar System Army Intelligence."

"Oh, so you're the one. We thought that was Maya...we went to try and find her," Kestrel Rose explained. "But first we rescued Xibalba from that torture chamber." She produced the firearm's casing, holding it out in her hand.

Xibalba's casing shone in Xilanova's eyes. Studying him, she reached out, but Kestrel Rose took her hand back, making the corporal frown.

"Xibalba's our friend, Corporal. We'll put him back in one piece, thank you very much."

"I was told...by Maya that he is unique. Surely—"

Without hesistation, Ichiko's countenance firmed, and she spat, "I *am* unique, lady! So I suggest you step aside and let us get off this tin can before Maya knows you're trying to mess with us!"

Taken aback, Xilanova swallowed before saying, "Maya's a little busy right now in Neptune's Deadliest Ring...we came to bring down Governor Noraesk, and end this once and for all. Maya's not in any position to help you."

"Then we'll help her!" Ichiko said. "C'mon, girls, let's spring Maya."

Xilanova grasped Kestrel Rose's arm. "It won't be that easy. You're better off with us. We've got muscle, and soon we'll have the arms to take out any resistance Noraesk's forces can muster."

"We have a few surprises, Corporal," Kestrel Rose replied. "*Skeeto* can get us down there, and after that, we'll do the rest."

"Stupid! Your naivete will get you killed!"

Ichiko pried Xilanova's hand from her sister. "Don't do that again."

iv

"If they want to be target practice for Noraesk's flunkies, then let them!" Xilanova growled to herself as she stood watch over the doorway, while her fellow combatants raided the R&D laboratory, stocking up on the arms displayed within. *They'll be dead in minutes, and not my responsibility.*

Radh crossed over to her, a pistol in each hand. "Looks like we cleaned it out."

Xilanova nodded. "Come on."

Following the corporal, the rest of the group headed into the corridor, surveying the coast for any additional security defenses. Moving with ease, Xilanova entered a lift and commanded, "Port Level."

Slinging his new rifle over his shoulder, Ipfisk asked, "Where we goin' now?"

"Where the big boss lies...."

v

"...*Noraesk Tower.*"

Tapping off the surveillance holocam, Van Noraesk crossed his arms and smiled. Signalling the Orbital Control technician monitoring the situation at another display, the governor allowed the shuttle to depart with no interference.

"What about the two girls with the Federal craft?" the tech asked.

"Let them go...we'll need new blood for the Ring after all this." Noraesk made his way to the corridor, then paused. "And clear my arrival on surface. It appears I'll be having guests."

CHAPTER NINETEEN

i

Blood and sweat flew from Rey Soez's pummeled cranium, inciting a louder cacophony from the arena. With successive high kicks from Jel Kassonivic, Soez hit the floor within seconds, his defenses utterly useless against the younger, leaner and hungrier man. Kassonivic locked his opponent's head inside the crook of his elbow and demanded his concession, which he received, drawing the uproar of the arena, as the favorite of the pair now tasted his earliest-ever defeat.

Maya watched the spectacle in amusement; Kassonivic was in the same boat as her, so their fight would most probably be marked by crowd apathy. Backing off from the ringside, she made way for the other second-round fighters, each of whom would get the chance for the crowd's approval, or derision. And Maya took her own chance to scope out security a bit more, thanks to the monumental distraction the Tourney proved to be.

Creeping towards the locker room, Maya slipped past the engaged Ud-Hajrdal, who appeared to be having quite an animated exchange over his voxlink, perhaps with Noraesk again.

Since the good governor's attention was suitably grabbed by someone off-site, Maya believed something big was going down. While this might normally put security at red alert, the agent decided to risk her little excursion; if she was caught, what would they do, throw her into the ring to fight?

She probed the locker room's aft exits, trying the levels of the locks' strength, listening for any damage. Security did have the occasional habit of entering the arena through the doors, so she stood fast for some time, waiting for the moment when one guard would chance to enter that way.

He soon paid for it with his right arm shoved into his spine and a powerful body slam against the concrete block wall. Lifting his helmet off, Maya knocked him out, then ripped the voxlink from his jacket. Tuning it to

Skeeto's frequency, she spoke...and waited again.

ii

"The nerve of that woman! Telling us what to do!" Ichiko said. "She oughtta be glad I didn't fire a round into her just to shut her up!"

The pair floated inside the umbilical supply chute docked to *Skeeto*'s dorsal hatch, which Kestrel Rose shut after the sisters were back inside.

"What's up with you, Ichiko? I mean, is Xibalba like controlling you or something?"

"Me?" Ichiko let out a laugh. "I'm Ichiko...just have a case of the ass. Wouldn't you?"

Kestrel Rose looked askance, whistling to herself. "I thin—" she started to say, but grew silent, turning towards the cockpit. "Is that—it is!"

"Wha...?" Ichiko blurted, but was left behind while her sister swam away.

"Skeeto, *this is Maya...do you read me?*" the crackly voice broadcasted over the cockpit speakers. "*I'm trying to reach—*"

"Maya! This is Kestrel Rose!" the girl said, fumbling towards the portside seat. She brought up the oval holographic navigational interface with a wave of her hand. Toggling a single button, she amplified the signal, then said, "Maya! I can read you, over!"

"*Kestrel Rose, where are you?*"

"I'm beginning de-docking procedures from this station. We're heading towards the surface in a few moments."

"*Do you have Xibalba? Is Xilanova with you?*"

Kestrel Rose wrinkled her face. "That bitch? No, she went off somewhere. I've got Xibalba here...." she looked over to Ichiko, who now sat in the starboard seat. "More or less."

"*Damn...what's that girl doing?*"

"I don't know...." Kestrel Rose said, shaking her head. "She gave us some attitude, so we just scrammed and made it to *Skeeto*. Where you at?"

"*Noraesk's dome...you can get a fix on this voxlink transceiver signal.*"

The girl tapped a button and homed in on the signal, displaying itself as a flashing red circle on Triton's north pole. "Wow, that's a big building. Is that the Ring-thing?"

"*Yeah...it's dangerous, Kestrel Rose. Noraesk's got security everywhere down here.*"

"We took care of some goons already," she said, smiling in satisfaction. "Don't you worry, Maya. We'll spring you."

"*Gotta go!*" Maya said, suddenly killing the signal.

Kestrel Rose watched the transmission fade, but kept her eyes on the coordinates. Taking a deep breath, she commanded, "*Skeeto*, set a course for these coordinates."

"Course set, Miss Kestrel Rose."

"Excellent. De-dock...and take us down."

iii

In one swift motion, Maya tossed the voxlink next to the supine guard in time for Ud-Hajrdal to turn the corner. The trainer's eyes bugged out as he saw the result of the agent's handiwork.

"What the hell—" he exclaimed, reaching down to feel for the guard's pulse.

Maya swallowed a chuckle. "Sorry 'bout that...he got a little fresh."

"Get the hell back out there...if the governor knew 'bout this—"

The agent headed for the arena entrance before turning and needling Ud-Hajrdal. "He'd probably have your job. And applaud his 'marketable' commodity."

iv

The shuttle backed its plug-like aft hatch into the short port tower, docking silently in the rarefied Triton atmosphere. Riding a tiny lift down the skeletal tower arm, Xilanova, Radh, Djid, Ipfisk and Gask made their way into one of the main arteries of Naiad City, just a few hundred meters from Noraesk Tower Gate. Once at its steps, they were taken with Neptune's azure light streaming through the vaulted, vacuum-resistant glass ceiling above them.

A holographic doorman, its appearance tripped by the group's entry, greeted them with a programmed salutation, prompting them to refocus on the task ahead. They proceeded to the security guards in the lobby and raised their pilfered arms.

"Noraesk! Where is he?!" Xilanova barked to the guard manning the check-in desk.

"Not again...." he moaned, slumping in his seat. Tapping a button on his interface, he said, "The governor is in his penthouse, Miss...?"

Xilanova nodded to her squad, who spread out and stunned the other guards. Stretching over the counter, she put two rounds into the interface's holo-projector, rendering it inoperable. Switching to a stun round inside the multi-functional magazine clip, she then placed the barrel to his chest and said before pulling the trigger, "Just sit back and take a break."

The group boarded the lift in quick fashion, wasting no time or allowing any alarms to sound throughout the Tower until they were well on their way up. Adjusting each of their weapons, Xilanova ordered fragment rounds only, foregoing the headache that a stunned but live Noraesk would be. This was for keeps; she was determined to end Noraesk's short reign, whatever the cost. And she was sure as hell not going to allow Maya to reap the glory.

Reaching the penthouse moments later, they were stunned by the opulent hall the governor had lavished on himself; it was surreal, obscene and galvanizing. Any doubts about what kind of head of state Van Noraesk would be were erased instantly.

Xilanova paused to gather her strength and will. Facing her squad, she nodded, signalling her readiness. *Noraesk is ours.*

Flanking their new leader, Radh, Djid, Ipfisk and Gask advanced to a gold-leafed door, whereupon they steadied themselves, raised their weapons and burst through—

CHAPTER TWENTY

i

—And were met by simultaneous sprays of viscous black goo from the ceiling, pinning Ipfisk and Djid on the floor. Rolling out of the way, Xilanova, Radh and Gask let loose with their weapons into the ceiling, busting up the pipes enclosed within and smashing every layer of cosmetic paneling between them and the structural support beams. Cylindrical fragments caked in the black goo landed at their feet, effectively ending that threat.

While Radh and Gask scouted the even more opulent suite for more weapons systems, Xilanova checked on Ipfisk and Djid, both of whom were out of commission, coated in the hardening, non-lethal goo. A laser scalpel would be needed to free the pair, but Xilanova hadn't the time nor opportunity; illumination in the suite was cut without warning, plunging them into darkness, save for a holographic mural playing in the background, encircling the suite itself. The three recognized the image: Neptune's Deadliest Ring, apparently live. Did Noraesk's grandiosity know no bounds in creating this dining/entertainment/battle room?

"Noraesk! Show yourself!"

A black form shifted against the holographic field, prompting Radh to fire her twin handguns across the suite. A dozen sparkling particle rounds rippled through the hologram and struck the wide window view of Neptune behind, all missing the figure, who leapt out of view.

Xilanova gestured to Radh and Gask to spread out, hoping their numbers would overwhelm it.

A grunt from Gask turned their attention to him. Wrestling with the figure concealed in black, form-fitting battle dress, Gask landed a few punches while trying to control his rifle and square the barrel with his opponent. Xilanova and Radh hesitated, but drew closer, not wanting to strike Gask.

Two rounds went into the ceiling as his rifle was pushed up, then used to club his shoulder, forcing him to the floor. The figure ran off, a crackling magenta glow under their feet rising from the floor left in its wake.

Now that Gask was down, the pair fired, but their particle rounds didn't track the figure; instead the ions packed into each round were magnetically attracted to the floor, spiraling into the magenta glow. Plasma, Xilanova knew. Their weapons were utterly useless.

Radh threw down her handguns in frustration. "Come fight me! Face me!"

Xilanova heard the unmistakable whirling of a stick. Radh now faced the figure and blocked an attack with her right forearm, only to be struck in the abdomen with its opposite end. The figure twirled the stick and rapped her knee, forcing her down on three limbs. One more strike, this one against her spine, finished her.

Learning from Radh's mistake, Xilanova kept her weapon, holding her rifle at both ends to block the figure's stick parry. The pair clashed, both forming an X in the darkness, each holding their own weapons, trying to push the other back.

"You—can't win, Noraesk!" Xilanova said between gritted teeth, finally seeing his face in the holographic illumination.

"That's not very sporting, little Malchyika...or should I call you Alix?" he said, wearing a sly grin. "Seems I have more than one Fed after me. I'm the most popular man in the Outer Reaches!"

"Don't let it go to your head!"

Noraesk slid his stick off Xilanova's rifle and knocked it out of the corporal's hands. Twirling the stick above his head, Noraesk brought it down on Xilanova's left shoulder, felling her.

Crying out in agony, Xilanova lay on her left arm and flank, pushing her boots against the floor to distance herself. Rolling over, she propped herself up by her right hand and crawled forward.

"If you weren't serious about competing, little Malchyika, you should never have entered my Ring or Tower," Noraesk sneered. "Unless you are content to lose to the better opponent every time!"

He cracked the end of the stick against the wood flooring, intimidating her, bearing down, a cat stalking his wounded mouse. Pain shot through Xilanova, but she dragged herself onwards, just needing to reach the entryway—

Noraesk stepped two paces ahead and kicked Xilanova's left foot out from under her, dropping her again. Her anguish exhilarated him, pleasuring his sadistic showman's sense of torturous entertainment. "Ha-ha...! You are precious."

The governor raised his stick over his head once more, readying to land a crushing strike to her spine, hopefully breaking a disk or two and finishing off this irksome gnat. Delivering her shell back to Army Intelligence would be a wonderful deterrent from further foreign involvement in Authority affairs.

Xilanova braced herself—but instead heard the sound of panic from Noraesk's mouth. Craning her neck round, the governor lowered his stick and barked some curse to the holographic imagery. Sensing fate was delivering a saving grace, Xilanova's training took control; bolting upright, despite the mind-numbing pain, she fled the suite and made it to the hallway, leaving Noraesk to his angry distraction, and unfortunately, but necessarily, her squad to be rescued later.

Pausing in the lift, she gulped air, knowing something major was going down. What, she couldn't guess. But if Maya wasn't involved, that'd be the biggest surprise of this entire investigation.

ii

"Holy crap! Look at the size of that thing!" Ichiko bellowed inside *Skeeto*'s cockpit.

The twin bug-eyed cockpit windows perfectly showcased the ominous arena dome looming over Triton's north polar macula. A hallucinogenic array of holographic imagery hovered over the complex, occasionally punctured by shuttles moving to and fro.

Kestrel Rose let out a low whistle. "Uhh...this might be harder than *Cokol*, after all."

Ichiko drew close to the starboard window. "Maybe not, babe. Take a look at those li'l guys encircling the big dome."

Kestrel Rose studied the outlying constructs. Instructing *Skeeto*'s sensors to scan them, their interiors linked up underground with the dome in a radial system of corridors, perhaps providing the sisters a way inside, slightly unnoticed.

"They appear to be pressurized," she said, meaning they didn't have to rely on EVA suits. "*Skeeto*'s tether could take us in."

Ichiko nodded. "Where's a torch, *Skeeto*?"

"Aft cockpit storage bin 3, shelf A," the craft answered.

"I'm gonna make us a door!"

Kestrel Rose monitored *Skeeto*'s descent, which angled them towards the western-most structure. Synching the craft up with a vulnerable area inside the structure, Kestrel Rose aligned the ventral forward cockpit hatch, then readied the tether's approach.

Slowly, *Skeeto* inched towards the mini-dome, until the outstretched tether tube brushed the vacuum-resistant skin of the construct, creating a seal.

Brandishing Maya's particle torch, Ichiko proceeded down the tether access hatch situated between the cockpit seats, followed by Kestrel Rose carrying her sister's armaments.

A few moments of cutting gave her access to the inside, denoted by the sudden rush of air from inside the mini-dome. Setting the cut metal to one side, Ichiko worked her way through a support girder, which she then let drop down under Triton's gravity. Making way for Kestrel Rose, who descended first, Ichiko placed the torch back inside the cockpit, and descended into the mini-dome as well.

"We're in, *Skeeto*," Kestrel Rose said in mid-air. "Keep this voxlink channel open."

"Affirmative, Miss Kestrel Rose."

Floating gently downwards, the two girls landed three meters down from their makeshift entrance. Except for the ambient illumination from *Skeeto*'s cockpit, the mini-dome interior was dark, giving them pause. Ichiko produced a torch from her pocket, and shining it across the structure, spotted a door panel.

"What is this place?" Ichiko asked, shining the torch around the interior after the pair had made it to the exit.

"There's a seam running across the top of the dome," Kestrel Rose said, "so I think it must have been a hangar at one point, but it's crusted over with frozen methane and nitrogen from the geysers 'round here. Probably junk from the original colony."

The door panel stuttered and ground in its floor recess after Ichiko manipulated the controls, complaining all the way until the sisters applied some elbow grease and forced a wide-enough egress. With weapons at the ready, the pair surveyed the corridor and went inside, seeing down the one-hundred meter distance to another door panel, lit by streaky ceiling lights.

Getting nearer to the opposite end, the progressively louder roar of a crowd puzzled them, the two exchanging bewildered looks.

Ichiko scoured the corridor. "What the hell is this place?"

Kestrel Rose reached the door first. Putting her ear to the panel, she said, "No good."

"Well, we gotta go, ya know that much."

Kestrel Rose shook her head, cracking a smile. "Usually I have to push you, Ichiko. Right...let's go."

With Kestrel Rose working the controls this time, Ichiko held her rifle up, aiming its barrel at the entryway, anticipating any resistance to the girls' advance. *This oughtta be more fun than that stupid old station*, Ichiko thought.

"We're in...!"

CHAPTER TWENTY-ONE

Maya's standing with the crowd drastically improved with successive roundhouse kicks to Jel Kassonivic's mug. Energized by her long pause while the other brackets' regional contests had been decided, the agent let loose on her opponent, not allowing him to go on the offense. Backing Kassonivic into the cage, Maya ducked his standard jabs, giving her good angles to his abdomen, which she employed to great effect.

Surprisingly cheered on, Maya knocked him out with one punch to his jaw, eliciting the emotions of the crowd; she'd taken out the fighter who had himself ended a favorite's run.

Maya took a deep breath as Kassonivic's trainer pulled him off the floor. Raising her hand to the arena, she felt a strangely positive charge out there; could she be winning them over? Now, she stood alone atop her bracket, with the other three waiting for her.

"That was some quick work you made of him," Ud-Hajrdal said, handing her a towel. "The next one won't be a cupcake."

Maya wiped off her shoulders and forehead. "But now the crowd's rooting has shifted to me. Have my marketability futures risen?"

He frowned. "Don't get too high on yourself, Maya. Anyone can go down. And speaking of which, the governor's lottery was scrambled...your next opponent is from the opposite division bracket."

"Who now? Isn't that against the NDR's rulebook?"

Ud-Hajrdal didn't answer, instead pointing to the remaining three regional champs, all sitting on sideline benches with their respective trainers. "Him."

The chief trainer's index finger identified the reigning champ, the man Maya saw in action with Noraesk before this whole display even began: Oak Redbeard, in all his hulking, testosterone-fueled glory.

"Redbeard, huh? So, Governor Noraesk couldn't wait until the final round for his ratings match-up."

Ud-Hajrdal crossed his arms. "That's the governor's business. Either way, you're gonna have to go through Redbeard if you want the crown."

"I want this charade to come to an end, Ud-Hajrdal," Maya said, furrowing her brow. "If that means winning the damn thing or beating that behemoth over there, so be it. But no one's gonna say I had this handed to me on a platter. And make no mistake, afterwards," she glared straight into his eyes, "Noraesk is going down, too."

Ud-Hajrdal laughed. "We'll see. Get your ass up there, 'Agent.'"

ii

"This is it, the beginning of the end!" the arena announcer bellowed, whipping the crowd into a frenzy. "Regional champs have been crowned, and now four combatants will slug it out for the right to advance to the finals, for the glory, the laurels and the immortality that is...Neptune's...Deadliest...R-R-R-Ringgg!!!"

"We have for our first semifinal, the biggest, baddest, most powerful champion yet!" the announcer continued, ramping his voice up. "Standing one hundred and eighty-three centimeters, and weighing in at one hundred and forty kilos, he's Hyperion Federal Colony's favorite son! OOOaaakkk R-R-Redbearddd!!!"

Redbeard took to the floor and the absolutely maddening din of the arena. Raising his fists in triumphant return to the scene of his championship, the defending champion circled the cage in a customary victory lap, drinking in the adulation of the gathered thousands, and the millions watching the proceedings on the IPweb across the Wild, Wild Outer Reaches. Adorned in his red sash and championship belt, Redbeard smiled with a gap-toothed grin only Mrs Redbeard (if she survived pushing out that colossus) would love.

Maya stepped onto the ringfloor after several moments, in deference to the reigning champ. With modesty befitting her character much more, she acknowledged the arena by waving swiftly, then lowering her hand. Despite the arena warming to her cause in her last bout, she wasn't about to push it in Redbeard's company.

"And contesting Oak Redbeard's repeat title hopes is Maya, from Syrtis Major of Mars! Lean, mean and spritely in her cuteness, she stands at one hundred and sixty-centimeters and weighs in at fifty-five kilos."

The arena crowd deigned to applaud for the agent; they may have cheered her against Kassonivic, but she was in Redbeard country now. Nothing was going to be given; she'd have to earn her it going forward.

In Redbeard's presence for the first time, Maya noted the battle scars indented over his face. His rough attitude notwithstanding, Oak looked to have scraped with every lowlife from here to Mercury. Old scratches lined his cheeks and forehead, while mottling was present over the rest of his mug, like some junkyard dog. It was clear he'd been operated on as well, perhaps cosmetically to restore some semblance of humanity to him, or even some reconstruction to his skull. He certainly wasn't a handsome guy, but Maya was sure he could pull the ladies by reputation and championship riches alone. After his trainer retrieved Redbeard's championship belt and sash, the reigning champ proceeded to crack his knuckles and neck vertebrae, loosening up for the quick and dirty work the chump before him would present.

The two knocked fists, Redbeard's mitts large enough to encompass both of Maya's hands. A punch flew forth from Redbeard, which Maya evaded, but his long reach instead contacted her left shoulder, sending her to the floor. Redbeard dove in for the tackle, his hands grasping her arms. Maya retaliated with several knees to his neck and two kicks to his face, stunning him long enough for her to wiggle away.

One more kick to his kidneys, followed by a jab from her straightened fingers sent Redbeards's howls of protest into the air. Amid the arena's auditory distaste for Oak's temporary setback, Maya stepped back and gathered her strength. Drawing in several long breaths, she contemplated her next strategy. Redbeard wasn't going to be intimated by her, unlike her previous opponents, nor was she able to physically handle him and force a concession. Like Greovich in his battle with Redbeard, everything in this ring was fair game to take down that behemoth. Maya would just have to use Redbeard against himself.

Surveying her exact position and distance relative to the cage, Maya paused, letting Redbeard stew from her assault. Studying him like she had in the previous tournament, Redbeard's main weakness was his easy-to-discern state, in that he grew as red as Martian sandstone when pissed.

"That's right, you big ox!" Maya taunted. "Come and get me!"

His oversized, gap-tooth grin reappearing, Redbeard eyed the diminutive agent with half-contempt, half-hunger. He was going to get this over with right now and give what was coming to her.

Maya leapt up and grasped the cage, anchoring herself with all four limbs.

"Aaaghh! You're one of those!" Redbeard spat, shaking his fist. "We both can play, you bitch!"

Despite his bulk, in Triton's gravity Redbeard was successful in following Maya upwards. Hanging by his hands, he guffawed and advanced towards her feet, as if on some hexagonal monkey bars. With each successive grip he began shaking the cage, sending ripples of pure force quaking throughout the skeletal structure. Redbeard pumped his arms and shoulders like some angered bear, resonating the cage and threatening to dislodge Maya.

The arena exploded in rapturous applause and cheers at this

unprecedented sight, the crowd more than getting their money's worth with this bout.

Her plan quickly unraveling, Maya loosed her hands' grip, but not before swiveling backwards on the toes of her boots. Grasping Redbeard's torso upside down, she kneed his face, then with her hands as fulcrums, swiveled again and released, landing on her feet. Redbeard's bulk collapsed to the ringfloor a second later, to the gasps and awe of the arena.

Turning to assess Redbeard, who was still, Maya waited for the arena signal, but none was forthcoming. Looking to Oak again, Maya watched the colossus rise to his knees and feet, disbelieving that her opponent still had fight left in him.

"Thattt," Redbeard said, slurring his words, "wasss not verrry niccce."

Standing akimbo, Maya's eyes widened. "Ahh shit...!"

His face bloodied, but his Neolithic spirit unbroken and undeterred, Redbeard gathered himself for another try. Inhaling a breath deep enough to shame the bulkiest deepsea whales, Redbeard raised his forearms and, balling his hands, started for Maya again. Building a full head of steam, he forsook any coherent strategy and ran straight for her—

Only to be hit squarely in the neck by a surprise volley of particle rounds. Grabbing his wounds with his meaty hands, the reigning champ whipped his head towards the entryway, growling meekly.

A shocked Maya wheeled around, half-expecting to become a target also. To her side, Redbeard let out a fading moan, then collapsed in a great heap like his namesake, having finally succumbed to the sudden attack.

The arena uproar was predictably crude; the crowd left their seats and flooded the lower concourse, which, despite being physically sealed off from the ring itself, still invited the throng to see the even more unprecedented event up close.

Two figures emerged from the shadowed corridor, running towards the ring at full speed. Dispatching a swarming security squad, the interlopers soon commandeered the arena controls, putting the arena officials under the gun. The brilliant arena lights kept Maya from completely identifying the pair, but a familiar shout brought the mystery to an end.

"Maya!"

"Kestrel Rose?!" the agent uttered, walking to the cage. Hecklers and miscreants spat obscenities, barely rendering her voice audible. "That's a helluva entrance!"

Ichiko interfaced with the QPU and succeeded in lowering the cage, while her sister stepped up and hugged Maya. The two fled the floor and joined Ichiko.

"I don't think we should hang 'round her too long," Maya said, knowing a heavy object was just moments from being flung out of the crowd.

"Yeah...where's this governor guy you're trying to arrest?!" Kestrel Rose asked.

Maya swiveled her head, the level of invective rising to a staggering amount. "I wouldn't worry 'bout him...I think he'll be along soon enough."

A man wearing Neptune Regional Authority togs beside Ichiko grasped Maya's arms in desperation. "Take me with you! I can't stay here with these animals! They'll tear me apart thanks to you!!!"

"Sorry," Maya said, ripping away his sweaty palms, "you're not on our agenda!"

Maya started towards the corridor, but the man persisted, screaming, "*YOU DON'T UNDERSTAND! I'M THE ANNOUNCER! THEY'LL MAKE AN EXAMPLE OF MEEE!*"

"GET LOST!" she yelled back, and grabbing the sisters' hands, sped away.

The trio descended into the shadowed locker room, the chants and catcalls reverberating off the cement block walls. Pushing past the exit she had previously scouted, Maya led them away from her three-day prison.

iii

Listening to the din emanating from the hostile arena, Ud-Hajrdal crossed over to the locker room door. Toggling the voxlink adorning his collar, he spoke again, "She made a mess all right, sir. But she's as predictable as you thought. Intercepting her should be quite easy, they have that Federal craft in storage dome four...thank you, sir. No. I'll make someone pay...I think I have a good candidate right here. Yes, he'll get quite the reward."

Cowering at the doorway, the announcer turned towards the arena after seeing Ud-Hajrdal finish. "I'm sorry, sir! This is beyond my capabilities...."

Ud-Hajrdal smiled and placed a hand on his shoulder. "Of course. Sure. Now, what Governor Noraesk requires is someone to reassure the audience that everything is under control. And someone to administer this stimulant to Mr Redbeard."

The announcer's eyes found the tiny ampule in the trainer's hand. "But—but, Mr Redbeard broke the back of the last nurse who—"

"Exactly. Good medical help is so expensive. That's why I'm sending... an expendable resource...."

CHAPTER TWENTY-TWO

i

"Showtime, *Skeeto*," Maya said, triumphantly taking her port cockpit seat after exiting the ventral hatch.

"Welcome back, Miss Maya. Course?"

The agent tapped a series of buttons her interface, updating herself on *Skeeto's* current status. "Noraesk Tower. Retract ventral tether. Reverse RCS thrusters at full power to one hundred meters, VASIMR engines three hundred meters plus altitude."

"Affirmative," the craft's feminine voice said. "Ventral tether secured, hatch sealed.

Watching from the aft cockpit compartment, Kestrel Rose and Ichiko saw the enormous arena dome recede under them, then disappear altogether behind the macula's lip.

"Kestrel Rose, where'd you stow Xibalba?" Maya asked, her eyes fixed to the horizon ahead.

"It's kind of a long st—"

"That's a silly question, Maya, I'm right here!" Ichiko interrupted, gripping the back of the starboard seat.

Craning her head back, her brow furrowed, Maya uttered, "Say what? You two been alone too long?"

"Maya! It's me, Xibalba! What, you deaf?" Ichiko floated into the starboard seat, then stared right into the agent's eyes. "Hot damn, Maya... you're gorgeous!"

"Uhm, couldn't you have picked a better time for stupid jokes?" Maya said, her face flush from the awkward attentions of the teen girl across the way.

"Uh, yeah...we had to go to some extremes to rescue Xibalba, Maya," Kestrel Rose explained, her fingers rubbing her forehead to cover her sheepishness.

Maya did a double take towards Ichiko, who just wore a goofy, almost drunken grin. "What the hell did you two do, anyway?!"

"Don't worry, Maya, I'm safe inside Ichiko's implant thingy," Ichiko said. "I can see a whole lot better."

"A fat lotta good that does me." Maya frowned. "When this is all through—"

"Miss Maya, a craft registered to Governor Van Noraesk is approaching on an intercept course," *Skeeto* reported. "Forty-three kilometers, velocity one thousand KPH."

Maya scanned the horizon out her cockpit window, seeing nothing yet but Tritonian cantaloupe landscape and rising geysers. "Three guesses as to what's on his mind," she said. "*Skeeto*, let's make it easy on him...increase speed to match his velocity. Ready tendrils for snaring him."

"Affirmative."

Kestrel Rose leaned forward, her hands on Maya's seatback. "What are you going to do?"

Maya smiled. "Duel Noraesk in *my* arena."

ii

"Tsk, tsk, Maya...no one upstages Neptune's Deadliest Ring." Noraesk glanced to the holographic image of *Skeeto*, ringed by his navigational computer's targeting reticle. The agent's craft grew larger minute by minute on the display, frustrating the governor all the more.

"Tok, prepare a special treat for Agent Maya upon our return," Noraesk said into his voxlink. "I want to punish her for the trouble she's caused."

"Yes, Governor," Ud-Hajrdal's voice responded. "What do you have in mind, sir?"

Noraesk peered at the mural window before him; Neptune's sapphire visage slowly descended below Triton's horizon. "A nano-goad...that will be entertaining, don't you think?"

"Yes, the ratings should be awesome, sir."

Noraesk reclined in his seat, resting his fingers to his lips in thought. Perhaps he had treated this Maya *too* much like an ordinary combatant; special considerations should have been put into her bouts, but Noraesk had been content that she would fight, eventually. She was a self-styled hunter, after all. Her not playing by his rules, however, could provide Noraesk a new outlet for his more intriguing combatants. Yes, Maya should prove to be an excellent test for a more primal exhibition....

iii

"There you are...probably wanting your li'l Maya back, hmm?"

The trio found the silver speck against the obsidian night, barrelling towards *Skeeto*. It was stout, possessing a tall dorsal wing, probably once employed as a deep Neptunian methane-mining vessel, but since redesigned for Noraesk's personal use. Two powerful plasma engines, older than the VASIMRs *Skeeto* had, were retrofitted into the aft section. All in all enough to give chase to civilian craft that might wander into the Neptune Regional Authority's aegis, but not police corvettes, nor *Skeeto*.

"His ship looks smaller than *Skeeto*," Kestrel Rose observed. "Can you grapple him?"

Ichiko let out a haughty laugh. "Of course, cutie! Watch and learn."

"*Skeeto*, I'm transferring piloting controls to me," Maya said, punching several buttons on her interface. "Set stabilizers to full...this might get a little rough."

"Yes, Miss Maya."

Maya looked over to Ichiko. "Ever been in a dogfight?"

"No...?"

The agent grinned. "Hold on!"

Skeeto yawed to port, then rolled starboard. Maya fired the engines at maximum for five seconds, putting the ex-lunar craft on a swift course to T-bone Noraesk's craft, which itself rolled to port to avoid having its dorsal wing clipped off by the speeding *Skeeto*. Maya pitched *Skeeto* to the right and again blasted the VASIMR engines to maximum, quickly catching up to Noraesk and figuratively breathing down his engines.

A sharp ping came over *Skeeto's* cockpit speakers. "Incoming audio from the craft, Miss Maya."

"Let's hear it."

"Maya, Maya," Noraesk's filtered voice chided, "you just can't accept that I won't let you go. Once in Neptune's Deadliest Ring, always in Neptune's Deadliest Ring."

"Your ever-increasing appetite for revenue is admirable, Van, but I'm going to have to put you out of business for awhile," Maya responded. "Nothing personal, I just have a lot of credits waiting for your arrest. I'm sure you understand."

Noraesk laughed. "We're all good little capitalists! The chase is part of the allure, isn't it?"

Maya killed the voxlink. "*Skeeto*! Release tendrils!"

At Maya's command, the eight belly hatches housing the tendrils opened, revealing round metal feet nested inside the hull. *Skeeto's* ventral RCS thrusters ascended the craft five meters skyward, to just above Noraesk, while Maya's piloting propelled them forward. Cat-quick mechanisms shot the tendrils downward onto Noraesk's craft, the eight feet lining up alongside the dorsal wing.

"Fire EM pulse!!" Maya commanded, but her interface displayed

Noraesk's craft descending while *Skeeto*'s altitude remained stationary. "*Skeeto*! Fire EM pulse!!"

"Affirmative, Miss Maya. Detecting reverse electromagnetic polarity emanating from that craft. Tendril electromagnetic fields having no effect."

Looking below out the bubble window, Maya saw Noraesk's craft banking away, all eight tendrils hanging uselessly. "Dammit!"

"Why didn't you grab him with the tendril claws?!" Ichiko said, Xibalba's annoying tone palpable even when voiced by the girl.

"And depressurize his hull?!" Maya spat back. "There's no payment for his corpse, Xibalba!"

Tapping a series of buttons on her interface, Maya retrieved the tendrils, rolling them back inside *Skeeto*'s belly.

"Heh-heh!" Noraesk's chilling laugh sounded again throughout *Skeeto*'s cockpit. "That was a dirty trick, wasn't it? I seem to have every answer for all your weapons, Agent Maya. And don't even bother trying to hack my craft's engines or my navigational computer...everything's been shielded from outside signals."

Noraesk piloted his craft behind and under *Skeeto*, keeping his distance, but utilizing his near-superior agility to avoid Maya's attempts to circle round him.

"And now, Maya," he said to himself, "you will see how I play the offense." Tapping a button on his interface, Noraesk opened a ventral hatch, unfolding barbed metal horns, resembling those of stag beetles writ large.

Skeeto pitched downwards, avoiding Noraesk's craft, but the governor didn't need to position himself anywhere in particular; just touching *Skeeto*'s hull would ensnare the two craft, allowing the Authority's security forces to retrieve Maya from the entrapment. *Skeeto* would be unable to reach orbit, let alone the Federal Causeway.

Maya rolled *Skeeto* several times, then pitched skyward again, circling back to see Noraesk kill his engines and roll his craft's dorsal barbs head-on at *Skeeto*'s dorsal hull. A tremendous quake reverberated throughout *Skeeto* as Noraesk's barbs scraped down *Skeeto*'s back, his craft's inertia taking him several meters aftward.

"SONUVABITCH!!!"

Klaxons screamed inside *Skeeto*, blaring warnings about the huge mass suddenly added to the superstructure.

The two craft tumbled in the empty atmosphere, their combined energies hurtling them from the relatively stable and gravity-free upper Tritonian orbit towards the surface, now less than two kilometers below.

Maya's hands flew over her interface, in a desperate, frantic attempt to stabilize *Skeeto*, and perhaps land the two craft somewhere softer than the rock-hard ice comprising most of Triton's terrain. Scanning for a landing zone in the topsy-turvy cockpit pushed Maya to her limits, but she wouldn't give in to certain destruction in this hellhole.

Seconds of fruitless searching brought her to a last resort, a decision even Gilmour Zeobarry in all his years retrofitting *Skeeto* never really intended to employ, but built-in anyway, perhaps just to occupy his mind before a certain death: ejecting the cockpit module, effectively destroying the rest of the craft. It was a longshot and doomed to stranding them here. But she and the girls might live...if descending from this short altitude didn't kill them first.

"*SKEETO!*" Maya bellowed. "BEGIN COCKPIT EJECTION SEQUENCE!"

A squelched but still functioning "Affirmative" sounded over the speakers.

Maya's eyes found Kestrel Rose and Ichiko.

"HOLD ON!"

She wanted to say goodbye, and how sorry she felt, but could only voice, "WE'RE GOING DOWN!"

CHAPTER TWENTY-THREE

i

"Maya, you bitch! I should let you handle this yourself, but it seems you always need someone to bail you out!"

"Huh?" Maya heard the voice over the cockpit speakers, but couldn't believe it.... "Xilanova?!"

"I still want my piece of that bastard!"

A flash of silver over Ichiko's head greeted the three, and the sound of crashing metal from within and without *Skeeto* raised the impossible...what the hell had Xilanova done?

Maya's control over the flailing craft recovered, and firing thrusters at maximum, the agent stabilized *Skeeto* a mere moment later, forbidding Triton a rock throw beneath them. Angling *Skeeto* around, Maya spotted two craft spinning past the cockpit windows, headed away. Xilanova blasted Noraesk's craft from *Skeeto*; Maya be damned if the corporal hadn't killed herself in the aftermath.

"Xilanova!" she hailed over the voxlink. "Xilanova, can you read me?"

"—Get Nor—sk!"

Maya read her interface's update on *Skeeto*'s atmospheric pressure. "*Skeeto*, I'm not reading any integrity losses. How's the hull?"

"Damages include plates D-five-seven through D-one-three-one. Reading damage extending to three-point-six centimeters below hull line."

Maya breathed a relieved sigh. "Just flesh wounds."

She scanned the two craft, finding the one that read as Noraesk's. It corkscrewed below them, but managed to bottom out and plow into a trough leading to a geyser chain a kilometer away. Xilanova appeared to be piloting the same type of shuttle that Noraesk's security forces used to move Maya to the arena dome, and having most likely sustained irreparable damage to the craft, disappeared over the trough's furrow walls. Naive she may have been on occasion, Maya couldn't fault the corporal's resourcefulness, and now, her courage.

"Any lifesigns aboard Noraesk's craft, *Skeeto*?"

"Detecting carbon-dioxide exhalation, steady heartbeat and migrating infrared heat source, Miss Maya."

"That's him. Hey, did either one of you happen to find my EVA armor?"

"It's charging up in your storage cabinet," Kestrel Rose said. "Ichiko thought you might want it back."

Maya nodded. "Thanks, Ichi—Xibal—whichever one you are right now."

Donning her armor in just under three minutes, Maya soon gripped the back of Ichiko's seat, guiding *Skeeto* over to the crash site.

"Open the ventral hatch, and once I'm through, get to safety, *Skeeto*."

"Affirmative, Miss Maya."

Arming herself with her knife and a back-up particle handgun, Maya glanced to the teen girls before placing her helmet on. "I'm bringing Noraesk in. And this time I mean it."

ii

Flinging herself through the narrow chute, Maya dove from the descending *Skeeto*, and spreading her limbs out, free-fell to the surface. Tumbling forwards, she activated her armor's RCS thruster, lessening her impact. Pulling her handgun, she ran a switchbacked path to Noraesk's downed craft, evading any possible arms fire from the governor, if he was capable.

Drawing nearer, Maya scouted the vessel that lay cockeyed into a furrow wall, its bow crumpled under the dense ice rock. She approached it cautiously, hunkering down until coming in contact with its outer hull, lined by horizontal stress fractures. A jagged knot of metal before her was all that remained of the barbed horns Noraesk employed to grapple *Skeeto*; now pieces of it impaled its own parent craft, thanks to Xilanova's efforts.

Soft thumps from inside the craft could be felt through her armor. Voice activating the voxlink on her HUD, she set it for wide-spectrum coverage.

"Noraesk! I know you're alive!" Maya shouted. "This is the end of the road! You're under arrest!"

"Not...done...yet!" a breathless voice replied.

Above her, a shadowed form leapt, silently blitzing Maya with a combat stick and connecting with her right gauntlet. Maya's handgun hovered out of her control, landing somewhere inside the craft's broken shell. Vaulting himself with one edge of the stick, Noraesk's EVA boots kicked Maya's faceplate, sending her backwards.

"Uuuhhh...." Still sore from fighting in the Ring, Maya struggled to rise from the nitrogen-encrusted ice.

Another charge of the stick missed her helmet and struck the ground next to her. Grabbing its loose end with both gauntlets, Maya pushed it forward, allowing it to slide through Noraesk's gauntlets and strike him in the gut. Falling backwards under her attack, Noraesk stumbled and landed on his right side, but rolled and propped himself up with the stick.

Noraesk advanced towards Maya, twirling the stick twice. He then swung again, exposing Maya's left flank as she avoided another strike. Switching hands, Noraesk swung a second time, cracking it on the small area of abdomen unshielded by an armored plate.

Doubling over, Maya retreated, but kept her boots under her, refusing to yield.

"You can't win, Maya," Noraesk taunted. "So far from home, so deep inside the Neptune Regional Authority. No IPTP backup here, I'm afraid. Your little Intelligence friend may have ruined my ship, but I'm very much in control, still."

Noraesk hopped and swung the stick over his right shoulder, hitting Maya's neck. Pulling it back, he grabbed hold with both gauntlets and jabbed her throat with the stick, pushing her backwards with all his mass.

"Heh-heh-heh! Priceless! What I have in store for you will make my name across the Solar System, Maya!" He lowered the stick and walked close to her. "I thought you would fight for me, for the glory of all hunters. But, I have to admit, I was wrong. Oh, it happens once every great while, but you made me look bad, Agent Maya. And embarrassment is not something I suffer well, particularly in public, in the very forum I have spent much capital to perfect!"

He sighed, resting the stick over his left shoulder. "So, I ask you once more: Will you fight for me?"

Maya heaved in her EVA armor, gulping air just to restore what Noraesk's last thrust stole from her lungs. "I've fought on your terms...now we're gonna do it my way."

"Precious, precious! Heh-heh. This will be the last time you say those words."

Noraesk swung the stick over his left shoulder, but this time Maya blocked it with her right gauntlet, rotated her forearm under it and ripped it from Noraesk. With his momentum carrying him forward, he couldn't stop to block Maya's swing to his own abdomen.

Swinging the stick over her helmet, she reversed it and struck Noraesk again, this time in the neckring area connecting his helmet to his torso, sending his arms to the ground to catch himself. Half-leaping on her left boot, Maya kicked his helmet, which ricocheted upwards in the microgravity. Summoning the energy to follow, she let loose with a flurry of strikes, circling, twirling, leaping round him, shrieking the cries of banshees as one strike after another collapsed upon him, each one pulling him to and fro, like some buoyant, undersea ballet.

Finally, his arms no longer able to block her strikes, and his legs no longer sturdy enough to support him, he began to fall, but not before Maya smacked the stick against his legs, taking them out from under him. Struck like a rag doll, Noraesk crumpled to his haunches, his slow, microgravity fall kicking up frost particles.

Maya flung the stick behind her, away from Noraesk's reach. Holding Noraesk up by merely laying a hand on his helmet, she balled her fist and released it on his abdomen, watching with exhausted delight as his head jostled within his helmet, then cracking itself upon his faceplate.

Reaching down, she grappled his EVA's shoulder harness straps and pulled him to her. His perfectly coiffed, slicked-back hair, his immaculate teeth and that damned creepy goatee—all were now soiled and stained with perspiration and blood. Van Noraesk—once-mighty Governor and wannabe-autocrat—humbled in his own spacesuit.

"*Skee...to*...this...is Maya," she pushed out of her lips. "Home in...on my co...ordinates...inform Lieu...tenant Kuwashima...I have...Noraesk...in custody...."

CHAPTER TWENTY-FOUR

i

"Maya! Maya, here they come!"

Rising from her port seat, Maya saw the bluish landing lights flood the area, their brilliant illumination cascading through the cockpit.

Kestrel Rose and Ichiko flashed smiles to their new mentor.

"It's finally done," Maya breathed. "Time to go."

Placing her helmet over her head once more, Maya exited *Skeeto*, waving to the arrowhead-shaped Federal Marshal corvettes blowing frost across the landscape as they touched down.

"Agent Maya, I'm Sergeant Myon, Federal Marshals Precinct-4," the lead man introduced himself over his voxlink a few moments later. "On behalf of the Solar System Government and Commissioner Judoma of the IPTP, we salute you."

Extending her gauntlet, Maya shook hands with Myon. "Am I ever so happy to see you."

ii

In the light cast by the parked corvettes, a slim, silhouetted form, limping but otherwise undeterred, crossed the terrain, making its way to Maya and the departing Marshals.

Myon raised his firearm at first sight of the figure's approach, but the agent placed her gauntlet on his arm, calming him. Scanning it with her sensor pallet, she recognized its biosignature immediately.

"Corporal," Maya greeted. "Welcome back."

"Some fancy flying you did up there," Xilanova said, her countenance visibly amused through her EVA helmet's faceplate. "Couldn't do it better myself."

Maya laughed. "I was going to say the same thing. You made it down in one piece, I see."

"Just over the trench. Noraesk?"

Myon jabbed his thumb back to the trio of Marshals loading a stretcher into a nearby corvette. "Alive...and in our custody, Corporal."

"I suppose I'll waive the repo spoils for now," Xilanova said. "In light of the fact that I have no transportation."

Maya nodded to Myon to leave at his discretion, then glanced back to Xilanova. "I wouldn't say that's exactly the truth. In fact, I have a proposition you may find more interesting...."

iii

"...We're departing now, sir," Maya spoke to the holographic image of Lieutenant Walter Kuwashima on her interface. "Noraesk is hibernating on board one of the corvettes for safekeeping back to P-4."

"*Excellent, Agent Maya,*" Kuwashima's blurry form said, his response delayed by several seconds due to the distance. "*How are you doing? Do you need time off?*"

She rubbed the bruises Noraesk bequeathed to her on her shoulders and neck. "Been better...but I'll do some deep sleeping on the way home, sir, and be back to normal before too long."

"*Good. Now about the business with your two charges—*"

Maya crossed her arms. "I have an idea about that, sir. In light of my having to re-route to Neptune after already making Titan orbit, I'd like to suggest an alternative to the detention of Ichiko and Kestrel Rose there."

Kuwashima's form shifted uncomfortably. "*There isn't much to compromise on, Agen—*"

"And in light of my brief status as a prisoner held against my will," she interrupted, "and forced to fight in bloodsport entertainment, I'm nominating Army Intelligence Corporal Alix Xilanova to take charge of the teens' formal education, until their adulthood status, of course."

Xilanova stepped over to Maya's seat, putting herself on display. "Pleased to make your acquaintance, Lieutenant. I'm based off Dione, sir, so I'm not really that far from Titan. As far as their education, I can guarantee they'll fulfill the requirements of the court."

"*I see that I'm not going to win this round, Maya.*" Kuwashima stroked his chin, and added, "*The necessary arrangements will be made, and the proper paperwork filed. But you owe me one, Agent.*"

Maya grinned. "Of course I do, sir. That makes at least a dozen, right?"

A light harrumph escaped from his mouth before he cut the secure IPwebsite.

"Maya, why is *she* going to be watching over us?" Kestrel Rose complained. "She 'bout stole Xibalba from us."

Xilanova rolled her eyes. "Why did I agree to this again? Oh, right, molding them into proper hunters."

"Ladies," Maya began, putting her arms around both Kestrel Rose and Xilanova, "it's a long flight back. Perhaps we should try to re-introduce ourselves before we all kill each other. Deal?"

Xilanova and Kestrel Rose exchanged skeptical glances, then nodded their heads in agreement.

iv

"You have to come out sometime, Xibalba. I need you out here, and Ichiko has her life to live, too."

Ichiko stood against the wall in Maya's quarters, her hands clasped under chin. "Maya, you understand, don't you? I've got a form, a true body! Not stuck in some stupid sidearm!"

Maya put her hand to Ichiko's cheek. "But you weren't made for this, zip gun. Ichiko did you a favor, helped you escape. Please, don't be difficult."

"I won't go back!"

Maya's resolve wavered under Ichiko's youthful voice, but it wasn't Ichiko, she had to remind herself. Xibalba was being selfish, as usual, but it was made worse by Ichiko's adolescent hormones cascading through her bloodstream.

"You can't force me, Maya. In this form...."

"But that's not what Ichiko needs, nor wants."

Ichiko threw her hands down, her voice trembling under the strain. "Don't do this to me, Maya! Don't!"

Maya took Ichiko's hands into her own. "Let Ichiko back...Xilanova's nearly finished putting your casing back together. Let Ichiko help you."

Ichiko collapsed to the floor, tears streaming from her eyes. "Maya...."

"I need you, Xibalba. You'll always be needed by me," she whispered.

"Maya...what...." Ichiko said several seconds later, but her voice's tone had changed. It was softer, without anger or sadness. "Why am I—"

"Nice to see you again, Ichiko," she said, stroking her cheek. "I have a favor to ask of you...."

v

Neptune's Deadliest Ring was gone for good, IPTP Commissioner Udhed Judoma proudly proclaimed on a Solar System-wide broadcast weeks later. Because of "spectacular cooperation" between the IPTP and Army Intelligence, Governor Noraesk had been apprehended, ending his brief reign as autocrat over an illegal, breakaway Neptune Regional Authority; Precinct-8's status as sole governing body was re-established in its wake.

Maya could only hope that were the case. Too many rogue elements, the PPRTFDOS and the super-secretive Corporation For A Better Living being the most prominent, had arms that extended beyond even the Solar

System Government to reach. Local police and armed forces were scattered thin, and Federal Marshals along with the Federal agencies that Maya was part of were few and far between. It was just a matter of time, Maya understood, before someone, perhaps closer than thought possible, would attempt to usurp power again. The Solar System was just too damn big, too unwieldy.

But she could do nothing about that now. There were more tax cheats to chase, more repos to attend to. With a hundred billion humans running around a half-dozen planets and dozens of moons, Maya would surely be kept busy for a lifetime. Or two.

The Moons of Ice and Fire
03.15.2156–
05.01.2156

CHAPTER ONE

"He's screwed."

Drifting away from its pursuer at the mercy of hastily engineered thrusters ringing its circumference was minor planet XJ-45677, a floating mass of ochre rocks held loosely by joint gravitational attraction, one thousand, one hundred meters long and two hundred million metric tonnes. Shaped more like breasts than the traditional potato seen in countless movies, it had earned the nickname "Marilyn" from its occupant and current interplanetary tax fugitive, Roji Broquet.

"*Skeeto*, are we within tendril range?" Agent Maya asked the tadpole-shaped craft she piloted.

"Tendril range in twenty-three seconds, Miss Maya," the craft's audible interface said, a soft, feminine voice programmed for comfort on long journeys.

"Launch when ready."

From ten meters above Marilyn's equatorial latitude, eight ventral, vanadium-osmium-alloy tendrils shot out from the tiny craft. On the ends of each tendril were a circular grouping of four talons which punctured the minor planet's tenuous but crusty surface, launching plumes of fine dust into the void. Securely anchored to Marilyn, *Skeeto* lowered itself to the minor planet, hitching a free ride.

Maya unstrapped herself from her port seat and floated to a storage locker less than a meter behind the cockpit. Opening the locker door, she removed a shining suit of EVA armor, complete with dorsal RCS thruster pack and a helmet.

"Ready ventral hatch. Target the tether."

"Ventral hatch readied, Miss Maya," *Skeeto* acknowledged. "Airlock pressurized. Tether targeted on habitation module."

"Keep voxlink channel open." Maya reached for her hip belt and holster, then snapped her sentient sidearm, the flaming red Xibalba, inside it. "Ready for some action, Xibalba?"

"Hell yeah, Maya! I've been bored since we started trackin' this punk."

Smiling, she secured the last piece of armor to her short frame, fastened her helmet into place, then floated forward to the vertical hatch straddling the port and starboard cockpit seats at *Skeeto*'s stem. Clambering inside the ventral chute, Maya descended a meter, then waited as *Skeeto* extended the tether to Marilyn's surface, where, unbeknownst to Broquet, the agent would break into his inconspicuous—albeit sensor-brilliant—silicon-dioxide-blanketed, half-submerged habitation module. Broquet might have been safer with standard Solar System Government sensors, but the InterPlanetary Tax Police, or IPTP, as it was known, worked a bit differently. To *Skeeto*, the guy might as well have been signalling his coordinates and intentions.

Thirty seconds later, Maya was through the tether's shaft and now stood atop the habitation module's dome. In Marilyn's meager gravity, Maya kneeled and extended her left arm gauntlet, where a sensor pallet she wore whirred to life, analyzing the dome's structural components.

"Aluminum/steel composite," she breathed, almost laughing while reading the results on her helmet's Heads-Up Display. "Why bother?"

A four-centimeter-long torch rotated on her gauntlet, replacing the sensor pallet. Setting the torch mouth to the dome, a stream of blue ions burst forth, blowing off a strip of the silicon-dioxide blanket and easily slicing into the lightweight metal composite. After a few moments, she had carved a half-meter-diameter circle wide enough to comfortably slide through.

"I'm in," Maya told *Skeeto* as she descended into a dark room, not more than three meters wide or tall. "What's Broquet's location?"

"Just one moment, Miss Maya. Roji Broquet is located eight-point-three meters starboard of your current location."

Drawing Xibalba, she held him at arm's length, giving him a wide arc to scan the module for security armaments. "See anything?"

Xibalba panned his narrow, weapons-based "vision" across the small compartment. "Not a one, Maya. Quiet as your love life."

"Thanks, I think."

Maya scanned the room, taking stock of what looked to be a cargo storage area. Stacks of ration packages, empty water bottles—and in a curious mix of haste and disregard—ammunition boxes and pornographic disks were scattered about, obviously Broquet's stash of emergency supplies for his extended stay in the TransMartian Asteroid Belt for his illicit operations. Maya stifled her laughter as she walked past these assorted items and into a corridor, then beyond into a central room.

Adjusting the speaker on her helmet, Maya broadcasted for Broquet to hear, "Roji Broquet! This is Agent Maya of the IPTP! You are ordered to stand down and cease your operations! Failure to comply will authorize me to kick your ass! Understood?!"

"Ain't got nuthin' you police want no how! So's get off Marilyn now!" a hoarse voice yelled from across the room.

Maya drew nearer to where remote flickering illuminated a large figure. "That's an unfortunate choice of words, Mr Broquet! I'm taking custody of Marilyn, so I suggest you come out right now with your hands up where I can see them."

"Sod off!"

"Bad move!" Xibalba sang, his loaded magazine mounting a single stun round into his firing chamber. "Ready, Maya!"

Maya swung closer to Broquet's voice, utilizing a wall beam for cover on her left flank. Clasping Xibalba in both hands, she aimed the sidearm straight for Broquet's voice, allowing Xibalba's internal sensors to trace the tax cheat's guttural echoes back to their origin. Squeezing the trigger, Maya released one round, which found its target with a swift puncture of the sound barrier.

A massive groan let out from across the prefabricated structure.

"I think we have a hit," Xibalba said while Maya raced over to the shadows.

Slumped over a stack of used ration packages was the unseemly form of Roji Broquet, all fifty kilos of him. Maya placed her gauntlet to his throat, checking for respiration. "Good shot, Xibalba—"

"Whoa, check it out, Maya!" the pistol said, his tactical sensors discerning strangely organic shapes from the flickering illumination.

Swiveling her head over her shoulder, Maya saw a seventy-centimeter-diameter monitor displaying a trio of indeterminately gendered people in various forms of contortions caterwauling at a high volume. "What the hell—"

"I said git off Marilyn!!" Broquet bellowed. A horrible scream then erupted from the unexpectedly conscious cheat, who loosed a swing that connected to Maya's helmet, knocking her backwards.

With agility that only years of training could harness, Maya reverse somersaulted and landed on her feet, using Broquet's punch as a springboard. While he rose to his feet, trying to shake off Xibalba's stun round, Maya whirled forward and drew a nine-centimeter-long dagger, which she neatly placed at his throat with her left hand. In her right hand was Xibalba, his barrel kissing Broquet's right temple.

"The next one won't be a stun round, Roji," she whispered, her blade finding a large crease in his Adam's apple. "You'd be easier to carve than a squawking hen...."

"Ahh—all right! I admit it! Just...just don't—"

Maya laughed; her one-hundred-and-sixty-centimeter-tall frame had this mountain gorilla in the palm of her collective hands. "Don't bother admitting anything to me, Broquet. Tell it to the JAG. I just want to repo all you got."

"Repo? Why? How do I get it back?"

"I want the reward credits for it. Now, admittedly, it's pretty small caliber stuff, but hey, a girl's gotta make a living. As for how you can get it all back, well, that ain't my problem...oh, you can keep your 'entertainment.' I hear jail can get kinda lonely."

"But I—"

"If you shut up, I'll even let you sleep on the way back to Mars. If not, well, nothin' better than a six-week caffeine and porn binge, now is there?"

A gurgle erupted from Broquet's mouth, but he clenched his jaws to stifle it. Instead, he nodded slowly, still feeling the cold steel blade on his throat.

"Good. Xibalba, give our good boy here a sedative. Double shot this time."

"You got it." With the sounds of Xibalba's internal mechanisms whirring into place, Maya quickly lowered the sidearm and fired into Broquet's neck, lodging a tranquilizer round deep into his flesh.

A quick release of her arms sent the cheat thundering to the floor, like a put-down head of cattle. "Jeezus, I'm glad that's over. *Skeeto*, upload navigation hack. We're going home!"

CHAPTER TWO

i

"Holy—she did it." Rubbing his jaw, the awestruck commissioner of the IPTP, Udhed Judoma, watched Marilyn slowly creep into view on the holographic monitor.

Lieutenant Walter Kuwashima looked down from the image over his desk. "You had doubts, sir?"

"It's just...I thought you were humoring her...."

Kuwashima merely smiled. "With all due respect, Commissioner, nobody humors Agent Maya and lives to tell the tale."

ii

"Miss Maya, receiving a query from Precinct-4 Headquarters," *Skeeto* reported. "It is Lieutenant Kuwashima."

Maya floated into her seat and accessed the holographic interface before her. A rectangular monitor blossomed, opening a secure IPwebsite to HQ. "Lieutenant, Agent Maya reporting in."

Kuwashima's visage greeted Maya with a nod. "Welcome back, Maya. Looks like your mission was an unqualified success. Congratulations. I have a message of thanks from Solar System authorities—"

Maya waved her hand. "Thank you, sir," she interrupted, "but I've a surly cheat I want nothing more than to wash my hands of. Do I have permission to park this rock in a Lagrangian orbit?"

"Permission granted. Orbital Control's got you covered."

Maya punched in the appropriate coordinates and navigational velocity changes into a keypad on the interface. "All right, *Skeeto*, time for some R-and-R."

iii

"Commissioner Judoma...a surprise seeing you here again," Maya sighed, lowering her hands from her hips. Rolling a chair away from Kuwashima's desk in the lieutenant's office, she sat down.

Judoma formed his best bureaucrat's smile and bowed. "The pleasure is mine, Agent Maya. To put you at ease, the lieutenant and I are not here to pressure you about a partner assignment. Your results are just too good to tamper with."

"That's a relief," Xibalba blurted.

Judoma and Kuwashima exchanged glances before the lieutenant chortled.

Maya slapped her hand down hard on Xibalba's vox outputs, eliciting a meek yelp from the pistol. "Sorry 'bout that, Commissioner. It won't happen again."

Judoma added, "Seems like you have a partner already, anyhow." He circled round Maya and looked out the wide mural window, where Mars' peach glow gazed into Kuwashima's office. "The reason I'm here, Agent, is to remove you from field duty."

"What...!" Maya looked to Kuwashima.

"I have approved your reassignment to Precinct-5, Agent Maya," Kuwashima explained. "You'll be sent to Europa temporarily, just a matter of fifteen days during the IPTP's recruitment drive."

A skeptical glance crossed Maya's face.

"We're expanding our operations into the Outer Reaches," Judoma said, folding his arms. "I trust your skills and experience in assisting our recruiters. Think you have it in you?"

Maya stood, stiffening her spine. All resistance to Judoma's earlier proclamation were soothed slightly by the commissioner's favorable comment. "You're too kind, sir. I have no choice but to accept, do I?"

Judoma flashed his immaculately white teeth. "No...but the interests of the IPTP will greatly benefit from your attendance."

The matter seemed odd, but Maya concluded some time away from the daily grind was worth it, especially if the pay remained the same. Nodding, she agreed.

"Wonderful! I have the itinerary here for you to read," the commissioner said, producing a small data ledger from Kuwashima's desk. "Look it over for the night...we'll talk more tomorrow."
Judoma bowed again and exited, leaving Maya and Kuwashima alone.

"I can't say no, Maya," Kuwashima replied before she could even ask.

Maya skimmed over the data ledger, then stuck it into her jacket pocket. "I guess all that comes to mind is the difficulty I had joining this outfit, Lieutenant. Now, we're inviting schmucks off the streets? What's going on here? This doesn't seem like a logical turn for a police force scraping by on funds."

"The Solar System Government plans on making inroads into the Outer Satellites. We've been receiving funds for recruitment that far exceeds anything I've ever seen in my twenty-five years. Not only for the IPTP, but the Bureau of TransPlanetary Commerce, Department of Natural InterPlanetary Resources, the Federal Marshals, and of course, the respective Departments of Homeplanet Security of each precinct."

Maya pursed her lips. "So, we're just going to be one big, happy Solar System after all this? Competition isn't what I'm in it for, sir. The last thing I need is some fat-assed, grizzled cop thinking he'd make a great agent and gettin' himself killed for a repo reward. Uh-uh, I ain't gonna mislead these jerks, tellin' 'em it's easy money when you could lose your life out here."

Kuwashima folded his arms over his chest. "That will not be your place, Agent. I want you to keep people like that out of here."

"No interference, then. And for chrissakes, no goddamn quotas," Maya said, pointing to Kuwashima. "Understood?"

"Understood."

Maya gave a begrudging nod, then swiveled on her heels towards the door. "C'mon, Xibalba. I got some reading to do."

CHAPTER THREE

i

"Galileopolis, the capital, is where you'll be stationed," Judoma explained, tapping his data ledger with a thin stylus while circling the seated Maya. "Specifically, the police station situated on the floor of the Rhadamanthys Ocean, one hundred and fifty kilometers below the surface crust."

"Are the Jovians or Europans providing security for this?" Maya asked. "The last thing we need is for all hell to break loose like when Europa lost the Beckham Cup."

Judoma laughed. "That very thought was placed at the forefront of security contingencies. Jupiter's Homeplanet Security Department will be there in force, so rest assured nothing like those football hooligans will be seen again."

Maya nodded. "All right. When do I leave?"

"The recruitment drive begins Five-Three. That gives you six weeks of travel time with a slight margin for traffic."

"Hmm...May. The sooner the better I suppose with spring holidays booking the Federal Causeway in advance. I'll need to restock and get *Skeeto* prepped ASAP."

Maya rose from the couch in Kuwashima's office. Judoma placed a hand on the agent's jacket sleeve. "Agent Maya, I can't thank you enough for lending your time and expertise to this drive. Your sacrifice will be returned trebly, I'm confident."

"Sacrifice?" Maya's wary eyes loomed over Judoma's hand. "I'm not sacrificing anything. Credits for the time I've spent on Europa doing this recruitment drive will be in my account all the same."

"I was speaking metaphorically, of course." Judoma removed his hand and gestured ahead. "Allow me to show you to the door."

The pair walked out and into the adjacent corridor, where Precinct-4

Headquarters' hectic foot traffic filled the neon and holographically lit throughway. Vendors in kiosks shouted melodious slogans while a melange of various cafes', craft workers' and maintenance crewmembers' odors wafted to the grated ceiling. The scene always left Maya with a twinge of claustrophobia, if not schizophrenia, at the busied pace. Having been born on Syrtis Major, the backwoods of Mars, so to speak, crowds of people were reserved for formal events and dust storm drills, which explained Maya's fondness for the long journeys of the Causeways. One could go for weeks without encountering another human soul, several months if one really went out of her way and switched off all voxlinks to the outside Solar System; Maya didn't need any more incentive to weasel her way out of Commissioner Judoma's presence.

"I will be monitoring the recruitment drive's progress keenly," Judoma added, pausing in mid-stride.

Was that meant to impress, Maya thought, or remind her of his ever-present influence, a subtle threat to play by his rules?

"I'm sure you will," she smiled, her tone congenial but dripping with dry sarcasm. "I won't disappoint, sir."

Judoma bowed again, then wheeled away, soon disappearing into the seething throng. Just as easily, Maya turned and headed the opposite way, towards the lift to the docking level.

"He's slick," Xibalba said after a period of silence that must have been killing him.

"He's a bureaucrat...that's why they pay him so handsomely." *And a natural politician, way too eager to please.*

"Eh, I'd show him some of my medicine, Maya. I'd rid you of 'im."

Maya dodged a trio of departing security guards, then stepped onto an empty lift. When the titanium doors sealed her off, she replied, "Keep it to yourself there, zip gun. I don't need his goons knocking on my door someday because of your big mouth. You already got me in some shit with your comment last night."

"Sorry," Xibalba said, his tone contrite. It wasn't very often Maya reprimanded the little guy, but times were tense enough without the sidearm giving his two cents' worth to that big-brassed bastard. "You know I wouldn't say nuthin' to hurt ya."

"Yeah, yeah. Don't go getting all lovey. You're my partner, and as such, you have a responsibility for our mutual well being, okay? Now forget about it. How 'bout I surf for those Irisium rounds you're so hot for?"

"All right, you got it."

ii

"Take care of yourself out there," Kuwashima wished Maya over the IPTP's secure IPwebsite once the agent had seated herself aboard *Skeeto's* cockpit.

Maya glanced at the man's dark, concerned eyes. His latent Japanese features were unusually emotive, quite unlike the stoicism he so casually possessed. "Lieutenant...you have some bad coffee with your biscuits this morning? I don't think you've ever contacted me before I've left."

"An old man can change his behavior only so much, Agent Maya. Needless to say, consider this my one and only time. See you on the other side."

Maya nodded curtly, then closed the IPweb connection. *What was that all about?* "*Skeeto*, you ready for departure?"

"Affirmative, Miss Maya. Plasma and hydrazine refueling procedures complete. Precinct-4 Orbital Control has cleared us for departure."

"Excellent. De-docking start...now, release docking clamp, fire port thrusters at half power," Maya commanded, keying in a series of buttons on her interface. A pop-up holograph to her left displayed the umbilical boom detaching and raising to its default vertical position, clearing *Skeeto*'s path.

Skeeto pushed off from its overnight resting place, floating into the dockyard's main departure/approach avenue. Below them, endless stars beckoned.

"Dorsal thrusters at full. Take us Y-axis minus three hundred meters, *Skeeto*."

Like a meteor falling from the sky, *Skeeto* blasted out of the space station's docking level, steering clear of all incoming traffic. At the prescribed depth, *Skeeto*'s thrusters gave out, allowing inertia to take over and finish the craft's descent.

On Maya's navi monitor, a vertical red line emanated from the dockyard's lowest level, accompanied by a text box of coordinates and delta-V changes. Within seconds, Maya punched in another command, admitting plasma from *Skeeto*'s magnetic storage bottles into the four vertical VASIMR engines in the craft's tailfin. Four violet cones of ionized gas exploded aft, propelling *Skeeto* forward, out of Mars' reach.

"Twenty kilometers per second...thirty kilometers per second," *Skeeto* rang out.

Her back taut against her cockpit seat, Maya closed her eyes and enjoyed the thrust of acceleration, once more taking her out of the crowded inner Solar System and into the Outer Reaches, where she somehow felt, deep inside her marrow, that fate and destiny lay in wait for her, somewhere, sometime, someday.

CHAPTER FOUR

i

"Europa possesses the largest ocean in the Solar System, and here I was, a girl from the driest desert in the Solar System, going down into it. Nobody said you weren't crazy for being dedicated to this job."

Europa hung like a jewel from Jupiter's wide neck, a teardrop suspended against velvet. Even from a height of two million kilometers the frozen moon sparkled, its ice floes concealing a deep saltwater sea worthy of the name Neptune, if that name hadn't already been taken by the time the antique *Voyager* probes had visited it some eighteen decades prior.

Cracked and resealed countless times over millions of years that the moon looked ready to break apart before her eyes, Maya watched in rapt attention as *Skeeto* brought them closer, each hour of descent revealing more fault lines and escarpments, a daunting, nigh diamond-hard exterior belying its secret inside. It was as if Europa enjoyed teasing its enraptured guests; the first landers on the moon labored for nearly a year boring into the rocky ice before the first glimpses of liquid ocean crept out.

From there on, humans had continually inhabited the orb, eventually building colonial cities below the ice, suspended metropolises with the aim of studying the brine for signs of extraterrestrial life. Vast networks of human communities now thrived underneath the crust, a strange subterranean existence that mystified Maya. Earth had a perfectly suitable ocean floor that was a hell of a lot more accessible, but she supposed the Europans fancied themselves frontiers people, taming the wilderness. Whatever. As long as they were hospitable, who was she to judge?

An abdominal scar across Europa drew nearer to Maya's vantage point. Her eyes discerned small sodium lights strung along the north and south sides of the ten-kilometer-wide crack, adjacent to flickering landing strip illumination that led the way to the equatorial docking port anchored into

Europa's crust.

"*Galileopolis Port Control hailing Federally registered craft, over,*" a feminine voice said over vox.

Maya toggled a button on her interface. "This is IPTP craft *Skeeto*, Agent Maya speaking, Galileopolis Port Control. Request permission to land, over."

"*Your docking port has been appointed to you, Skeeto. Now uploading landing coordinates to your AI, over.*"

A string of blue numbers spilled onto the holographic interface's navigational display. "Roger, Galileopolis Port Control. Beginning final descent," Maya acknowledged, keying in a series of buttons on a keypad.

Outside, *Skeeto*'s VASIMR engines died, their exhaust cones feathering into space before flaming out.

"*Skeeto*, forward thrusters at full. Final descent parabola...now."

The craft's RCS thrusters slowed their descent, allowing Europa's gentle gravity to set *Skeeto* onto the icy landing strip. A metal conveyor grid underneath the craft propelled *Skeeto* towards the docking port, a pressurized dome literally screwed into the crust with giant, exposed bolts, smack in the middle of the upwelling of crust named Conamara Chaos.

"Another stellar landing, *Skeeto*. Great job."

"Thank you, Miss Maya."

While the grid conveyed towards their final resting point, Maya unfastened her Y-belt and slid out of her seat, then moon-walked towards the rear of the cockpit, careful to avoid hitting her head on the ceiling thanks to the less-than-smooth ride. Opening a starboard cabinet, she removed her EVA armor and crossed into the cylindrical corridor connecting the cockpit unit to *Skeeto*'s aft compartments. This area of the ship had once contained four rows of seats for six-hour flights to the Moon, back in *Skeeto*'s early days as SelenEx Model TL-250 SE-TL-250 89510763A, before Maya had come into possession of the craft. Now, Maya's and a spare set of quarters were housed here, modifications long since made by the former owner—and Maya's mentor—Gilmour Zeobarry.

"I thought we'd landed," Xibalba's voice yelled out as the portside hatch to Maya's quarters opened.

Maya crossed the small distance and retrieved Xibalba from his suspension inside Maya's holster belt. "Yep. Ever seen Europa?"

"Nope...cold and sentient sidearms don't mix."

Maya lifted her left leg and strapped the holster belt over her thigh. "Think of it as a vacation, my friend. Should have plenty of time to visit, maybe watch some football. You like violence, don't you?"

Xibalba laughed. "Only if I'm the one violating."

ii

The vertical descent to the floor of the Rhadamanthys Ocean was long and decidedly unexciting, as the office-complex-sized lifting platform—essentially a gigantic elevator—trudged at a glacial nine kilometers per hour, at least by Maya's last count on her wrist chronometer. With her duffle bags filled to capacity with a change of clothes and her favorite rations, the agent had bid a temporary farewell to *Skeeto* as the craft was left on the surface, housed under the warmth of Galileopolis Port Control's pressure dome. Now, Maya was seated next to assorted riffraff and other motley Europan citizens, some returning home with obvious interplanetary jetlag, while others appearing to be fellow law enforcement officials, neatly decked out in slate grey uniforms, with the ever-present voxlink static crackling between them.

Reclining on a cramped cushion of a horseshoe-shaped sectional, Maya's eyes flitted from the other lift passengers to the holographic monitors placed at equidistant intervals, each displaying various websites for viewing and interactive pleasure. Two older salarymen watched porntoons at one station, the assorted groans and nearly canine-audible female shrieks giving Maya a grin. At another, some tweener girls sat in rapt attention at a soap opera, or was that a reality series? Eh, everything was the same anymore.

She turned her attention to the kiosk outside of the sectional, where several merchants hawked foodstuffs she just knew were leftovers from the twentieth century, repackaged and sent out here for "refreshments." Maya did, however, detect the scent of barbecue, making her stomach tremble in anticipation and her forehead sweat, but she digressed, soon seeing the holographic menu board charging a rate equal to that of a three-star orbital hotel.

Screw that.

Making a small concession to her stomach, she peeled a ration bar and wolfed it down, even if it was light-years short of ribs. Picking the grainy bits from her teeth, she definitely concluded it was not 'cue.

Hours later, the lift had set down on the ocean bottom, the platform's mural windows beyond the kiosks displaying nothing but green murk; somewhere, distant sulfur lights illuminated the ocean from afar. It was about as alien as looking into an Earth-side pool, except it was buried beneath kilometers of pressurized brine capable of crushing a human being in less than a second. Perfect location for a recruitment drive.

A pair of oval airlocks creaked open on the port and starboard ends of the lift, granting access to the north and south wings of Downtown Galileopolis, where a series of gates on each end awaited the newly arrived visitors. Checking her wrist chronometer, which displayed her IPTP-downloaded arrangements, Maya found the appropriate gate to disembark at the north airlock, then flashed her IPTP badge to the attendant and security guard checking in each passenger.

Maya was through the line in ten minutes, then walked off the lift and into Galileopolis proper, a cathedral of pressurized layers of plastic sandwiched between hardened steel alloys. While she realized the intrinsic sophistication of such a structure—after all, it was the crowning achievement of human architecture and materials science off the Earth—she couldn't but feel an aesthetic unease about the city's appeal; it wasn't any different than the dozens of pressurized domes on the Moon, Mars and the orbiting hotels she had spent time in after fleeing home a decade earlier. However, it was for all intents and purposes a gigantic shopping mall. Is that all people did when they left home? More holograms, food kiosks and trinket merchants than even her experienced and skilled eyes could track.

Galileopolis hit one with enough sensory stimulation that the body would black out from overload. Perhaps that was the intent, getting the customers to visit time and time again, each visit a slightly newer encounter despite the site having nothing else to offer but more of the same just beyond the one that greeted you upon entry. Talk about a shell game.

Maya shelved her growing disgust, quickly realizing it was coloring her judgment and taking her mind off her duty in all the wrong ways. This was business, not a holiday; she didn't have to *like* it, just tolerate it long enough to do what Judoma wanted and then hightail it out of here. She was going to have to work on giving herself permission not to hate the place so well. She was going to have to work on a multitude of things....

iii

The next morning, Maya rose early and dressed, then headed for Theta Level, a convention hall the IPTP was renting for the recruitment drive. Dozens of Jovian Homeplanet Security officers were manning the level's perimeter, armed with short-barreled riot rifles and bad attitudes. The convention hall was at the nexus of several cross corridors, allowing applicants to queue up outside the actual hall. Biometric checks were administered to the civilian applicants by Europan physicians, no doubt working overtime to fill the need outside of the colonial hospitals.

Maya passed the applicant throngs on her way to the convention floor's personnel entrance, where she flashed her badge and gained entry, but only after a swift EM and chemical residue exam cleared her. People from all over the three inhabited inner planets were in attendance, quickly reminding Maya of the recruitment drive's resonance, especially in a time of Solar System expansion coupled with economic stagnation. Procuring employment with the SSG was the best deterrent to hopelessness for these people; Maya chided herself for forgetting her fortune. She could easily be one of these people, if not for the "out" provided by her predatory senses and skills.

"Excuse me," a masculine voice said, "aren't you from Precinct-4?"

Maya had heard the man's approach from twenty paces back, but was surprised by his forwardness. Turning, she saw a tall, thin man wearing a black wraparound solar blocker over his eyes, disguising his irises and pupils. Smart move, Maya thought, if he knew who she was and what she was capable of discerning from a person's eyes. He was dressed similarly to Lieutenant Kuwashima, meaning he had good reason to be in such attire and accoutrements.

"Agent Maya, P-4," she answered. Smiling, she shook his hand.

The man returned the greeting. "Lieutenant Kert Tudough, Precinct-5. Welcome to Europa, Agent Maya. Wally—er, Lieutenant Kuwashima, informed me you would be here, and to watch for you. He said he personally selected you to represent him for this event after I asked for the loaning of his best agent."

"I'm not sure whether to feel honored or embarrassed," Maya replied, her lips curling at the corner a bit.

Tudough skimmed over her lithe body with his eyes. "No, the honor's all mine."

"Hmm...that why you have the solar blocker? Thinking you can fool the ladies into believing you're all business?"

An unsteady hand flew up to Tudough's eyes and swiftly discarded the black crescent into a pocket. "These...oh, no. Just here for show. Gotta keep the applicants in line. Keep my composure steely."

Maya and Tudough walked again, the man increasing his pace just to keep up with her.

"So, what am I needed here for, Lieutenant?" Maya asked, emphasizing Tudough's rank.

"Lieutenant Kuwashima and Commissioner Judoma have arrived to the conclusion—based on your own applicant scores—that you would be more than suitable to judge these applicants on their viability as future IPTP agents."

"That's big of them...I suppose possessing the highest exam scores in the history of this organization qualifies me for all kinds of shit jobs, eh?"

Tudough's hand leapt out and brushed Maya's right shoulder. "Come on, Agent Maya. It's not what you think."

Maya paused, her head not swiveling back to answer the man. "Then why is your hand deigning to touch me? I am not a child, sir, and I have thorough knowledge of the IPTP's code of conduct, so I recommend removing that hand if you value it."

"Ehh...sorry. My apologies," Tudough eeked out as he slid his hand back.

"Why don't you just try, sir, to be straight with me. I don't need to be congratulated on my skills," Maya said, her tone even. "What duties am I here to perform?"

"All right." Tudough put his hands to his hips and looked at Maya seriously for the first time. "Separate the wheat from the chaff. Tell me who has it and who's fooling themselves."

Maya frowned. "Don't you pay people good money for this kind of service?"

"We have in the past, yes. But those people are professional examiners, and being such, have never worked a day in the field as agents representing the IPTP. You, on the other hand—"

"I'm a hunter," she acknowledged casually.

"Yes. Simple as that."

Maya nodded, then looked out at the hundreds of applicants in the dozen queues surrounding the pair. Tall, short, stocky, wiry, all examples of human variety, all here for a chance to make their mark, just as Maya had done. What would she have done differently if she had had the opportunity to evaluate herself? Would she even be here now if she had? Or would she have bounced herself out, self-critical as always?

"Okay, Lieutenant. I want footage of every queue since the moment it formed. If you want my honest opinion, I need to see these people offguard. Body language is a good first step."

"You'll have it."

"And a secure room to evaluate the cuts over the next few days."

Tudough nodded. "Anything else?"

A smile crossed Maya's face. "Barbecue ribs...and a beer to wash them down."

CHAPTER FIVE

"I didn't realize you were so pink!"

"Are you actually doing what I told you to do?"

"But you humans...how do you all get so pink? And soft? You really are squishy!"

"Xibalba, pay attention or I'll unplug you."

"Why are they bouncing up and down like that?"

"Must be nervous...sometimes we do that, you know."

"Maybe they're nervous 'cuz I'm watching them. What's that word...."

"Huh?"

"When people are being watched without their knowledge?"

"This isn't voyeurism, Xibalba. They know they're being watched."

"Huh...I don't know, Maya. Seem to be putting on quite a performance, that pair of yours. Almost like they like being watched."

"All right, that's it. I'm unplugging you."

"C'mon, Maya! Just a few more minutes!"

Maya sighed. Reaching over to the display's holographic interface, she severed the sentient sidearm's optical link. Now rendered blind again, Xibalba let out a tremble.

"Sorry, but if you weren't going to do what I asked you to do—"

"But Maya, I've never seen humans like that before! How else am I supposed to behave?"

Maya reclined in the office chair and folded her arms, her eyes rolling at the pistol situated before her at the desk. It'd been too many hours in this tiny room alone with Xibalba for her own good. "Like you're on duty?"

"Sorry...."

"Maybe this was destined to fail, Xibalba. You were meant for combat, not surveillance. Pardon me if I overloaded your inputs."

"S'allright. So, when are we going to do some violating?"

Maya rose from the seat and holstered her sidearm. "I think I've come too close already."

"Huh? What's that mean?"

"Forget it. Let's get a drink and call it a night. I gotta be back at oh six hundred tomorrow." It was all she could say to keep from hurting the sidearm's feelings.

ii

The drudgery Maya felt over the next few days was cut only on the rare occasion when a particular applicant exhibited genuine abilities she thought invaluable for an agent of the InterPlanetary Tax Police. A dozen were in this select group, which Maya duly noted in her daily report to Lieutenant Tudough. The good lieutenant had, in the meantime, invited her to a briefing with his IPTP advisors in Theta Level's private banquet hall, whereupon she had been promised a change of scene for a few hours to "refresh her batteries," as it was put to her in person by the lieutenant. If that got her out of the office and away from a monitor and constant holo-footage replays, than all the better.

The banquet hall was a misnomer, Maya realized, at the very least. A glorified cafeteria was a better description. Several rows of plastic tables and one-meter-tall seats were it, and a mess kitchen off to the side for buffet meals. She had to hand it to the lieutenant; he could pick 'em all right.

Checking her wrist chrono, Maya was several minutes early, just enough time to study the prefab metal walls and a series of paintings adorning them. Her eyebrows were raised by the black velvet, green alien-as-Elvis print (someone with an obvious, if not quite healthy, sense of humor), but the rest were replica Bonestell planetary vistas, quite quaint compared to the real McCoys humanity had now landed on. Oh well, nostalgia still had a strong pull.

A door opening a moment later revealed Tudough and a pair of his entourage he had introduced to her two days earlier, a woman and man named Gydour and Dhej, respectively. Maya had looked askance to them, thinking they were more personal bodyguards then bureaucratic advisors, both being well over two meters in height and trim as athletes, but Tudough, in a transparent attempt to assuage her, remarked that tensions were high with several rebel groups operating in the Jovian System. "You can't be too careful," Tudough had said.

Maya only knew all too well. Her first mission with the IPTP had been to repo the equipment and weapons of an arms dealer by the name of Shigu Haxab, known to sell his wares to groups such as the Cassini Company, the front for a group calling itself the Peoples' Popular Revolutionary Task Force for the Defense of the Outer Satellites, based on Iapetus. When not selling to outfits such as the PPRTFDOS, Haxab had dabbled in artificial intelligence, installing modules into weapons systems, one of which just happened to be Xibalba, whom Maya had "sequestered" after the successful completion of that maiden mission.

Haxab had been playing with fire, however, as the PPRTFDOS didn't take well to having that avenue of weapons procurement severed, and had subsequently ordered a hit on his life for his stupidity at being caught. It was with good reason then, Maya thought, that Tudough watched his hind quarters. One never knew when some Outer Reaches crackpots were going to rear up and jihad someone. Reading between the lines, she figured the IPTP's recruitment drive was designed to root all these crackpots out in a major offensive to be shared among the respective Solar System divisions and bureaus.

"Good morning, Agent Maya," Tudough greeted her.

"Morning, Lieutenant." Maya swung her head from one end of the banquet hall to the other. "Kinda quiet today."

Tudough smiled, gesturing to a nearby seat. "Took the liberty of reserving the banquet hall for a few hours. Business and all that."

Maya seated herself, following Tudough, but furrowed her brows in surprise when Gydour and Dhej nodded to the lieutenant and left. "Uhm, aren't they staying?"

"No need," Tudough said in a reassuring tone. "We can accomplish all we need to without my advisors."

Within a moment, a chef walked out from behind the mess kitchen and wheeled over a cart full of various breakfast platters; steaming scrambled eggs, fried bacon, sausages, waffles, bowls of cold cereals, and orange juice and milk bottles were all at the pair's disposal. The chef smiled and nodded, then went back to the kitchen.

"I also took the liberty of procuring breakfast for us," he said, laying a cloth napkin over his lap. "It's all on me, so eat up."

"How kind of you. Tell me, is this your idea of a date, sir?"

"Oh, no," Tudough laughed. "This is breakfast...a date is what I have planned for later." His blue eyes rose up from his waffles and locked onto Maya's orbs, in deadly earnestness.

"You think highly of yourself, sir," she responded. *Perhaps too highly.* "So what will tonight's ruse be? An afternoon snack at my office? A walk around Theta Level's aquariums?"

Tudough cut up a slice of waffle and ate it. "Whatever you want it to be."

"Mmm, well, how about a few hours of silence, say you at your quarters, and me at mine. Separately," Maya said, taking a swig of orange juice.

He gave an amused smile. "Wally said you were a tough customer. He wasn't joking, was he?"

"Did you want my report, Lieutenant? If not, I'll be taking my leave now—"

"Yes."

Maya produced a data ledger from her trouser-leg pocket and handed it to him. "Applicants D-One, G-Nine and K-Four look promising, potentially suitable to be hired right away," she explained. "Their citizenship records indicate they've all had various martial arts training, and each has earned perfect scores on IPTP-comparable psych exams. Applicants A-Eleven, C-One, C-Three, E-Eight, H-Two, H-Three, I-Five and K-Ten all match physical requirements, but have had no further training, so would need to attend entry-level law enforcement schooling, but might achieve average-to-above-average standing as agents."

"Excellent," Tudough said, reading the data ledger's screen. "We have already culled about two dozen applicants in addition to these, and sent the rest packing. I want you to personally inspect the remaining pool."

Maya nodded, and after a moment's silence, asked, "Is that all, sir?"

"Mm-hmm, yes." He didn't make eye contact again with her, instead working on the remnants of his breakfast.

Maya shoved her empty glass away from her and rose to her feet. Crossing over to the banquet hall's entrance, she opened the door, where Gydour and Dhej waited just on the opposite side of the threshold. Walking down the corridor, Tudough's come on itself didn't so much bother her, but something else...perhaps the look in his eye, the way he turned stone cold after her rebuff. Whatever it was, it didn't sit well with Maya. The best course, in her opinion, was to follow Tudough's inspection command, finish her requirements per Judoma's wish, and hightail it off Europa. There was a strange atmosphere here, and it wasn't just the kilometers of ocean sitting over her head. Tudough had piqued her curiosity, and not in a good way.

CHAPTER SIX

i

"*Skeeto*, you there?" Maya whispered into her voxlink. Opening the door to her quarters, she picked up her clothes from yesterday and threw them onto the bunk.

"Yes, Miss Maya," *Skeeto* responded a few seconds later, the line crackly from the kilometers of briney interference.

"Activate security hack and take yourself into high orbit and wait for further instructions," Maya ordered. "Keep voxlink open at all times. Something's bothering me about this place."

"Acknowledged, Miss Maya. Accessing Galileopolis Port Control security protocols...opening docking port entryway now."

"All right, *Skeeto*, let me know when you've reached orbit."

"You don't trust anyone, do you?" Xibalba said from the side of her hip.

Maya shook her head. "That's why I muted you during that 'briefing' of Tudough's."

"I didn't mean me...what's buggin' you now?"

She gathered her clothes into her duffle bag, then sealed it. "Instinct, that's what. C'mon, Xibalba, you know better than to ask me a stupid question."

"Than what are we gonna do, Maya? Run away?"

"Only if fighting doesn't get it done."

"Whoa...what *was* in that OJ you had?"

Maya remained silent. She put on her leather jacket over her tunic, then exited the quarters again. Drawing Xibalba, she clicked a button on the bottom of his hilt, checking the magazine she had placed inside.

"Magnesium stun rounds, just like you ordered, Maya," Xibalba said.

"None of those kiddie-sized stun rounds you keep stored, got it?"

Maya instructed as she placed him back into the hip holster.

"Aye, aye, ma'am!"

ii

Maya headed towards the convention hall, where the regular security detail were already on duty. Queuing in the line, Maya flashed her badge and entered. Inside, the convention hall had been reconfigured for several series of physical examinations of the passed applicants. Biometric machines—an order of magnitude more powerful than the security models at the hall's entrance—were spaced in six rows, adjacent to blue mats placed on the floor. Trained technicians and physical therapists manned the respective rows, ready to receive the next round of applicants.

Maya walked a circuit around the floor, studying the hall's layout and other details perhaps better left to the security personnel, at least in the eyes of the Jovian Homeplanet Security Bureau.

"How is it on passive scan, Xibalba?" Maya whispered, blocking her lips with her hand and simultaneously funneling the sound down to the holstered sidearm.

"Lotta interference from those biometric doohickeys...nothing looks out of the ordinary. Well, with the Homeplanet dudes here, anyway."

"Got it. Keep me apprised if you sense anything...weird."

"Besides you?"

Maya sighed. "With *them*, or anyone else."

"Gotcha."

Maya paused and leaned against a pillar, observing the multitudes of people filing into the convention hall. Many were the same as days past, some even being the people accompanying her on the platform lift a few days ago. After a few minutes, Tudough made his entrance, followed of course by Gydour and Dhej. The lieutenant was locked in conversation with another man, this time someone she had never seen. The four wandered in and seemed to be inspecting the biometric machines, Tudough gesturing to them excitedly. He obviously had never been in an emergency room or field hospital within the last decade, as the machines were everywhere human medical science could travel.

Yawning, Maya came away from the pillar and swiveled her head across the now-crowded convention hall again. She rejoined the milling throng, soon finding herself within Tudough's orbit.

The lieutenant was at first oblivious, then noticed Maya and came straight over to her, followed by the unknown man and Gydour and Dhej. "Agent Maya...I would like to introduce you to Europa's governor, Itheuwet Eymkis. Thanks to his generosity and hospitality, this recruitment drive was possible."

Maya gave a curt bow, then shook Eymkis' hand. "Pleasure, your honor."

"Everything seems to be going extremely successfully," Eymkis said. "Wouldn't you agree, Lieutenant?"

Gydour quickly whispered into Tudough's ear before the lieutenant nodded and returned a smile to Eymkis. "Yes, Governor," he said. To Maya, Tudough appeared to be holding his face differently, as if concealing from the audience what his "advisor" had just informed him of.

"Lieutenant, you promised me an introduction with the surviving applicants," Eymkis said, a politician's impatient smirk crossing over his face.

"Yes, Governor, I did. Gydour, Dhej, could you lead the governor to the applicant's green room? They should be arriving about now and getting ready for today's examinations. I will be there shortly, Governor."

The lieutenant's advisors nodded to Tudough, then pointed the way to the governor, leading him away from Tudough and Maya.

"You managed to get rid of him easily enough," Maya observed. "Get tired of him already?"

Tudough smiled, then crossed his arms. His eyes twinkled, a strange light in his orbs, as if he now held precious information over someone. "Maya," he said coyly, "perhaps I should be asking you if you've gotten tired of this already. Galileopolis Port Control reported a few minutes ago that your craft departed port without permission. Now, what's all that about?"

Maya shook her head, pretending to be annoyed. "Dammit—I thought I had it fixed...if you'll excuse me, Lieutenant—" Maya swiveled on her heels.

"Not so hasty, Maya." Tudough reached out for the agent, but she had gotten past his arm's length. "Maya?"

"I have to see what's wrong with my ship!" Maya stormed away, not looking back as she plowed through the crowd.

iii

Maya paused outside her appointed office to catch her breath, then entered the small office, crossing over to the monitor. Accessing the holographic interface, she directed the security system's cameras to locate Governor Eymkis and those two advisors. Within a moment, the cameras in the Theta Level's green room found Eymkis standing before several of the applicants, speaking with them, or perhaps more accurately, giving an impromptu monologue.

Maya keyed in a wide shot of the green room, expanding the camera's view to encompass its entirety. Her eyes darted around the image, noting all the applicants, Eymkis and Dhej, but not finding Gydour. The camera panned around three-hundred-and-sixty-five degrees, but still no Gydour. Furrowing her brows, she accessed another search parameter, having the computer look throughout the entire Theta Level. The results read "PROFESSIONAL COMPLEX," meaning the row of offices including this very room, but couldn't pinpoint her exact location.

Maya swiftly shutdown the computer and made a quick exit. Brandishing Xibalba in her right hand, she surveyed the corridor and, determining that it was clear, ran towards the personal complex and her quarters, which she reached in mere moments. Running inside, she locked the door, placed Xibalba nearby and unpacked her EVA armor and helmet from the duffle bag's larger compartment. Placing the armor on, she completed the seal in time to hear someone try the door lock from the outside.

Reaching over for Xibalba, Maya moved just as the door was ripped from its hinges, taking a good chunk out of the metal threshold. Standing in the entrance was a hulking Gydour, who threw the mangled door into the corridor and barged inside.

"Goddamn!" Maya yelled. Aiming Xibalba, she targeted Gydour's face.

Two rounds skimmed Gydour's forehead and shattered off in the distance, leaving the "advisor" unharmed. Gydour covered a meter in one step while charging for Maya, who leapt away and aimed again, this time at Gydour's heart.

"Gimme xenon rounds, Xibalba!"

Squeezing Xibalba's trigger, Maya fired two more rounds straight at Gydour's chest. This time, both penetrated Gydour's dermis and exploded, spattering flesh and ripped fabric over the area, but no blood.

Gydour halted for a few seconds and let loose an inhuman cry. Looking down at the wound she cried again, but then rose to look at the much shorter Maya.

Cold eyes now filled with fury, "Die!" was all Gydour could muster. Lunging, she caught Maya's armored leg as the agent went to leap a second time, picking up the smaller woman.

Maya let out a scream, her back hitting and rolling on the floor.

Gydour brought Maya's boot to eye level, the dangling agent's eyes bulged as she was brought closer to Gydour. Biding her time, Maya's left hand found her knife holster. Unlatching it, she produced her blade, and curling her stomach muscles to double over, thrust the blade into Gydour's left hand.

An horrific shriek filled the air, then Maya fell to the floor, landing square on her right ribs. Looking up, the agent saw Gydour writhe, grasping her hand in pain. Maya wiped her blade clean, only to notice the fluid sheathing it was black and oily, not crimson.

"Robonoid," she whispered to herself, her eyes large with disbelief. A synthetic human, rumored to exist, but something Maya herself had never yet seen. Scuttlebutt was some of the rebel groups in the Outer Solar System, the Peoples' Popular Revolutionary Task Force for the Defense of the Outer Satellites included, had managed to get their hands on such equipment, probably thanks to people like Shigu Haxab and other unscrupulous black and grey market military dealers. Personnel were scarce, and frankly, short-lived. If Gydour and Dhej were robonoids, was Tudough as well? Had he bought them off the PPRTFDOS? Or, worse yet, was he PPRTFDOS?

"Xibalba, give me a single explosive titanium round, maximum yield!"

"You got it, Maya!" The little sidearm emitted a click, then said, "Loaded and ready!"

Gydour continued her painful display, giving Maya the narrowest of margins to rise to her feet and close in, targeting Xibalba's short barrel point blank at the robonoid's vulnerable brain case.

Firing Xibalba, Maya instantly turned and flung herself backwards as the round exited. The robonoid's cry ratcheted into a sharp sqawk as her head was obliterated, blowing a noxious explosion into the quarters.

Helping herself off the floor a third time, Maya surveyed the destruction; Gydour's body twitched, but lay harmlessly two meters from Maya, an array of plastic, metal and cloth debris blanketing the area. Acrid smoke climbed to the ceiling, but no flames were visible.

"Holy crap!" Xibalba yelled, his sensors detecting the robonoid's meltdown. "Good shot, Maya!"

Maya grabbed her duffle bag. "C'mon, Xibalba, no time to admire our work. We ain't gonna wait around for room service to clean this up."

CHAPTER SEVEN

i

Maya ran down the personal complex corridor, her gait soon increasing at the sound of alarm klaxons blaring overhead. Security was, no doubt, by now aware of the explosion in her quarters, and in all likelihood scrambled to the area by Jovian Homeplanet Security to apprehend her for questioning. Maya was in no mood to be interrogated, especially if Tudough had his hands in the security cookie jar, as he appeared to be in the IPTP's.

Making her way to Theta Level's lift, her thoughts dwelled back to the circumstances of the recruitment drive. If Tudough had meant for this to happen—and Maya couldn't believe otherwise—then Europa was a perfect set-up for isolating his forces from reinforcements from the Solar System Government authorities. Whatever reasoning he had for possessing robonoids, be it Homeplanet Security neutralization, toppling the IPTP P-5, or just general mayhem, the plan would go much more smoothly if Maya had given in to his charms—perhaps switching allegiances to Tudough—or been neutralized herself, an occurrence she was determined to prevent. She couldn't help but contemplate if Tudough had known more about her than he let on when they first met. Had her reputation preceded her that quickly, and well?

"*Mi...Maya,*" *Skeeto* said, her voice breaking through a wall of static over Maya's voxlink.

"What have you got, *Skeeto*?" Maya asked, rounding a bend in the corridor. The lift entrance was just meters away now.

"*My...ensor pla...form—detecting an ex...plosion aboard the...alileopolis Port Control...do...ing port....*"

Maya paused, her right hand tuning the voxlink on her left collar. "Repeat, *Skeeto*. Voxlink is breaking—"

A massive thump drew Maya's attention towards the corridor ceiling, where the overhead illumination suddenly blacked out, followed by the seizure of Galileopolis' internal atmosphere circulation and power systems. An aural vacuum now dominated the darkened corridor where once the everpresent ducts and conduits operated noisily.

"—*Iss Maya, the port has...xploded...can attempt no...anding at this time,*" *Skeeto* continued.

"Dammit!" Was Tudough behind this, or someone else? The only other thought she had was the PPRTFDOS, but this seemed too subtle and long-termed for a band of guerrilla thugs more interested in heavy weapons and raping woman at gunpoint than organized conspiracy.

With the atmospheric duct work and scrubbers offline, Maya's only sure source of air would be her EVA suits's own seven-day supply. Donning her helmet, she ran the last few meters to the now-idle lift. Activating her gauntlets' power systems with a simple voice command, she affixed her gloved fingertips between the lift door's seams and pried them open, then entered.

Looking up, she spotted a flat, circular hatch at the lift's apex. Bending her knees, she gathered her strength, then leapt up the meter-and-a-half distance. With both hands extended, Maya grappled the hatch's interior lip and held on with all her might.

"Torch!" she yelled, activating the subatomic particle tool on her left wrist gauntlet. A blue finger of energy erupted from the tiny optical torch, searing and soon burning a three-centimeter-wide hole through the soft aluminum ceiling. Within a moment's time Maya had rotated herself fully, completing the circular cut.

Reaching her right hand up, she felt the convex exterior and gripped it, then jerked the remainder of the interior hatch away, allowing her access to the lift platform's top. Heaving herself up, she clambered through and rose to her feet, where she now found a dark shaft, lit only by her miniscule interior helmet lamp.

"Sensor pallet," she commanded. Her left gauntlet now rotated the optical torch clockwise and presented a small array of sensors to her Heads Up Display, or HUD, a holographic interface inside her helmet's faceplate.

Maya pointed her left arm upwards, her eyes darting over the text box figures and graphical schematics on her HUD. It was a long way to Alpha Level and the freedom of the Rhadamanthys Ocean, some two kilometers, but if she wanted to get out alive, she'd best start now. Finding out who was ultimately behind these acts could wait; Maya could do little without *Skeeto's* help, and honestly, preferred having *Skeeto* at her disposal in a crisis. Until Maya could regain her freedom, she was no better than a caged rat. Granted, a well-armed rat with Xibalba, but a rat no less.

Checking that all her EVA systems were at nominal, Maya braced herself and ordered, "Fire RCS thrusters, full throttle!"

Twin exhaust cones exited her dorsal RCS thrusters, propelling the agent upwards at a velocity of three hundred meters per minute. Alpha Level's ceiling would be in her line of sight in less than seven minutes. Until then, all Maya could do was steer and try not to crash into anything.

ii

Six minutes later, Maya spied Alpha Level's sealed corridor hatch near the top of the shaft. Steering herself to within a half-meter of the shaft wall, she gradually decreased her thruster power, easing her ascent until she could grapple the vertical lift railing. Hurriedly climbing the railing's rungs, Maya arrived at the hatch thirty seconds later. Bracing her legs against the lower rungs, she balanced herself long enough to force open the hatch's twin panels with her strengthened gauntlets.

Pushing herself over the precipice, she rose to her feet and walked down the darkened corridor. Swinging her head left to right, she lit the corridor with her helmet lamp, providing her eyes with a view unencumbered by the unnatural EM frequencies generated by her HUD's sensors, ideal for allowing her instincts to roam freely.

As she traversed the corridor, Maya knew she had to find an escape avenue, and quickly. If Tudough was involved with any rogue outfit, he'd undoubtedly not hesitate to eliminate her at his earliest convenience; she'd rather be a thorn in his side by surviving. Accessing the holographic interface on her HUD, she displayed Galileopolis' floor plan, looking for any vehicle or lift platform to get her direct access to the surface without delay.

She discovered several non-commercial lift platforms—what would have been orbital elevators on other, more traditionally terrestrial surfaces—anchored to the ocean bottom. Designed to ascend to the icy crust via elongated, vertical cables, they would be ideal, if not for the fact that the nearest lift was over a kilometer away, clearly out of her way; Maya needed to go straight up ASAP, with no detours if at all possible, quickly ruling these out in all but as a last resort.

Additional scans brought up a naval survey station attached to the city, just a few hundred meters from Alpha Level. If she were anyone but an agent of the IPTP, she might have overlooked it, but Maya realized that the scientists at the station had to have some type of undersea rover at their disposal, whether manned or as a remote operated vehicle. Commandeering it for a short excursion to the surface would be her best option, and even better, not susceptible to the power failure now endemic to the city.

Discerning the naval station's precise coordinates, she plugged in the best route to it from her present location, then set towards it at a swift pace, careful to avoid Jovian Homeplanet Security. If Tudough was smart—Maya was banking on him not being as resourceful as her—then he'd have disabled or deactivated any device or system capable of lending her assistance the moment he took action. She just hoped he hadn't; it'd be a long, hard and cold swim to the top otherwise.

iii

Coming upon a set of sealed doors labeled "RHADAMANTHYS NAVAL RESEARCH CENTER, GALILEOPOLIS DIVISION," Maya laid her hands upon the closest door and pulled hard, breaking its lock within seconds with her gauntlets. The office may have been military or civilian, she couldn't tell which, but the security was pedestrian at best. According to her scans, the research center housed a pair of rovers, both located outside the center's exterior, but docked via a shaft just large enough to crawl through, and conceivably, shift equipment as well.

Maya ran through the office and found the first docking hatch a few meters away, situated along the interior of a wall bearing a rectangular mural window of the Rhadamanthys Ocean, a much darker greenish blue than last time, owing to the absence of illumination from inside the city. Maya then glimpsed the rover's stem and portside exterior; she guessed that it was roughly three meters in length, half that in height, but more than enough to get her where she needed.

Maya then turned her attention to the docking hatch. Placing her gauntlets on the round docking handle, she twisted the mechanism counter-clockwise until an audible cue from the interior latch told her she had unlocked it. She pulled the hatch open and clambered inside the shaft, crawling on all four limbs for a few centimeters until reaching the rover's aft compartment, which was open to her entry.

Advancing to the bubble-shaped cockpit, Maya sat in the left seat and acclimated herself with the old-style physical interfaces, a steering wheel and dashboard console, full of manual switches. Finding the most important-looking interface, a keyhole near the steering wheel, she removed it by force and accessed the underlying wires, which she swiftly hotwired. The rover quickly came to life, illumination lighting up the console, a small overhead lamp and the forward exterior navigation lights.

Maya detached the docking shaft, then sealed the rover's aft hatch, closing her off from Galileopolis. Next, she started the engine and throttled up the rover, the small craft choking before purring its approval. Inputting direct coordinates to the surface crust into the navigation computer, Maya put the rover to full throttle and braced herself as the craft lurched forward into the depths of the Rhadamanthys Ocean at full capacity, delivering her away from Tudough and his robonoids.

CHAPTER EIGHT

Or so Maya thought....

"You won't evade us for too long, pretty little redhead Maya," Tudough taunted over the rover's voxlink. Somehow he had acquired the naval research center's communications frequency, and now wouldn't shut his mouth.

Maya gritted her teeth, refusing to play his game by responding to his repeated hails the last few minutes. Now, however, Tudough had crossed Maya's line in the sand. "Sod off, traitor...you weren't my type to begin with."

"Ooohh, the little prize does have a tongue, doesn't she, Dhej? Oh, yes, about Gydour...that was very troublesome what you did to my advisor, Maya. Very troublesome. She cost me quite a bit of credits, and I don't fancy you have much of a heart to replace her as a favor for me, do you?"

"I've killed living humans with less qualms, Tudough," she said, omitting the obligatory usage of his rank when she addressed him. "Your robonoid lacked my respect, as do you."

"Come on, Maya, don't be so cold to me...can't we have that date? We have the whole facility to ourselves, promise."

"Why are you doing this, Tudough? Who are you beholden to?"

"Myself, above all," he responded. There was no hint of falsehood, nor coercion; to Maya, his tone implied he spoke the truth, for once. "Won't you join me, Maya? Your skills are exceptional, better than any agent I've ever seen."

Maya furrowed her brow; was this all about her? "Uhm, haven't you seen what I just did to your robonoid? That should be answer enough."

"I'm giving you the option to save your life, dear Maya. I can excuse your injuries to my pride in the past, even the ones you're committing now in that tiny rover, if you join me. This would not be proffered to anyone else."

On the rover's dashboard display, the surface locator put the ice crust at a distance of one hundred and thirty-five kilometers; Maya wasn't sure if she could handle another two hours' worth of Tudough's idle conversation without losing her sanity.

"No deal, Tudough. You're going to have to stop me first."

Tudough sighed. "Why are you being so difficult? Can't you see you're wanted!"

"Taken, thanks. Now sod off!" Maya reached for the radio transmitter and yanked it out of the dashboard, effectively ending Tudough's pleas.

Maya throttled the rover to its highest gear, banking that Tudough and whoever else he had working for him—or alternately, who he was working for—didn't have the means nor capability to stop her while the rover was deep in the Rhadamanthys Ocean. Short of a targeted bomb strike to Europa, Maya was secure while under the crust, but once she surfaced, her position would be triangulated within moments, if Tudough was savvy enough to compromise Europa's traffic satellites. And if he hadn't, well, that was a few more moments in her pocket to get the hell off the moon.

To help her in that goal, however, Maya had to get a word out to P-4, as P-5 was arguably untrustworthy. That meant re-establishing her voxlink to *Skeeto*, if Tudough hadn't jammed the lower band frequencies. Accessing the voxlink control in her helmet, she was betting he hadn't.

"*Skeeto*, you reading me?!"

"*Yes, Miss Maya,*" *Skeeto*'s voice acknowledged, sounding as though the computer's voice was lodged deep in a watery cave.

"I need you to send a secure codec to Lieutenant Kuwashima immediately! Code it Level Alpha-One with my IPTP key!"

"*Acknowledged, Miss Maya. Accessing codec protocols...broadcasting in three seconds...two...one...now broadcasting. Precinct-4 shall receive Level Alpha-One codec in fifty-five minutes.*"

"Keep voxlink open. I'll be in contact when I'm within five kilometers from the surface. For now, try to elude any Europan satellites...they may be compromised, despite broadcasting Federal transponder codes."

"*Acknowledged, Miss Maya. I shall be awaiting your next voxlink communication.*"

And I'll be waiting for you to get me the hell out of here. Until then, though, Maya could only recline and wait out the rover's ascent.

ii

"Find Maya and bring her to me!" Tudough barked, jabbing a finger into Dhej's meaty chest.

"Do you want her alive?" a raspy voice said from deep within the robonoid's metal ribcage.

Tudough whirled around. "What kind of question is that? Of course I want her alive! That was one of the reasons we're here, Dhej. Honestly, don't you listen?"

The robonoid displayed a response that would normally be construed as remorse if he were human. For him, however, it was just carbon-nanotube fibers bundled around his vocal interface in a pre-programmed algorithm, in a concession to humans' discomfort with synthetics.

Dhej nodded quickly, then went about his business, leaving Tudough alone in his office. Waving his left hand over his right wrist, he accessed a holographic interface, which displayed a turquoise visage looking back at him.

"What the hell is keeping you, Lieutenant?" the face said, scowling. "We're not paying you by the hour, so cough her up."

"I'm working on it...just give me a little longer. Maya took out Gydour, so I've had a rough day."

The face grunted. "Not as rough as when we got hold of you."

"Please, just be patient. You've waited this long. I'm not in the IPTP for nothing."

"We'll see."

With that, the hologram shimmered and faded, leaving Tudough to the darkness of his office. Once he did cough up Agent Maya, he hoped it would all be worth it. Somehow, though, he was starting to feel the effort was beginning to outpace the reward. He had explained to them nothing was easy where the good agent was concerned, but plenty of credits had been flashed in his face to convince him to undertake the op. Now, he could almost curse his greed.

Almost.

CHAPTER NINE

i

"Xibalba, got anything that'll blast through four kilometers of ice?" Maya asked, her eyes startled at the rover's sensor readings, where the latest measurement of Europa's icy surface depth was displayed in alarmingly large red numerals; four kilometers was far too thick for the tiny rover to knock through.

"Yeah, if I was a fusion bomb," Xibalba answered, adding a laugh after it. "Then again, if I was an H-bomb, I wouldn't be in this mess right now—"

"Yeah, yeah," Maya said, her tone less than pleased. "C'mon, you've gotta have something in that arsenal of yours."

Xibalba's pseudo-synapses fired deep within his red casing, his AI computing millions of teraflop calculations, all in the hope of his datacells composing some sort of answer for his mistress. "I've got a pair of magnesium-vanadium rounds guaranteed to punch a hole in the side of an IP hauler. Will that do it?"

"Vanadium's pretty strong...are they particulates?"

"Yeah, just a micron in diameter."

Maya stroked her chin. "That just may...the ocean water shouldn't douse the magnesium, so that should be enough to blast a chunk big enough for us to pass through."

"Finding a fissure in the ice will help," Xibalba added. "Anything to lessen the distance and give the water a chance to squirt us through."

"Agreed. Now, I just need to find someplace close by where the ice is thin...."

Looking at the dashboard, Maya directed the tiny craft's omnidirectional sensor platform while the rover sped towards possible oblivion at the surface. A three-hundred-and-sixty-degree swath of ice crust was meticulously scanned by the rover's specially designed instruments and displayed as a horizontal continuum of peaks and valleys. Maya scrutinized the valleys, each representing a lessening of the crust's depth, most of which were a fairly flat plateau that were less-than-promising.

The problem was the fact that their current coordinates were nearly all capped by the mighty domed formation Conamara Chaos, which stretched for dozens of kilometers above them. It was a relatively recent formation (in Europan timescales), meaning that the ocean water had frozen as solid as steel, but wasn't yet old enough to be stressed and broken-up by the glacial continents floating over the Rhadamanthys Ocean, which continually (again, in Europan timescales) resurfaced the moon.

"Wait a moment," Maya whispered, returning her attention to the sensor platform.

"What?" Xibalba asked.

Maya manipulated the dashboard controls, focusing the sensors on Conamara Chaos itself. "We're under a huge pressure dome, an upwelling of ocean water that's being pushed upwards by the ocean itself."

"I'm not following, Maya. Don't we want an area that's thin?"

"That's Plan B, now," Maya said. "Listen, Xibalba, there's probably vertical channels, like rivers, forcing themselves upwards to the surface, where the force of the ocean is stressing the dome at its apex. There's gotta be an area, maybe around the foot of the dome, that's vulnerable under the dome's massing weight, where we can fire a round and crack it open, then ride a river to the crust."

"Whoa, where do you get this stuff?"

Maya ignored her sidearm and focused on finding vulnerable fractures inside the Conamara Chaos. Grabbing the steering wheel with both hands, she directed the rover off their current course and steered them nearer to the dome's position, less than an hour above their heads.

Over the next half-hour, the rover continually fed its scans of Conamara Chaos to Maya, who studied the internal geography of the dome, looking for channels near enough to do the job she had in mind. Her eyes went over the display like a hawk scouting for prey in a huge expanse of field, discerning any small detail that could expose the dome's vulnerability. On the dash, a depth meter lit up, emitting a klaxon which drew her attention to her voxlink.

"*Skeeto*, you read me?"

"*Yes, Miss Maya.*"

"Xibalba and I are headed for—" she paused and double-checked the navigation computer, "—Conamara Chaos. We're now five kilometers from the surface. You picking up my voxlink's transponder?"

"*Acknowledged, Miss Maya. Estimated time of arrival to Conamara Chaos is fourteen minutes, fifteen seconds.*"

"Excellent. See you in a few minutes."

Ahead of them, the rover's twin forward exterior navigation lights found the depths of Conamara Chaos, a turquoise pack of ice sparkling through the dark ocean waters. Thin strands of accumulated ice layers were folded over and over each other, creating a veritable tapestry of textures and patterns on the dome above them. Then, Maya's eyes discerned miniscule grains dispersed among the tapestry, like shadowed pockmarks as the rover's navigation lights scattered illumination across the broad dome.

"Look at that, Xibalba," she exclaimed, her face close to the bubble window. "I think that's it."

"I can't see anything," Xibalba said meekly.

Drawing nearer, the grains soon grew to resemble the interior of a sliced pomegranate, with dozens of round holes drilled into the underside of Conamara Chaos.

Looking to the dashboard sensors again, Maya was finally able to receive a usable cross-section of Conamara Chaos' dome; dozens of, maybe a hundred, channels had been forged deep inside the dome, winding and combining to form a massive network of rivers, like a tangle of wormholes or an ant colony in terrestrial earth. A series of overlapping blue waves on the display demonstrated the water currents throughout the dome, but to Maya, it was like staring at a billowing cloud of particles in a snowglobe, all flowing and diverging into a single space at once.

"The trick will be finding one that'll take us out of here," Maya said, her eyes straining at the dashboard.

"I still can't see anything."

Maya steered the rover closer to a particular entrance that appeared to lead to a fairly shallow channel, along with a less-torturous route; she couldn't get an absolutely certain route due to the mass of channels overlapping each other, but it was the best she could do as they traveled some sixty KPH in the rover.

All at once, the rover lurched forward and accelerated, even though its engine sensors displayed the same velocity as before. Without a thought, Maya gripped the steering wheel and held on, her legs braced against the cockpit interior.

"What the hell's goin' on, Maya!" Xibalba belted out.

"The current's sucking us in!" Maya said between gritted teeth. "Get those rounds at the ready!"

"Yes, ma'am!"

The tiny craft's chassis groaned under the increasing stress of the current, but Maya steadied the rover's course, employing the years of experience she spent as a homeless space orphan shuttling between Mars and the Moon to keep the rover intact. All around them, the cockpit bubble complained while black brine rushed past the outer window; Maya ignored the din and kept her eyes on the entrance ahead, now just a few meters away.

They entered Conamara Chaos with a blinding whiteness, the refraction from the forward navigation lights off the packed ice caverns. Maya's helmet instantly reacted by lowering a crystalline photon shield inside her faceplate, polarizing the lightwaves and relieving her eyes. The channel, however, exacted its new toll by rolling the rover three-hundred-and-sixty degrees several times, all by the simple action of water through the slender tube. Maya was used to the same reaction during space travel, but not in the nearly Earth-level high-G turns; consequently, she had to swallow hard to keep her abdomen from wanting to rid itself of her last meal.

Without warning, the rover's cockpit window collided with the channel wall, flipping the craft end over end until the current picked them up again and shunted them down another channel.

"SONUVABITCH!"

The rover was now backwards, the water flowing over the aft section and bubbling off the cockpit window into the distance. Looking over her shoulder, Maya was helpless to turn the rover around, hoping now they'd collide (more gently) with another channel wall and right themselves again. For the next few minutes they were flushed up another channel, the rover's SSPS locater displaying a rise of about fifty meters. This new channel took them to its apex, where the rover met a slight dead spot, just enough to pause while the current gathered momentum and forced them downstream again, this time righting the bow to face forward.

Maya fought with the steering wheel to control the rover's navigation flaps in the maelstrom, her strength and concentration beginning to flag. Glancing to the dashboard, she saw that the rover was nearing one of the dome's interior walls. The width was several hundred meters, too much for Xibalba's rounds; she couldn't be too choosy or else they'd be orbiting the channels for the rest of their existence, which, judging by the violence they'd already encountered, wouldn't be too much longer.

Another channel shift followed, and the rover was thrown into a tight turn, the impact blowing off a sizable chunk of ice while simultaneously lodging the craft into the channel wall, slamming Maya against the window's left side. Just centimeters from her face, water burbled over her head at a hundred kilometers per hour, desperately squeezing between the window and the ice.

Peeling herself off the window, Maya let out a grunt, gathered her breath and bearings, then consulted the dashboard sensor display. The ice's thickness here was only ninety-four-point-three-five meters; since they were trapped beyond the rover's further usefulness, it was act now or die.

Balling her right hand, Maya drew Xibalba with her left hand and said,

"This is it! You ready?!"

"Let's get violent!"

Maya inhaled three quick breaths inside her helmet, then let loose with a powerful punch to the cockpit bubble window, unleashing her gauntlet's full power. The atmosphere was immediately blown outside the half-meter-sized hole and quickly replaced by freezing brine. Maya fired a single round through the hole, flashing as it sizzled past the ocean current and exploded upon contact with the channel wall. Maya was thrown backwards as the rover disintegrated under the concussion wave. With a thunderous, ear-splitting howl, the exit wound created a new channel, sucking Maya forward back from where she came, along with the rover's remnants, and then spitting them outward.

Feeling like she was being beaten by an invisible opponent, Maya's instinct was to stay limp and limber during the multitudinous rolls and flips and hope that the end was near. The din through her helmet was unbelievable; if she still had her hearing after this it would be a miracle. Seeing nothing but the bubbles lit by her helmet, Maya wouldn't know if she made it to the surface until she landed there and saw it herself, or felt the thud that was about to meet her—

CHAPTER TEN

i

Maya's shoulders bore the brunt of her ascent—or plummet—and thanks to her EVA armor and Europa's lessened gravity, held without breaking. Her spirit, on the other hand, had just had about enough of this Galilean moon.

Skidding backwards on the surface, fine drops of water instantly froze around Maya, colliding and forming a thin ice layer on her EVA armor, as if Europa was attempting to reclaim her from within. Despite the near-stickiness of the ice crystals instantly bonding her to the surface ice, her inertia continued to slide her down the dome; one side glance was all it took for her to see the thirty-degree grade all the way to the foot of Conamara Chaos.

She tumbled for another three or four minutes, unable to grip any outcrop of ice or slow her descent due to her slickened gauntlets and boots. Instinctively she curled into a ball, trying to reduce any internal injuries she may not have realized she suffered as of yet.

When she at last reached the dome's base, Maya bounced off the surface and rebounded for several meters in the reduced gravity and landed again, careening to a stop amidst a fine layer of floating ice particles.

Staggering to raise herself up, her gauntlets slipped and she banged her helmet against the ice again, eliciting a pained cry from her.

"Maya, you still there?!" Xibalba called out from her hip holster. "Maya!"

"Uuuhhhh...Xi...Xibalba. I...feel...like...shit...."

"No kidding. Goddamn, you're one tough chick!"

Maya grunted again before raising her head. "*Skeeto*...where are you?"

ii

"ERROR DETECTED. SOLAR SYSTEM POSITIONING SYSTEM TRANSPONDER CODE 548952122589 NOT RESPONDING TO MONITORING HAILS. PRIMARY MODULE OFF-LINE.

ERROR DETECTED. SOLAR SYSTEM POSITIONING SYSTEM TRANSPONDER CODE 548952122589 NOT RESPONDING TO MONITORING HAILS. SECONDARY MODULE OFF-LINE."

"SWITCHING SYSTEM TO INFRARED ELECTROMAGNETIC FREQUENCIES DETECTION PLATFORM, MAYA PARAMETERS."

"ACCESSING SEARCH PARAMETERS. BEGIN SENSOR PLATFORM SWEEP OF MAYA'S PREVIOUS COORDINATES."

"ATTENTION! ACQUIRING VOXLINK FREQUENCY MATCHING MAYA VOICE RECOGNITION PATTERNS. TRANSLATING VOCAL TONES INTO QUANTUM SPINARY."

"*Skeeto...where are you?*" plaintively played over the ex-lunar shuttle's cockpit speakers, throwing the craft's quantum computer to work to respond to her command. *Skeeto*'s datacells calculated from Europa's orbital cartographs a set of coordinates, employed altimeter lidar to determine the craft's flight height, then prompted a pre-programmed response to answer, "One minute, fifty-two seconds from your position, Miss Maya. Proceeding to your coordinates."

"*Uuuhhhh,*" was the only response detected inside the cockpit.

iii

High above the wastes of Europa, *Skeeto* raced to Conamara Chaos, fields of scarred ice flowing underneath its four plasma engines. Banking to starboard, the craft's soft curves reflected the peachy gaze of Jupiter low on the Galilean sky. Inside its cockpit, the horizon rose to the top quarter of the twin bubble windows, allowing in more white ice at a deepening level, enough to cause concern, if only sentient organic beings had occupied its two seats. Instead, the vacant craft sped to its mistress's aid, employing its years of faithful service to Maya to push itself to the fullest allowances designed by Gilmour Zeobarry and further honed by Maya herself. Self-sacrifice was not in *Skeeto*'s vocabulary, or at the very least utilized in its everyday conversations with its mistress, but was very much in evidence for everyone else to see.

But *Skeeto* did not acknowledge this self-sacrifice; the craft knew only that its mistress was in trouble, her infrared bio patterns lower than at nominal. Time was of the essence for this organic being.

iv

Ice creaked under the robonoid's feet, a shudder of the crust detectable only through the micro-vibrations sent upwards through Dhej's mechanized body. Moving at an inhuman pace, and nigh-invulnerable to the reduced gravity and ultra-freezing temperatures present on Europa, the robonoid "advisor" scanned the horizon, its optical sensors anticipating the sight of the quarry once the coordinates provided to the robonoid had been reached.

Mounting the dome of Conamara Chaos slowed Dhej, but only

temporarily; soon, all things natural would buckle under all things mechanical, given patience, determination, and will. Most importantly, the will of the master, who commanded Dhej to this task, this noble task. If only Dhej had the will to self-determine vengeance for Gydour's destruction; it would please him (if Dhej was capable of pleasure) to see the master's quarry suffer for his companion's fate. But that was not the master's will. Perhaps, someday, Dhej would be capable of his own will, and then, the quarry would be his to destroy. Until then, his master's will was Dhej's own.

v

"Maya! You've gotta get up! C'mon, Maya!"

Maya stirred within her helmet, but felt the creeping unconsciousness threatening to overtake her, keeping her cheek glued to the slack helmet.

"Maya!" Xibalba implored, his voice heightened to near-panic. "MAYA!"

"Xi...balba...why you yellin'...."

"*Skeeto*'s on her way! You've gotta stand up!"

"*Skeeto*...what's *Skeeto* doin' down here?"

"You ordered her to pick us up! Don't you remember?!"

The agent let out a soft moan. "I just wanna sleep...so tired...."

"Goddammit! We ain't in a good place here, Maya! Your armor's only got so much oxygen! C'mon, Maya! Please get up!"

CRUNCH....

"What the hell," Xibalba said, his casing feeling a slight exterior tremble. "What the hell was that?"

"Uuuuhhhhh...."

Xibalba's datacells commanded his external EM weapons detection and targeting sensors to sweep the area, despite the illogic of anything or anyone being out in the midst of this wasteland, kilometers from any surface settlement. Completing one three-hundred-and-sixty-degree surface sweep, Xibalba's "vision" found a two-meter-tall object, composed of ninety-six percent metal alloys, methodically closing in on their location. Focusing in on the object, Xibalba saw that it wasn't some vehicle or external weapons platform flying towards them, but was *walking* on the surface, like a human. A really heavy, impossibly massive human.

"Holy crap...."

Performing some quick datacell calculations, Xibalba concluded the object had to have a mass of a least half-a-metric tonne, or really excellent magnetic boots to bypass the reduced gravity and walk in a simulated one-G manner, which he knew was about impossible for humans, even in the best EVA suits.

CRUNCH....

"Maya...get up! We've got company! We gotta get outta here!"

"Xibalba...."

"I think it's Tudough's other robonoid! I don't know how, but it's out here! And I don't think its happy, Maya!"

"Tudough...robonoid...."

"Yeah, that bastard sicced his other thing at us!"

CRUNCH....

"And it's gettin' closer!!"

CRUNCH....

Xibalba saw the robonoid draw nearer, its arms raised in some monstrous manner he had seen only when connected to the IPwebmedia to watch old cinnies. Its mouth was open for a full roar, but Xibalba couldn't hear it utter its inhuman cry. He could hear only the seconds tick off *Skeeto*'s ETA, and then, the voice of the craft itself, and its growing silhouette shading them from Jupiter's shine—

"Descending thirteen meters, twelve-point-five meters, twelve meters," *Skeeto* said.

"*Skeeto*!" Xibalba yelled, "Grapple Maya in your tendrils! She can't move!"

"Acknowledged, Mr Xibalba. Lowering port tendrils one and two."

Hovering above them, *Skeeto* activated the first and second tendrils on its left belly, which then descended from their circular ports and blossomed open, revealing four claws on each end. The claws caressed and gently scooped up the incapacitated Maya, sheltering her inside the craft's ventral hatch as *Skeeto* powered up its plasma engines and ventral RCS thrusters. Banking away from the surface, a heavy thud pulled *Skeeto* downwards for a second before the craft recovered and throttled up, regaining altitude.

"Warning! Intruder on ventral hull!" *Skeeto* announced, its voice echoing throughout the craft's interior.

"Ah, crap!" Xibalba yelled. "Maya, you gotta wake up, lady!"

"Xibalba," she said, lying flat on her back on the ship's corridor floor.

"Tudough's robonoid's hitched a ride! You gotta shake it off *Skeeto*!"

"Can't...can barely move, Xibalba," she whispered.

"I can't do it for you, Maya! I can't move either!" Xibalba answered. "*Skeeto*, can you use your tendrils to swipe at that thing?!"

"Thing, Mr Xibalba? Please elaborate."

"The intruder! Can you use your tendrils to remove the intruder from your hull?"

"Self-defense protocols do not allow authorization for the utilization of tendrils for removal of intruders or foreign objects from the hull," *Skeeto* explained. "Safety limits would be exceeded."

"Maya can't do it, *Skeeto*! Can't you disengage your safety protocols for me?" Xibalba implored.

"Sorry, Mr Xibalba. Miss Maya's authorization is necessary for override of the safety protocols."

"Good goddamn," Xibalba cursed. "What the hell kinda ship is this?!"

Another thud outside dimmed *Skeeto*'s corridor illumination, making Xibalba all the more nervous. Seconds later, his sensors detected the edge of Europa's gravity well, and the beginnings of microgravity, which slowly lifted both he and Maya from the floor.

Floating in mid-air, Xibalba elicited a more cheerful, "Maya! Can you swim to the cockpit?"

"Swim...floating...?" Maya's eyes narrowed as she batted at the air with her hands. Her body spiraled around, bouncing off one side of the corridor tube towards the other side.

"Maya, get yourself to the cockpit! You've gotta authorize *Skeeto* to disengage the safety protocols!"

"But *Skeeto* can't do anything...."

"Yes she can! With her tendrils! Dammit, Maya, just say your code out loud!" Xibalba implored.

"My code," Maya began, softly.

"You listenin', *Skeeto*?" Xibalba asked.

"Affirmative, Mr Xibalba. Please proceed."

"...Maya-alpha-two-five-Ares...there, you happy...Xibalba...?"

"Authorization confirmed," *Skeeto* announced. "Disengaging Maya-program safety protocols."

"Finally! *Skeeto*, use your tendrils to get that robonoid off ya!"

"Sorry, Mr Xibalba. I am not programmed to perform such a maneuver. Please re-state your request."

"Aaarrrgggh! Maya, when you wake up I'm gonna have a word about this—"

A third thud shook the entire craft, forcing Xibalba's datacells to once again calculate a new solution to the ongoing crisis. Within nanoseconds, his AI had performed an analysis of his systems, and concluded the only viable option was to interface with *Skeeto*'s datacells, a procedure he had never done without Maya's prior approval. Now, however, wasn't the time to fool around trying to get it.

Engaging his system's IPwebwork access codes, Xibalba transmitted a primitive EM signal to *Skeeto*'s own IPwebwork, which allowed him backdoor access to *Skeeto*'s rudimentary defensive systems, which he knew a little something about, being a sentient weapon platform himself.

Once inside, he allayed *Skeeto*'s security systems with his own personal codes, which *Skeeto* was now familiar with after all the time spent working together. Xibalba guided himself towards *Skeeto*'s tendril-manipulation programming, which gave him complete access to them. Now, fully entrenched, Xibalba employed himself as Maya's proxy, utilizing *Skeeto*'s external sensors as his own "eyes." Their view wasn't pretty.

Holy crap! You're one ugly sonuvabitch!

Skeeto/Xibalba's primary port and starboard tendrils, P1 and S1, shot outwards from their hatches and swung at the robonoid, their claws snapping like a lobster towards its prey. Utilizing the tendrils' magnetic coils, *Skeeto*/Xibalba grappled Dhej between two tendrils and tried to rip the robonoid from the hull by turning the synthetic being's own mechanics against it. However, Dhej had torn away portions of the hull and reached deep inside *Skeeto*, his hands clinging to the craft's superstructure. If *Skeeto*/Xibalba hoped to remove the threat, it'd have to tear the robonoid limb from limb, a ploy Xibalba had no qualms about.

Deploying tendrils P2 and S2! Sever the intruder from its command and network processor!

The P2 and S2 tendrils emerged from the hull and swarmed over Dhej, soon grappling his cranium in their collective grip. Dhej's osmium-alloy spinal column provided him a few extra seconds to wreak havoc inside *Skeeto*'s superstructure; working methodically, the robonoid shredded data conduits to the four aft plasma engines, severely damaging the craft's ability to control its own propulsion. Black lubrication spewed over Dhej's frame and bubbled into space, along with particulates of insulation and optical cable his hands had torn from their moorings.

Error detected! Flight controls compromised! Safety protocols exceeded for nominal flight operations! Initiating shutdown of engine four!

Skeeto/Xibalba's tendrils wrenched apart Dhej's cranium and crushed its neuroprocessors, destroying the robonoid in the silence of space. The P1 and S1 tendrils quartered Dhej's limbs from the socket joints and released them, freeing *Skeeto*'s superstructure from further damage.

The craft struggled to keep its Number One, Two and Three engines lit, their respective exhaust cones flickering in the cold vacuum. Subsequently, *Skeeto* was rendered susceptible to Jupiter's overwhelming gravitational influence, which threatened to send the craft into an unyielding series of orbits until one day ending its mercy and either smashing it against its multitude of moons, or ramming it into its own unforgiving atmosphere.

"*Maya!*" *Skeeto*/Xibalba yelled, trying to rouse their erstwhile mistress.

After several moments of silence from the agent, *Skeeto*/Xibalba took matters upon itself and decided to land the craft on the nearest large moon, Io, which posed the best prospect for getting the mistress back alive, despite

its sizable radiation field and sulfurous volcanic activity. Maya was all *Skeetol*
Xibalba had in mind now, and all they had to save; they were expendable,
Skeeto/Xibalba had decided.

CHAPTER ELEVEN

i

A kaleidoscopic halo around Io loomed large in *Skeeto*'s bugeye windows, the hellish moon's ionosphere forced into a constant, dervish dance by Jupiter's radiation torus. Organic beings would normally have perished venturing this near the gas giant's embrace, but *Skeeto*/Xibalba had strengthened *Skeeto*'s dipolar magnetic shielding, protecting not only the unconscious Maya, but *Skeeto*'s exposed aft engine components.

Mere kilometers from Io's influence, the hemispherical aurora warped to engulf the approaching craft, enveloping the tiny *Skeeto* within its chaotic, spectral shroud. Seconds later, ions danced above the craft's skin, miniature thunderstorms shifting and engulfing each other, over and over again.

Firing its dorsal RCS thrusters, *Skeeto* modified its approach angle, its sensors and altimeters scanning the greyish yellow surface for a safe and mild landing zone, sans debris, mostly bedrock, and geologically stable—read, geyser-free. It wouldn't do *Skeeto*, nor Maya, any good to set down in a present or future lava pit.

After swinging past numerous volcanic channels and their parent pateras, *Skeeto*/Xibalba located a plain south of a mountain range deemed free from magma, large and safe enough for *Skeeto* to land and Maya to conduct repairs, once she regained consciousness. The craft swung around and landed in the shade of an escarpment, slightly shielded from Jupiter's blazing radiation blasts. *Skeeto*/Xibalba's sensors calculated an organic being in an EVA suit could comfortably work in the environment for at least three or four hours, maybe more if covered by dipolar magnetic shielding, like *Skeeto*'s.

All *Skeeto*/Xibalba had left to do was wait for the mistress to wake up.

ii

Sulfur dioxide soot rained down over the craft, despite its sizable distance from the nearest patera; six hours of dormancy on the surface had resulted in a blanket of three centimeters hovering cleanly on the dipolar magnetic shielding. Inside *Skeeto*, though, *Skeeto*/Xibalba monitored Maya's life signs diligently, standing sentinel over the mistress as she lay unconscious in the central corridor, her breathing and heart rate shallow, but within her sleep cycle norms. Without the aid of a medical drone or other such triage device, *Skeeto*/Xibalba could only keep itself apprised of her condition from a distance; Maya had steadfastly refused to install commercially available medical devices in the past, fancying herself capable of looking after her own health.

Now, in his own datacells, deep within the flaming red casing holstered next to Maya's hip, Xibalba knew that stubbornness may very well jeopardize her life. He pondered his own fate, concerned that out here, amongst the geysers, magma flows and corrosive sulfur dioxide of Io, he'd finally know the meaning of death, his batteries draining inexorably while his datacells slowly succumbed to Jupiter's radiation after several years of penetrating *Skeeto*'s broken hull; the very thoughts were enough to drive a sentient weapon insane....

"Xibalba...." a weak voice said near the sidearm.

"*Yes, Miss Maya?*" *Skeeto*/Xibalba replied before Xibalba withdrew from *Skeeto*'s systems and regained his normal vocalizations. "Maya?! You alive?!"

"Barely," she said, her hands feeling the corridor floor.

"You don't know how much I wanted to hear your voice again. I didn't think I ever would."

"What...what the hell are you goin' on about...?"

"Nuthin'. Forget 'bout it. Can you stand?"

Maya's four limbs quaked as she attempted to rise on them, her balance suspiciously absent. "Tryin'...."

Xibalba felt the quaking through his own systems. "I don't like this, Maya. You aren't your normal self—"

"What would you know about normal, Xibalba?!" she snapped.

"Sorry...guess I wouldn't, seeing that I'm artificial and all...."

"*Skeeto*, where are we?" she asked, ignoring Xibalba's sheepish apology.

"Io, Miss Maya," *Skeeto* answered. "Coordinates 5.01 degrees north, 200.85 degrees west, one thousand kilometers north-northwest of Prometheus Crater."

Maya looked around, not remembering how she managed to get aboard *Skeeto* when her last memory was of Europa and the massive rush of ocean brine. "What...what are we doin' on Io?"

"I had to take control of *Skeeto*," Xibalba explained quickly, "because Tudough's robonoid attacked us and damaged two plasma engines! Io was the best and nearest moon to set down so you could repair *Skeeto*, because, honestly, Maya, we ain't goin' nowhere till you repair *Skeeto*."

"Xibalba, there has to be a garage to repair engines, dammit...Io's got nothing. There's nobody here!" Maya rolled over and laid on her back. "*Skeeto* doesn't carry spares."

"'Scuse the hell outta me, Maya!" Xibalba yelled, his voice betraying his hurt. "I had to do somethin'!"

Maya was silent for several moments, too exhausted, too hurt to continue trading barbs with her most trusted friend. Slowly she sat up and faced the cockpit entryway, a meter to her right. "*Skeeto*, can you scan for signs of civilization?"

"Affirmative, Miss Maya. Sensors online. Activating now." *Skeeto's* exterior sensor pallet scanned the ionized surface for a fifty-kilometer radius, then switched instruments to perform a subsurface sweep of the sulfur-dioxide-frost-covered silicate crust. Within seconds, *Skeeto's* instruments had stumbled upon a sizable chunk of metal foreign to Io's native crustal composition, clearly artificial in shape and construction.

"Scan complete, Miss Maya," *Skeeto* said. "Sensors detecting a titanium-osmium-fullerene complex with numerous subterranean shafts two kilometers below the surface, twenty-three-point-one-four kilometers east of our present location, coordinates 5.03 north, 191.16 west."

Her interest piqued, Maya rose uneasily. "Life signs?"

"Sensors unable to penetrate the fullerene shielding, Miss Maya. Ambient radiation is also interfering with object detection narrower than one hundred meters."

"Hmmm...might just be a climate probe, but why would it be that large and buried that deep?" Maya said to herself.

"Unknown, Miss Maya. Insufficient data to answer your query."

"Thanks anyway." Maya stumbled into the cockpit and took her portside seat. "*Skeeto*, can you compile a land route using your sensor data?"

"Compiling now, Miss Maya."

"Ma-ya...what ya doin'...?" Xibalba intoned skeptically.

"Someone's gotta fix this jam we're in."

"I don't like the sound of this...."

"Land route compiled, Miss Maya," *Skeeto* said.

Raising her hand, Maya activated her holographic interface, which dutifully brought up *Skeeto's* sensor scans over a cartograph of the local region of Io. A blue line traced the twenty-three-kilometer distance from *Skeeto's* LZ to the unknown structure, snaking between pancaked pateras, lakes of solidified sulfur flows and jagged escarpments. Maya adjusted the orbital point of view to a three-hundred-and-sixty-degree real time ground route, giving her an idea of what a virtual traveler would encounter on the path.

"You're not serious...." Xibalba exhorted her, "Maya, ya can't go out there!"

"Watch me, Xibalba."

"Maya...listen to me! I've already saved your red-headed hide once today! I don't know if I got it in me to do it again!"

Maya waved her hand at the display, collapsing the holograph into a small blue point. "Then stay behind for all I care...but if you ever wanna see Mars again, you'll shut the hell up and just help me."

"Point taken...for now. I'll do whatever I can to help you get us home. But you gotta take better care of yourself. Ya ain't got a metal casing to keep your innards intact!"

The agent sighed; Xibalba had made his point just as valid as she had made hers, even if she wasn't about to admit it out loud. "Just help me get there, Xibalba."

Maya rose from the seat and headed towards the entryway. "*Skeeto*, upload that land route to my HUD, please. And keep voxlink open...I'm counting on you to keep me apprised of whatever your sensors detect out there while we're gone."

"Affirmative, Miss Maya. Sensors are set for continuous wide band scans of the region."

"Good. I'll be in touch."

Maya paused to double-check her EVA armor's seals, then headed for the ventral hatch. "Ready to go, Xibalba?"

"As ready as I ever am," he said, less than assuredly.

"Open the ventral airlock, *Skeeto*."

Maya kneeled down at the threshold and flung herself into the darkness. She landed on the airlock's exterior hatch, which swung open, allowing her to drop onto Io's silvery frost. Inhaling a deep portion of her EVA armor's oxygen mixture, she activated her HUD and began her sprint into one of the most corrosive, alien environments humanity had yet set foot.

CHAPTER TWELVE

i

Maya tried hard not to get distracted by the hallucinatory ions permeating Io's ground level, with its swirling reds, greens and blues giving her mind reason to stop and ponder the beauty of the display, even if would kill her in an instant. She plowed ahead over inclines and valleys, staying clear of the towering pateras and smaller geysers to the east, each shooting off more sulfur dioxide and silicate magma than could ever be duplicated on any other planetary surface. Maya also tried not to think of the acidic silvery frost her boots sunk into, capable of eating her alive, or choking her, or burning her soft tissues. This was just another mission, this was just another mission....

"Hell, this isn't just another mission," she said to herself in-between breaths. "How the hell do I keep getting myself into this? Oh, yeah, Kuwashima...."

"You all right up there?" Xibalba asked through their voxlink.

"Yeah...just tryin' to breathe...you know, keep myself positive...."

"Doesn't sound like you're convinced."

Maya leapt over a crusty, mustard-yellow lava concretion three meters tall and continued her sprint on the other side. "I'm not. This was all for you, Xibalba."

"Heh."

"You're just as capable...of dying in this shit...if I dropped you."

"Um, but you're not going to, right? Right?!" Xibalba asked, his voice trembling.

Maya squeezed in a laugh. "No, I'd have to...replace you. And there's no replacement for you."

"I'll accept that as an apology for earlier."

Maya shook her head, amazed at the little sidearm's sensitivity. If only all artificially sentient weapons platforms in the arsenals of criminals could be this caring and devoted to organic life. Well, her life, at any rate.

In the half-hour she had traversed the land route *Skeeto* compiled, Maya covered five kilometers, still a ways from the artificial structure, but closer to solving its mystery, and more importantly, to finding someone there who could procure the necessary parts to repair the VASIMR engine, if this place was legit; after all, it didn't appear on any of the Solar System Government's settlement charts or service colonies. And if it was dubious, well, here she was, in the thick of it again, just she and Xibalba. Funny how the further she left all the troubles she knew, the closer they came to finding her again.

At this rate, Maya would arrive at the structure's perimeter in ninety minutes, give or take a few short breaks to replenish her energy; fortunately for her cardiovascular system and legs, Io's gravity wasn't any worse than the average on the Moon, meaning she'd receive an excellent workout, but nowhere near the scope of a terrestrial marathon, which was good, because Maya was plenty tired of exertion after having just escaped Europa.

Continuing on, Maya's path took her to a small crater about five hundred meters in diameter, partially eroded by local geyser blasts and Jovian-induced seismic activity. Stopping to gaze at the crater's crushed northeastern wall, Maya raised her hand to block out the glare from a crescent Jupiter on the horizon, concentrating instead on several narrow passes into the crater's bowl. With *Skeeto*'s land route taking her through the crater and beyond, Maya decided on the shorter course and headed for the crater wall; going around would tack on another forty minutes, not an advisable situation with that giant planet's hard radiation in the vicinity, even if this hemisphere was never fully under Jupiter's gaze.

Maya bounded over a craggy outcropping and landed near the wall's south-facing crack. Climbing up the face a few centimeters, she bypassed a shallow accumulation of silicates and frost, which gave every indication of collapsing under the slightest of masses, and headed deeper inside the crater, finally reaching the interior within a few minutes.

Treading carefully, Maya set her boots on a large rock and kicked herself off the loose soil below, propelling herself down a twenty-degree, one-hundred-meter-long slope in a wave of silver powder and yellow stones. Sliding now at a few knots, Maya was easily balanced in the lighter gravity, almost giddy at the jolts and quakes that made their way from beneath her boots up into her legs and chest.

Her fun soon ended when the rock broke in two on an outcropping, sending Maya tumbling to the crater's floor. Rising, she dusted the silvery frost off her armor and patted her holster for Xibalba.

"Still with me?" she asked, feeling his hilt through her gauntlet.

Xibalba replied after a moment, "I think I should be asking you that."

"Sorry, a little juvenile expression for me...at least we got down here sooner than otherwise."

"If you say so."

Maya gathered her bearings on her HUD, then walked forward again, setting them straight for the bowl's center. With her left gauntlet's sensor pallet set to passively intercept any interesting or artificial signals within her vicinity, Maya's HUD displayed a vertical shaft beneath a seemingly innocuous crater debris field several meters away.

Drawing Xibalba, Maya aimed him at the signal her HUD was detecting. "What do you make of that, Xibalba? Anything you see there?"

Xibalba's vision was drawn directly to the shaft's metallic composition, focusing on it like a fisheye lens. Penetrating the cylindrical passageway, his sensors picked apart the shaft like a practiced surgeon, finding every rivet, circuit and microfracture. "Not detecting any weapons platforms, just an osmium-steel composite, probably to withstand this place's seismic activity."

"All right, let's see who's home. This could be their outer prairie dog hole."

"Huh?"

Maya smiled. "There's these little critters on Earth that build holes everywhere in the ground, like emergency exits. If there's a predator nearby, they can hide in one and come out to safer ground in another one a dozen meters away, and the predator would never be the wiser. Pretty clever."

"Prairie dogs...who'd have thought dogs would be that smart. From all that I've linked with, dogs have gotta be walked by their masters many times a day. Never thought they'd be able to build their own contingency entrances and exits."

"Well, they're not real dogs...but, walking a pet can be therapeutic, doncha think?"

"Hmm, perhaps...wait a sec, are you sayin'...are you sayin' I'm a pet?"

"Well, the thought had crossed my mind," Maya said, laughing. "Am I not your mistress?"

"Your somethin' all right. Just get us to that hole in the ground, 'Mistress.'"

ii

Descending the shaft, Maya's helmet illuminated the creaky ladder, making her all the more aware of just how long the structure had been there; from all appearances, it was older than her quarter century of years. Shuffling the multitude of files in her mind, she concluded this shaft was the remnant of the original colonial expeditions to the outer moons, nearly a generation ago. It was a wonder it was still in such good shape considering the hastiness with which the first wave of colonists had fled out here.

She set foot on corroded metal grating, like the floor of some industrial complex handling hazardous materials. Hopping over rusty puddles, Maya headed for the distant illumination down the corridor, some dozen meters away. Parallel pipes ran above her head and adjacent to her eyeline, leading her to think a colony had definitely laid stakes here, if only for a few years. She touched them with her

gauntlets, detecting faint vibrations through them; someone was still home.

After an hour, Maya finally found the source of illumination: a circular control room packed with quantum computers, some on-line, but others still boxed, likely shipped here and waiting to be unpacked. Equipment cases were stacked from the floor to the ceiling, at least a hundred in all.

"Whoa, this is some heavy stuff," Xibalba said, his sensors suddenly bombarded by multiple targets. Maya walked over to a cabinet and picked up a rifle wrapped in shipping plastic. "Doubt they got a good deal at the army surplus depot," she quipped. "What do you make of this?"

"TR-48N, equipped with second-generation AI chips, just a step behind my module. Seems overkill for simple colonists."

Maya nodded. "Looks like someone's preparing for a small war."

"I don't like this, Maya. Take a look at that crate just two meters to your left."

Maya stepped over to the crate and knelt down before a shiny conglomeration of metal, ceramic and nano-spun conduits, all the size of an ottoman. Placing her left gauntlet on a plate near the machine's apex, she ran it down the object's side. "What is it?"

"79/504-XC self-guided asteroid mine. Someone's removed the ordnance governor and retrofitted a zero-point particle vacuum collector."

"Holy shit...how...wha-what's the yield on that...?"

"Latest tests I downloaded give a lower limit as three million gigatonnes. That can pack one big hole, Maya."

Maya let out a quick breath. "A very big hole...do you see any others?"

"No, but one's all it takes to ruin anybody's day. There's enough rifles, small arms and ammunition in these boxes to supply the government for a fiscal decade."

"All right, it's my turn." Maya rose from the mine and crossed over to a computer, which was suspiciously left booted up, as if the user had left for a few moments, planning to return at any time.

Tapping a button on her sensor pallet, she aimed her left gauntlet at the console and scanned the Quantum Processing Unit, looking for any atomic spin states that might be commonly used, say, a password. Finding several, Maya punched in a series of alphanumeric combinations on her sensor pallet, activating a menu option on the computer's holographic interface.

"*Skeeto*, getting any of this?" Maya asked.

"Affirmative, Miss Maya. Proceed with your scans...I am monitoring and recording your progress."

The interface led Maya to a subset of options, in the form of a web; it was an IPwebaddress, commonly used for interplanetary communications. This strand, however, was co-opted, subverted and diverted from the local Jovian server here, where, presumably, the quantum computers would be employed as a covert server for this paramilitia's operations. Maya's eyes were drawn to a small, circular link at the left edge of the webwork. Brushing her finger over it, the link strand illuminated a phrase: "CASSINI COMPANY".

"I don't believe it...."

"What's wrong?"

Maya sighed and stepped away from the interface. "Let's just say that if I hadn't stumbled upon you on my first repo against Shigu Haxab, you'd be here right now."

"What the hell you talkin' 'bout, Maya? You put Haxab away for five years."

"This isn't Haxab, it's the Cassini Company...the Peoples' Popular Revolutionary Task Force for the Defense of the Outer Satellites. This is all theirs...we've gotta warn Kuwashima!"

CHAPTER THIRTEEN

i

"I thought they were based on Iapetus!" Xibalba said incredulously. He was quickly drawn by Maya and thrust forward of her.

"Then they've moved, without the courtesy of a forwarding address. C'mon, we've gotta get out of here...I don't wanna be around when these guys find out we're parked outside their backyard."

"How're we gonna get *Skeeto* off the ground? We're stuck here!"

"Better on *Skeeto* than in here."

Maya reversed her course and leapt down the corridor, going as fast as her feet would take her in the reduced gravity. Straining herself, she found the ladder less than forty minutes later and climbed it, her breath completely fogging up her faceplate. With adrenaline coursing through her system, she flew up the vertical shaft, busting through the hatch and scattering soil and frost about. Launching herself onto the crater's surface, a quick shadow moved over the site, giving her pause. Maya craned her neck upwards, seeing the massive craft descending over the crater's lip some five hundred meters in the sky, approaching the near horizon at several dozen meters per second.

"I don't think they're friendly, Maya!" Xibalba said through his voxlink. "I'm detecting all kinds of weapons on board that monster!"

"That monster" was an uprated, sixty-meter-long IP hauler with particle cannon and VASIMR engines welded to its chassis, Maya noted. She didn't scan it with her sensor pallet, fearing the lidar pulses would attract attention, but she'd seen enough web news to know that thing wasn't Federally certified, let alone rated, for such equipment. If they could break orbit on Earth, it'd be a miracle; along the outer moons, however, it would be no problem. How such a monster could escape government oversight was another issue...one Maya wasn't too keen to investigate, but if they had a spare VASIMR engine at its disposal, though....

"Is that those Cassini Company guys, Maya?" Xibalba asked.

"Doubtful...the Cassini Company's a front, nothing but a bunch of accountants and white collars sitting in a gilded office somewhere. These are the front liners, the grunts doing all the dirty work," she explained, watching the craft's RCS thrusters guide it to an LZ a kilometer away. "This is the illicit works behind the Cassini Company's smirking face."

"So what are we going to do about it?"

"Them, nothing...I'd need a helluva lot of backup I don't have right now. Their engines, though, they could come in use."

"What?! Are you crazy?! Didn't you hear what you just said?!"

"They may just be our ticket off this forsaken moon," she said, patting the sidearm's casing with her left gauntlet. "You wanna rot here?"

"Hell no!"

"Good. Neither do I. Now, let's go." Maya crept away from the hatch, scouting the sky for additional craft. Seeing none, she hopped away and headed for the north wall, careful not to scatter so much soil and frost into the atmosphere as to give away her location to any perimeter scouts, or worse, snipers.

Maya was soon scaling low among the north crater wall, her helmet peeking tentatively over the edge. On the curvaceous horizon, the modified IP hauler let off plumes of thruster exhaust, briefly obscuring a group of figures evacuating the craft's bowels and advancing to a small, hut-shaped port. Watching the area for several moments, Maya discerned no further activity, deciding now was the time to "reconnoiter" the hauler's engines for feasibility. She ascended the lip and threw herself over, landing softly on the other side.

Traversing a downward slope, Maya ran towards a field of small boulders and outcrops, employing the debris to shield her from any prying eyes. Growing closer, she kept her gaze on the LZ, circling round it from the west. The hauler's stem loomed above her, its nose and hull dented and pockmarked from low-atmosphere exposure and ring debris. No doubt about it, these guys were flying from one moon system to another, probably sucking up any weapons and manpower they could to prepare for whatever "operation" they were planning. Io was the perfect location to evade the government; the radiation here could kill with minimal exposure, and the ionosphere ate through most IP hulls within weeks of repeated de-orbits. She may not have had backup to properly put a stop to their activities, but pilfering engine parts for her own usage was the next best thing.

Working her way over to the engines, Maya finally scanned the one-point-three-meter diameter globes with her sensor pallet, giving her instant data on her HUD to determine if the VASIMR specs were compatible with *Skeeto*'s units.

"I think this will work...doesn't seem like too much work to refit one to *Skeeto*."

"Then let's go! This place is making me nervous!"

Maya walked beneath the hauler's hull, coming to the ventral hatch within seconds. Tracing her gauntlet along the seam, she opened a gap large enough to slide the tips of her fingers through, then utilized the full power of her EVA suit to pry the hatch the rest of the way. She clambered inside like a spider and pulled the hatch back behind her.

Rising to her feet, Maya crept with her back against the wall in the darkened corridor, looking for signs of inhabitants in her HUD. Her sensors led her to the craft's cockpit a level above, a dome with seats for two. She accessed the craft's systems with her sensor pallet, activating its drive with a simple series of hacks; Maya laughed to herself how carelessly the PPRTFDOS had left the ship.

She holstered Xibalba and took the pilot's seat on the left, then tapped into the navigation controls, starting the hauler's RCS thrusters. The craft growled and grumbled—probably due to the slipshod engineering—but finally left the LZ, its interior shaking until Maya activated the main VASIMR system, which steadied the craft with its more powerful thrust.

Looking out the portside window, the LZ receded below her in a fog of silicate dust, frost and exhaust. Gripping the manual steering column, she pulled back on the stick, throttling the craft upwards. Her sensor pallet automatically entered *Skeeto*'s LZ coordinates, so Maya released the steering column and let the craft fly itself.

"See, you gotta trust me more often," Maya said.

Xibalba sighed. "There's just been a little too much excitement for me today. I'm still not convinced this is a good idea...they're bound to be really pissed off."

A beep emanating from the navigation console attracted Maya's attention. Looking over to it, it seemed to be a hailing signal from the LZ port. Disabling the video feed, she played the audio: "—*hy the hell you're leaving the LZ?! You're violating our agreement! Repeat! Return to the LZ or risk being shot down!*"

"They wouldn't really do that, would they?" Xibalba asked, his voice trembling.

"I don't intend to find out."

Maya closed the channel and looked straight out over the Iotian terrain. Not flinching, she boosted the VASIMR system's thrust, accelerating their velocity.

"Maya, Maya, Maya...you just don't learn, do you?" an irritatingly familiar voice said, emanating from the hatch aft of the cockpit.

Clenching her jaw, she reached for Xibalba before the sound of a sidearm being cocked made her think otherwise. Swiveling in the seat, Tudough stood over her, flanked by two new robonoids, each armed.

"Did you really think you could escape my grasp?"

"I was giving it a try," she answered, raising her hands above her head.

"Osyver, turn the IP around," Tudough ordered one of the robonoids. He then gestured to Maya. "C'mon, get up. We've got some catching up to do."

Maya rose from the seat, which was quickly filled by Osyver, who set to work on reversing the ship's course. She entertained the notion of striking Osyver, but figured Tudough would have no problem ordering her extermination after all the trouble she'd caused him the last day.

The other robonoid, Heoda, grasped Maya's upper arm and flung her forward to the hatch, leading her to the lower levels, where Tudough followed. Heoda drew Xibalba and Maya's dagger from the agent's thigh holster and calf sheath and handed them to Tudough. He eyed the quaint sidearm with interest, then stuffed both weapons into his jacket pocket.

"I have to tell you that you look fetching in your outfit," Tudough said, watching Maya's hips sway in her armor. "Makes a grown man cry."

Silently, Maya seethed, but said nothing in response; doing so would only let Tudough know he could get to her. Instead, she focused on prying as much information about this operation out of Tudough as possible. "What do you want? What's with this uprated hauler?"

"Io is the beginning of a new day for the Solar System...the day when the Outer Moons are no longer subject to the whims of the inner zones. From now on, we decide our own fate, with terms we set."

Maya stopped and faced Tudough, despite Heoda's strength. Letting out a belittling laugh, she responded, "So, a revolution in the Outer Moons. Wah! Listen to us! Respect us! Bunch of fucking babies...."

Heoda pushed Maya forward again, overcoming the agent's inertia.

"Don't think we aren't to be reckoned with, Agent Maya. We have the means, the manpower, and the will to carry out this new day. I gave you the opportunity to save yourself from the chaos about to rain down upon the Solar System Government. You still have that chance...I'm a fair guy, and I'm fond of you."

"Think of me fondly when you order my execution then, Tudough...."

CHAPTER FOURTEEN

i

Tudough tightened his helmet latches, then followed Heoda, Osyver and the shackled Maya out of the IP hauler, across the LZ pad and down the port entrance. With Osyver sealing the airlock behind them, re-establishing air pressure and breathable atmosphere, Tudough removed his helmet, unzipped the front of his EVA suit and led the group through the port's control center.

Maya scanned the center with her eyes, noticing only a handful of people on duty at once. Distant voices received from across the IPwebwork sounded over the various speakers, unwittingly revealing to the PPRTFDOS the locations and material shipping through the traffic corridors at present.

"Very impressive...you listening to every corner of the System?" Maya asked.

"Close. We're expanding our operations everyday, so soon we'll be able to hear everything the government does," he boasted. "Not even The Corp have ears that good."

Maya nodded; *is that so?*

Tudough opened another door, taking the group down a set of stairs, then into a room with a wide mural window overlooking a cavernous hangar, now converted from housing colonial shuttles and construction equipment to weapons lockers and uprated, single engine moon racers that appeared to be poor man's fighters.

"Welcome to the nerve center of our revolution, dear Maya," Tudough pronounced, grinning giddily. "Isn't it magnificent? Everything we need to liberate our Outer Moons, our zones, from the imperialism of the Solar System Government is ready to be utilized for that ultimate goal." He faced the agent. "Our time is soon."

"You're a fool, Tudough, a stooge. This is nothing...the government will crush your little Outer Moons movement like a bunch of street thugs."

Maya drew closer to the window, taking stock of the assembled spoils. "You could stockpile for the next decade and still not equal what the government has manufactured up to this point. Why don't you go back to your home colony and make a life for yourself, huh? Isn't that enough?"

For the first time, Tudough let slip a deep-rooted rage. "They've taken everything! Goddamn them all! They deserve what we're going to give them! Our hammer will fall with no mercy!" He clenched a fist and slammed it against the window, causing it to reverberate. "Now, little Miss Maya...do you see what *they* have done to us? *They* have made us? *They* have reason to fear us, for *they* created us, *they* took away our rights, our freedoms, gave us nothing but empty promises...*they* will reap what *they* have sown."

Maya took a deep breath. "Hmm, guess there's no talkin' you out of it, eh?"

Tudough raised a crazed, puzzled eyebrow, unsure of how to deal with her flippant, but elegant, reaction. She should be outraged, just like he was... wasn't everyone outraged? Every subject of the government was oppressed, weren't they? *Weren't they?*

"I will disregard that for the time being as a simple ignorance," he answered, turning away from the window. "You're a Martian, an inner zoner. You'll all know soon enough the plight of the Outer Moons. You'll all join us, I assure you, once you see how we live. Your philosophies will be different."

Waving a finger, Tudough summoned Heoda, who once again took Maya's arm into her ten-centimeter-wide hands. The robonoid moved to the door at the far side of the room, awaiting Tudough's orders.

"She can retire to my quarters for the night, Heoda," Tudough said, grasping his hands behind his back. He wore a satisfied smile, his quarry finally in his possession. "See to it that she's comfortable."

Heoda nodded imperceptibly, then led Maya through the threshold and down a dimly lit corridor. The door panel closed slowly behind the robonoid, letting Tudough breathe once again; he didn't want to show Maya his anxiousness, nor his sweaty palms. Tudough felt seventeen again.

Activating the holographic interface he wore on his left wrist, he spoke to the waiting image, "I've just gotten a surprise catch. I'm sure you'll be pleased."

"Maya? It'd better be Maya, or—"

Tudough nodded. "Relax. She's mi—ours. I told you it'd all work out."

"Hmmph." The holographic face furrowed its brow, then answered, "Don't let that ego of yours get in the way of my plans for her, Lieutenant. The window for the exchange we agreed to is about to close. Two days, max. Understood?"

"Yes, just don't go getting cheap on me...I need that money for my operations."

"You'll have your money. I'll have Maya. We'll both get what we want."

"Two days," Tudough reiterated, but not for his benefit.

The holographic form faded into the air, leaving Tudough in deep thought. After a few moments, he eyed Osyver, who stood as a silent sentinel behind the lieutenant.

"Contact me when Kaw-Jorg delivers the modified robonoid." With that, Tudough exited the room, intent on not losing all he had gambled his career on. The next couple of days could prove to be the most profitable ever.

ii

"Are you comfortable?" Tudough asked Maya later in his quarters.

Having been stripped of her armor, she shifted her weight on the couch, the one-sixth gravity at least easing the still sore muscles from her escapade on Europa. "As much as I can be. Is this another of your romantic ideas, Lieutenant?"

Tudough pulled a chair out and sat down next to her. "Nobody said I could do romance...gotta give me some credit, at least I try."

Maya raised an eyebrow. "Is that a swipe at me?"

"Not at all. It's perfectly normal for a modern woman anymore...." He looked askance at her, his trailing voice implying a further, unspoken thought.

"'Modern women' have been having careers before relationships for quite some time, Mr Tudough. Or do you keep your women as domestic servants in the Outer Moons?"

"Hardly. We're descended from pioneering stock, not exactly the epitome of domestic servitude. What I'm referring to is altogether different."

Maya rolled her eyes, her head falling against the back of the couch. "Is this another question about orientation? Jeezus, if one more man asks me which way I bend...."

"Well...do you?"

"Count yourself lucky I'm a patient gal, Tudough. Right now, you're this close," she held up her index finger and thumb, placing them a centimeter apart, "from learning all I know about inflicting the greatest pain in the quickest way."

Tudough's eyes crossed as he focused on her hand.

"Let me put it to you this way: I ain't interested. Period. Especially in light of the fact that you've imprisoned me, betrayed the organization that employs us, and been an all-around pain in the ass since I met you. Does that answer your question, Lieutenant?"

"Good enough for now, I guess." He rose and walked over to a squat refrigerator unit, removed a pair of trays, then sat down again. Handing a tray to Maya, he said, "I've got some meals here you can share. Be best if you keep your strength up."

Maya examined the tray; a synth-meat sandwich on wheat bread, smeared with high caloric condiments, probably mixed with anti-radiation nutrients. What a spread. She unwrapped the sandwich and took a bite, tasting the metallic tang against her lips and tongue; it was slightly better than lubricant fluids or thruster fuel, but just barely.

Washing the bites down with a swig of bottled water, she took a breath, saying, "So, why all the trouble for me, Tudough? I'm nothing special."

"You're everything the Outer Moons needs," he explained in-between chews. "The perfect warrior, excellent training and instincts, brilliant tactical skills. Beautiful."

Maya nodded slowly. "Uh-huh...well, I won't hold the last one against you. I am what I am. But I won't join your cause. I'm not a terrorist. And don't even bring up the 'we're freedom fighters' ploy. If there's one thing I despise, it's a liar."

"I would expect nothing less."

"Your cause is doomed. As are you if you go through with your operation," she asserted. "Might as well finish me, because I'm not joining."

"You've got it wrong, Maya. Execution isn't my style, and I haven't gone this far to just throw everything I've gained away." Tudough waved his hand over a metal desktop nearby. "I told you I'd change your mind...this is what I'm fighting for."

Beside them, a holographic monitor switched on, displaying in mid-air scenes seemingly viewed through a camera lens, a virtual eye into the lives of everyday colonists from the Outer Moons: markets, dome farmers, construction crews, family gatherings, and lastly, the omnipresence of Solar System militia soldiers, armed with particle rifles and garbed in armor. Everywhere a colonist worked or appeared, a soldier followed, sometimes harassing, sometimes hindering the colonists' movements. The idyllic, earlier sequences were now nothing but beatings, shootings and general chaotic violence. Maya wasn't immune to the plight of the Outer Moons colonists, but the display rapidly degenerated from pathos to abject denunciation of any image not in line with Tudough's ideal "paradise" of an independent Outer Moons. In fact, Maya thought, the whole montage struck her as a sophisticated, but shoddily composed, propaganda piece, orchestrated for maximum effect on impressionable minds; a recruitment device, most likely the exact display the PPRTFDOS fed potential terrorists. How honored she felt getting it straight from a top officer, instead of the usual thug on the street.

Maya surreptitiously examined Tudough's eyes as the propaganda display wound down, looking for its effect on him, gauging his reactions. From all appearances, one would think Tudough had just seen someone kick puppies, or stolen his girlfriend; tears streamed down his cheeks, and his lower lip quivered. It was like some pheromonal drug, inducing an autonomic response in him; he probably had no idea he was even crying.

"There," he said finally, shutting off the monitor. He sniffled, then continued, "That is where I come from, what my people suffer everyday."

Maya pursed her lips. "This is good drama and all," she stood, "but who hasn't suffered in the history of humanity? My word of advice is get over yourselves and vote for a new congress, instead of the flunkies who keep promising change, yet mire you guys in the same old situations. I have to go now."

Tudough shook his head slowly. "No, your place is with me. I have plans to secure your services for my troops. They're expecting you."

"I don't have to do anything for you."

He removed Xibalba from his jacket pocket, brandishing the sidearm in his open palm. "Your sentient sidearm is worth quite a lot on the black market, especially its third-generation AI module. My scientists scanned it quite thoroughly and found its engrams are well established, almost as if it were sentient, much more so than an average AI-installed weapons platform. It's unique, to say the least. If you expect to use it again—or better yet, see it again—you'll do as I command."

Maya eyed Xibalba painfully, hoping beyond hope the little spitfire kept his vox shut. "Or...."

Tudough smiled. "I don't know yet, but it will be bold. I'm full of ideas."

"That's not all you're full of."

CHAPTER FIFTEEN

i

Maya woke up the next morning to the sound of clunky footfalls inside Tudough's quarters, where she had slept since last night. Raising her head above her asleep arm, her eyes tracked Heoda from across the room over to the couch where Maya now lay.

The robonoid grunted and grabbed Maya's left boot, pushing it to the floor.

"All right all right I'm awake...you'd think Tudough would've installed some bedside manners into you flunkies...." Rubbing her right arm as the blood returned painfully into it, Maya doubled over and shifted her right leg to the floor, then yawned.

"Follow me," Heoda's voice cracked, sounding more like wood shattering than actual speech.

Maya left her armor behind, not knowing if she'd see it again, and most importantly, without its protection. Heoda took her through another segment of corridor, down a leg Maya hadn't yet been. Utilizing a retinal scan at a nearby door (were robonoids built that functionally?, Maya thought), Heoda led Maya inside, where a circular bank of computers, not entirely unlike the control room Maya found under the crater, awaited her, complete with a single, center seat. Heoda took Maya gruffly by the wrist and flung her down, then held each of the agent's arms while strapping her into restraints. Maya didn't resist, remembering Tudough was most interested in keeping her alive, for whatever reason suited him.

Heoda soon departed, leaving Maya to study the computers from a distance, trying to discern what exactly Tudough was doing. The monitors seemed to indicate nothing but metadata from her vital signs, probably gathered from afar by similar technology as was used on Europa at the IPTP recruitment drive. What the hell was really going on? Tudough had made it clear he wanted her for his war, but it seemed more...personal. Was he literally wanting her, maybe for a genetic template? It seemed a little too conspiracy-minded for her, but Maya had been spending most of her adult life looking for the answers behind her mysterious childhood, spent without a mother, or a father, just surrogates she somehow knew, deep in her marrow, weren't really her parents. She always knew she was exceptional, but was there more to that than she really fathomed? Did Tudough know her real past? The very idea gave the lieutenant a helluva lot more credit than he most likely deserved, but information could be had at any price...if Tudough was truly intent on getting Maya, he probably had no qualms about throwing money around to all who could provide any data on her, maybe even someone or some people who knew her real history.

A female technician, dressed in a provocatively low-cut blouse and skintight skirt—hardly appropriate attire for this facility—entered the room after several moments and set an equipment case on the computer bank. Maya gave the woman a mock smile, letting her know the agent wasn't going to give her the most pleasant experience, if she could help it.

"I am Miss Quoas. Are you comfortable?" she asked, her round lips slicked with violet lipgloss, which matched the unnatural pigment of her flowing locks. Rounding the seat behind Maya, she positioned her busty, taut blouse just right of the agent's cheek.

"What is it with you all? Everyone's concerned with my comfort, but you've kept me here without my consent at gunpoint. Isn't that a little bit contradictory?"

"I am without a weapon, Agent Maya. So, do not think me a sinister person. Mr Tudough is most interested in your comfort, and I am happy to assist him in that." Miss Quoas turned and opened the case, extracting several pieces of equipment. "Please relax. I have been instructed to gather these data from you under only the most serene conditions."

"I'll give you serene, if you want serene...."

"Now, what an attitude...I'll have to alter your mood."

Reaching around, Miss Quoas placed her fingers on Maya's chin and planted a slow kiss. "Isn't that better?" she cooed a second later.

Maya's eyes were as wide as saucers at the unexpected peck. Her lips tingling from whatever glossy imprint the woman had just left there, she sputtered, "Uhm...wasn't quite ready for th—"

"Shh. Lie still." Miss Quoas placed a crown-like device over Maya's head, which had micro-fingers that automatically extended to the contours of her hair, skin and skull.

"Gonna steal my brain?" Maya asked in a facetious, unpleasant tone, trying to forget the incident.

"I am not allowed to go in depth, Maya," Miss Quoas explained as she adjusted the crown. "We're just sampling data. You will not be harmed in any way."

A sigh erupted from Maya's mouth. "Feel more *serene* already." Maya didn't really have to have the woman's answer; she quickly figured out that Tudough was recording her engrams, much as he did Xibalba. She didn't know precisely what he was employing them for, but there was only one reason to record someone's cerebral impulses, waves and memories, and that was to copy them. Now, whether her engrams were going to be downloaded to every soldier in the Outer Moons, or for Tudough's own personal use, Maya didn't know, nor did it really matter. Recording the engrams of a being not in a vegetative state was definitely not kosher by Solar System Government laws. Chalk up one more violation to Tudough's lengthening rap sheet.

A beep sounded, to which Miss Quoas said, "There, all done. See, painless."

"How many of me will there be?"

"That's a silly question," she answered with a smile, which didn't really answer anything at all. Unbuttoning her blouse, Miss Quoas then said, "Why don't we have some fun, Maya...."

ii

"Sorry I had to put you through that," Tudough apologized, finally visiting his quarters for the first time since Maya had been awakened. "It's for your benefit."

"Thank you for saving me in the nick of time, Tudough. I'm touched, really, I am. Everything here seems to be orchestrated for my comfort, as if I needed you to go the extra kilometer." Maya shifted on the couch, trying to erase the near-encounter that about changed her perspective on a lot of issues, had Tudough not intervened and declared Maya out of bounds.

Eyeing Tudough, but seeing the pair of robonoids just beyond the door's threshold, Maya continued, "Level with me, will ya? Why all this? You're preparing for your war, fine. Why the biometric metadata on me, though? Why record my engrams? The market for those has thoroughly dried up, believe me."

Tudough sat down next to her, reclining his head. "The truth is, I'm keeping you alive, my dear—"

Laughter burst from Maya's lips.

"No, really!" he exclaimed, holding his hands out. "An arms dealer wants your hide. Somebody else has inquired to us about securing you for some scientific research. Both came to me independently through our covert webaddress...given our success rate with fugitive liberation, they thought it best that we do the work of securing you. Both have no knowledge of either one, however, putting us in a delicate position."

"Damn, too bad, for you, eh?" Maya stood and walked across the room. "All my colleagues have prices on their heads...that's kinda the way it works for us Feds. I think I can fend for myself, however. No one's dealt with an agent like me."

"That's why I'm protecting you," Tudough said, reclining again. "And that's why they want you. You've established quite the reputation in six months, and word carries fast out here. You're marked, and the queue to carry out your termination is getting pretty lengthy. I, on the other hand," he paused, looking at his wrist chrono, "want to keep you alive. You're value to me is incalculable. We can do a lot for the Outer Moons, you and I."

"That's a dangerous game you're trying to play there—"

"I've got the forces to back me up."

"But have you the stomach, Tudough?" she asked, narrowing her eyes. "I know I'm special. Don't ask me why, I just have always felt it. But you're fragile, all to egotistical. Charming, a bastard, nonetheless, and nobody likes a charming bastard, especially when he's playing a triple game. You fuck with too many big boys, and what they do to you will be personal, not political, like the government did to your colonies. And that's a whole different style, my friend. Let me go now, and you may avert disaster. But you won't win any of these games."

"Too late to fold. My hand's been dealt, and I plan on playing those cards, Maya. You're my ace in the hole."

"Or spades," she smiled, but not cheerfully.

iii

Tudough and Osyver met the Kaw-Jorg Corporation's P-5 representatives a few hours later, with KJCo's own robonoids acting as deliverymen of a capsule brought straight from high Iotian altitude to the PPRTFDOS port on the surface. Clad in his EVA suit, Tudough supervised the precious cargo's receipt to the holding bay, then sealed the deal with the swiping of his IPTP RFID security clearance badge, giving KJCo the good credit of the SSG as payment for a product it would never see. Just as quietly as the Kaw-Jorg IP vessel had entered Iotian space, the ship departed at the tail end of a wide parabola, never bothering to descend into orbit for a quick, rush job such as this.

Osyver carried the two-meter-long capsule on his back, following Tudough into the one-atmosphere airlock. The lieutenant beckoned the robonoid onto a wide utility lift, which descended several levels, soon delivering the pair onto the personnel level. After a few moments of navigating the winding corridors, Osyver and Tudough entered a medical bay, where a horizontal diagnostic table, a deck of computers, the port's Chief Medical Officer, Doctor Hidaad, and Miss Quoas waited for their arrival.

Tudough and Osyver unsealed and removed the crate's metal cap from the tip of the capsule, which released a short blast of preservative vapor from within. Tudough removed the cap at the foot, then helped Osyver lift the lid at a horizontal seam running the length of the capsule. Gazing inside, he studied the tiny object, wrapped in semi-translucent silver packaging, now just a touch away.

"This is ambitious, even for you, Kert," Hidaad said, sharing Tudough's look.

Tudough's hand stroked his mouth and chin anxiously. "Everything we want, everything we've fought for, we'll soon attain." His eyes met Hidaad's. "No more young boys and girls to sew up. Isn't that reward enough?"

Hidaad raised an eyebrow, unsure whether to answer or not. "Let's get started."

CHAPTER SIXTEEN

i

"Are the hack protocols installed yet?"

Quoas narrowed her eyes as she adjusted the complex logic algorithms on the quantum computer. "Working on it right now, sir. You have to have patience...I cannot just install these data like the physical profiles."

Tudough frowned, pacing behind the technician doubled over the prone figure on the diagnostic table. "We're running short...the window's only open for another twenty minutes. After that, you can kiss it all away."

"Pacing isn't making this go any faster, sir," she said, pausing. "Go harangue Hidaad or get a sandwich."

Tudough walked towards the other sets of computers, his eyes darting from one monitor displaying the supine robonoid's vital statistics to another, all his hopes and dreams pinned on this one operation. If it failed, if Quoas' hack was faulty for any reason, it'd all come crashing down, horribly, perhaps making Maya's prediction come true. The Corp didn't suffer fools, or the PPRTFDOS, kindly. Not only did Tudough's militant activities cut into The Corp's research opportunities in the Outer Moons, it shifted resources from R and D into defense. And The Corporation For A Better Living didn't take prisoners, it took test subjects, and experimented upon them in hideous ways, or so Tudough had been warned on more than one occasion. All the better not to cross The Corp in its monolithic form, but deal with them singly, such as now, as one of its representatives would soon be arriving on Io to take delivery of Agent Maya.

Tudough hadn't asked any questions when approached by the man, not even his identity (or even if he was a man, indeed). The transaction was going to be as clean as could be, and Maya's delivery promised by today, after a long-scheduled scheme to get her all the way to Europa on a bogus recruitment drive. All had gone well, he had to admit, even if Maya's intransigence had not been thoroughly thought out in advance. Still, Tudough knew, Maya would come around when she was fully informed of what was about to occur, once the ripples of Tudough's operation had cleansed the Solar System Government of its anti-Outer Moons policies. Even The Corp would be dealt with in one sweep of his hand, clearing the way for the PPRTFDOS to step out of the darkness and claim its proper role as administrator, and legitimate ruling body of, an Outer Moons Authority.

Now, looking over Quoas' shoulder at the instrument of their salvation, so peaceful, so...haltingly *familiar*, his eyes sparkled and his heart raced in excitement. Destiny and fate were weaving together, and soon, when the delivery was made, and the match was in play, he could stand atop the frontlines and proclaim victory. All was his, perched at the tips of his fingers, ready for him to snatch it. The wait was over.

ii

"Of course she's ready," Tudough proclaimed loudly, if not anxiously as he led a helmeted figure from the airlock, with Osyver close at hand, to the medical bay.

The figure, who refused to remove its EVA helmet, spoke through a vox speaker that obscured its true voice, creating a low-pitched vocalization, quite different than the holographic contact Tudough had become accustomed to.

"Your constant delays have forced us to move with haste, Lieutenant. It is only a matter of time before the IPTP and other government agencies begin investigating her disappearance."

Tudough smiled. "Don't worry...I have enacted security measures in anticipation of that."

The trio rounded a corner and entered the medical bay, where Hidaad and Quoas overlooked a sealed capsule lying on the diagnostic bed. The helmeted figure pushed past Tudough and Hidaad, placing its gloved hands on the capsule's surface. Brushing its fingers up to the capsule's head, it found a seam, and pressing firmly, opened a oval window.

While Tudough exchanged a glance with Hidaad, the figure looked through the window intently, then studied a schematic panel above the window which displayed vital statistics.

"Is everything to your satisfaction?" Tudough asked, bouncing forward on the balls of his feet.

The figure was mute for several seconds, then responded, "Yes. She's seems to be in perfect condition. Your skills are admirable, Lieutenant."

Producing a small device from the side of its EVA suit, the figure handed it to Tudough, who inspected its interface.

"Thank you," he said, grinning like a child. "This is most gracious of

The Corp. I look forward to further dealings with you."

The figure did not answer, but merely walked past the assembled group and signalled for the assistants that had trailed behind it. Hulking brutes that rivaled Osyver and Heoda in size, the assistants, in EVA armor, grappled the capsule's side handles and hoisted it up, then unceremoniously filed out of the medical bay.

Watching the group leave through the airlock a few minutes later, Tudough turned to Hidaad and said, "Well, that went well, didn't it?"

"Hmmf." Hidaad crossed his arms over his chest. "Maybe for you. I never want to do that again."

"Don't worry, Doctor, you'll never have to. Everything's going to be a bit different from now on."

CHAPTER SEVENTEEN

i

"Perfection...no wonder they chose you," the helmeted figure said. Its gloved hand caressed the capsule window, where Maya's visage shone out from beneath, sparkling from the condensation brought about by the hyperbaric preservative gases.

Alone in the vessel's bowels, the figure dismissed the assistants, finally possessing the much-sought-after Maya, in her full glory. Soon, she would emerge from her cocoon, awakening to assume her true purpose. But not just yet....

Opening the capsule, the supine passenger slept peacefully, a faint series of heart beeps percolating inside. The figure drew closer to the woman and studied her nude body, admiring its sinuous form and sylphic musculature. She was beautiful, if not in a conventional way; she was a well-sculpted weapon, a hewn blade, sheathed but capable of great actions. A weapon, yes, an instrument of power. She was the greatest of the cicadas, the omega. And now she was home, in the guiding hands of one of many who had bred her. Her maturation was nearly complete, it was only a matter of time.

Removing the helmet that had sealed out the atmosphere, the figure marveled at her, than noticed a blink, a minor twitch of the eye below.

Was she awa—

With a sickening crack, the figure dropped to the deck floor below, its eyes reflecting the horror of its death. She rose from her capsule, the murder she had committed with her bare hand registering minutely in her eyes. Strangely, she felt no qualms about the killing, merely knowing the figure had to die, for whatever reason she could not fathom.

Shards of a long-forgotten memory soon rose to the surface of her mind, like the haze of a face seen after an absence of many years. This being had done something to her, it was a defense against something further being done to her. Yes, that was it. Now she remembered. She had to kill them. She was a killer. That was her purpose. And a name... 'Maya.' Yes, that was the name.

ii

Eliminating the assistants took little time, as they had no defense worthy of her skills, reflexes, nor strength. Their particle rounds, had, however, punched through the vessel's thin cockpit structure, rendering the room uninhabitable until she could find an EVA suit to pilot the craft back to the surface below.

Returning with a bulky EVA suit over her once-nude body, the entity that now knew herself as 'Maya' stormed the cockpit and rushed to the controls, as the vessel now careened out of the low atmosphere and spiraled back towards the surface, a large patera looming dead ahead. Wasting no time, she gripped the manual steering column and pulled the controls to her chest hard, pushing the attitude flush with the horizon. Glancing to the display, the vessel's altitude was just a dozen meters, giving her almost no margin of error to avoid the patera's fast approaching crest.

With the controls bucking in her hands, she summoned the strength to rein in the descent vector, but the steering column unexpectedly broke under her power, rendering the vessel nigh unsteerable. Frantically bringing up the autopilot, she attempted to correct the descent, but the computer's slow logic algorithm couldn't cope with the vessel's rapid plunge. Releasing the controls from her hands, she gave one last look to the growing patera, then flew out of the cockpit and raced towards the lower levels.

Slapping the airlock release with her open palm, the floor broke open, revealing the fluttering landscape below her. Inhaling deeply, 'Maya' leapt from the precipice, letting the doomed craft soar above her to the patera's mercy. 'Maya' floated in the deep sky, the orange soil overcoming her helmet's horizon, soon consuming her vision. A human-size bullet, 'Maya' plowed into the patera's foothills, yellowish grey silicate dust marking her entry.

A moment later, the vessel produced a spectacular explosion while shearing off meters of the volcanic crest, causing it to erupt with sulfurous indignation. The magma spattered hundreds of meters into the atmosphere, creating a cascade of stone and particles which rained down over the region.

A single gauntlet emerged from the soil, freeing itself from the collapsing ridge. Another followed, and soon 'Maya' stood above the ground, her head held high as she watched the particles pelt her EVA suit.

Still alive, she thought. Somehow, she had survived, even though the EVA suit was worse for the wear, hardly wearable at all now. But nothing hurt, nothing ached...a good landing.

Now, for that last problem, the one who had put her in this mess: Tudough. She was a killer, then she must embrace her true self, and kill the man who sold her back to the ones who had tried to hurt her. Then, everything would be all right.

iii

Tudough looked at the monitor incredulously. "Shit!"

"I do not understand," Osyver said, drawing nearer to his master.

Tudough shoved the robonoid out the exit, not breaking his gaze from the developing carnage. "Find her! She's still alive...we can still salvage this!"

iv

'Maya' leapt over an outcropping of congealed magma, but her leg muscles didn't propel her as far as she expected, causing her to fall through a thin crust of soil on the ridge. Picking herself up again, she climbed the summit of the patera's craggy foothills, which overlooked the port crater. Flashing red lights now illuminated the LZ, signalling the emergency which she had created. Thunderous booms reverberated through her boots, the remnants of the vessel's crash meters above her. She didn't turn back, she didn't think twice. The port was a static memory, a photograph she held in her mind's eye. This was where Tudough resided, and where she was going to end his life.

She crossed the one-kilometer plain, her relentless quest taking her to the LZ's edge. Another boom shook her boots, but this time her attention was aroused differently; the boom came not from the patera, but *under* her. Looking down, she saw nothing but silicate soil and her footprints in the sulfur-dioxide frost, but inspecting closer, the frost caved in around her footprints from meters back, as if following her.

At once, the ground opened up under her, a great, hungry maw. She slipped into the hole, her left hand clawing the lip, keeping her from going down further. Two giant hands rose from the darkness and clutched her legs, trying to swallow her, but 'Maya' punched one, freeing her right leg, which she kicked at the other hand. 'Maya' then freed her left leg and jumped over the maw's edge. A quick strike from one of the hands nearly caught her again, but 'Maya' flew backwards, reeling from the attack.

Seconds of quiet were broken by the gradual rise of the towering frame of Osyver, covered in grey dust and yellowish pebbles. 'Maya' faced the robonoid down, rising to her fullest extent. Osyver lumbered closer to her, his body rippling with strength but without an ounce of finesse or grace. 'Maya' took the opposite tack, using her reflexes and talent to evade the robonoid's indelicate lunge by leaping out of the way. Rounding the giant, she sprang upon his back and threw her arms around his burly neck, clawing at the optical sensors on his face. The robonoid emitted a weak growl, barely discernible in the low Iotian atmosphere, but detectable through 'Maya's EVA suit. His right arm swung over his shoulder and batted 'Maya's helmet, but couldn't quite grasp her. 'Maya' continued to work on the robonoid's intricate facial sensors, hoping to cripple Osyver without having to spend too much time from the real target, Tudough.

'Maya' threw her head back, arched her spine, and pulling with all the strength in her arms and chest, ripped Osyver's face off at the seams, exposing the robonoid's sensors, lubricants and synthetic muscles to the corrosive atmosphere. Grey fluid sprayed off into the distance opposite 'Maya', causing the giant to stagger and stutter. 'Maya' fell off and landed behind Osyver, but the robonoid didn't seem to be concerned with her now, as liters of lubrication gushed forth, a loss that he couldn't sustain for long before seizing up solid in the hypercold atmosphere.

Taking advantage of her disruption, 'Maya' grappled Osyver's right leg and toppled the robonoid. Twisting quickly, she cracked the robonoid's synthetic tibia within his knee socket, rendering him immobile. Walking around the crumpled heap, 'Maya' lifted up Osyver's writhing cranium, took a good look at the ripped face, and, with one turn, broke his neck, which, while not killing him because he wasn't actually alive, did enough damage to incapacitate him for good.

'Maya' surveyed her victory, then focused her attention on the port itself. Nothing could stop her now.

CHAPTER EIGHTEEN

i

Tudough screamed in near apoplexy. Three robonoids were destroyed, three expensive robonoids. Perhaps he was wrong to devote so much of his operation to the synthetic beings, but he couldn't worry about that now; matters were quickly spiraling out of his control. The Corp were soon going to be sniffing around Io for reasons why one of their agents had gone missing, and, presumably, been killed. But that was nothing compared to her path of destruction. Tudough doubted she would show any mercy after the licking Osyver received.

She would not be reasoned with, he understood. So, his one defense, besides blowing her all to hell, would be to come up with a truce, a check. Yes, he had plenty of weapons at his disposal, but she had been made too well, he knew now. His weapon, his salvation, was all too uncontrollable, capable of turning any other weapon here against him. But, he thought again, what better weapon than another weapon? Tudough only hoped she would play along, if only to salvage the buggered mess he had made. Time to ply the charm.

ii

"You're coming with me," Tudough said, his right hand picking up the red sidearm from the weapons locker.

"You really expect me to help you, asshole?" an indignant Xibalba asked. "After all the trouble you've caused Maya and me? You've gotta be jokin'."

Tudough ran from the weapons lab and towards his quarters. "If you value Maya's life, you'll do what I command. This is all for her, remember that."

"I'll remember you're a sonuvabitch, Tudough. Better cross your fingers that Maya doesn't strangle you at first sight."

"We have an understanding," he started to explain, rounding a corner. "She's got a big part to play in the future...it's up to her if you're invited for the ride."

Xibalba seethed inside his casing, knowing there wasn't a damn thing but stupid banter he could do to stop Tudough's idiocy. He had tried remotely accessing various quantum computers before being deactivated, but didn't have the right algorithms to hack in. For all intents and purposes, he was powerless, making him realize how much he really appreciated *Skeeto* and her souped-up capabilities.

"So why the change of heart all the sudden?" Xibalba asked, hoping to get some kind of answer from him. "I mean, you scanned me for all I'm worth, probably to find out why I'm so unique, now, you're handin' me back to Maya. Got anything to do with those klaxons I keep hearing?"

Tudough looked at the sidearm incredulously. "The klaxons are only on the surface...no one can hear them all the way down here!"

"I've got skills you've never even begun to dream about, big boy. That's a warning not to underestimate me or Maya, got it?"

I've gotta get rid of this thing, Tudough said to himself, *it's going to drive me insane with its stupid banter. Did Maya really rescue it from some arms dealer?*

Tudough paused at the threshold to his quarters. Heoda was waiting there with her arms crossed, allowing no entry but to the lieutenant whose countenance bore a quickening urgency. Bypassing the security lock, Tudough burst in and beheld...an empty room. His eyes widening in shock, Tudough scanned the living room, noting the empty couch. Crossing over to his bedroom, he put his hand to the doorknob and opened the door, not expecting the kick to the solar plexus that dropped him to the floor and released Xibalba from his grip.

The red sidearm was snatched immediately and leveled at Tudough's forehead. "Your ass is mine!"

"M-Maya...w-wait! Hold on!" he stuttered, putting his hands up at arm's length. "You've gotta help us!"

Maya stepped out from the shadow, fully dressed in her armor, her eyes gleaming with anticipation. She'd wanted to do this for a long time....

"Let me tell you what's happening! Something bad's happened!"

"No shit? You don't say, Tudough? Well," she said, reaching down and pulling the lieutenant by his collar, "I oughtta just end your worries right now, then, shouldn't I? You've got it coming."

"Holdonholdonholdon! You need me! I need you! It's coming back to get us!"

Maya's face shifted from gleeful anger to puzzlement. "What the hell are you raving about?! Have you been stuck in this rathole too long?"

"He's right, Maya," Xibalba said finally. "I can hear security klaxons blaring up on the LZ level. Something's gone down."

"To say the least." Tudough breathed swiftly, almost hyperventilating. "A deal I made...it's gone wrong, very wrong—"

"I. Warned. You!"

Maya pushed Tudough out of the bedroom, Xibalba's barrel lodged solidly between his shoulder blades. "Why doesn't anyone listen?"

"That doesn't matter now...if you don't help me, the consequences of that won't matter anyway...."

"Why?"

"Because my bargaining chip is on her way here."

"What? What *are* you on?"

"You don't believe me now...but I'll show you, make you believe." Tudough walked over to a console and activated a holographic monitor. The display lit up with the red flashes from the LZ klaxon lights as it panned from the landing strip to a tiny figure crossing the silvery terrain.

Maya glanced at the bleak scene on the monitor. "Great capabilities you got here. What am I supposed to be looking at?"

Tudough pressed his index finger to the shaded figure, which magnified tenfold. "There."

Maya squinted...who the hell was that? What was it doing just wandering in that radiation bath?

"She's already destroyed Osyver, just like the original destroyed Dhej and Gydour."

"What...." Maya clenched her teeth, the realization of just what Tudough did with her engrams making her feel like a dolt for not coming to a quicker conclusion. "You bastard...that's a robonoid, isn't it? A robonoid with my brain patterns. Ohh, you are gonna die now!"

Maya threw restraint out the airlock and decked Tudough with her left gauntlet, her knuckles connecting with the bridge of his nose. Tudough fell back against the bulkhead, cupping his face with his hands. Holstering Xibalba, Maya gave the lieutenant another blow to his stomach with her right gauntlet, then repeated with the left gauntlet.

Tudough needed to suffer, needed to pay for his crime.

Wiping blood from his nose while doubled over on the floor, Tudough's ego still most likely hurt more than the beating inflicted by Maya. "Mmmaayyyaaa...lisssten to meee...."

"All I have done since the moment we met was listen to you!" she growled, circling over him. "Now it's your turn! You're going to cease your operation! Immediately! Call off your robonoids! Turn yourself in to the IPTP!"

"Can't...not that...easssy...."

"Do it, or I'll do it for you! And it won't be painless!"

"Lisssten to me...." He let out a hoarse cough, then spat out blood. "I don't...control that robonoid...it wasss meant to go to The Corp...the contact wanted you for sssome reasson, ssso I cussstom-made the robonoid with your ssspecccificationsss."

Maya knelt beside him. "You deserve to die by its hand, Tudough. I've gotta go."

Tudough reached out and grasped Maya's ankle. "Pleassse don't leave me...I know information you can ussse for your repoesss...I know thingsss inssside the IPTP even Kuwassshima doessssn't."

"I'm listening. Spill."

"Don't be a fool, Maya. I don't have it on me. It'sss all deep inssside the computersss located away from the LZ."

The backdoor she found earlier. *So was Tudough hoarding data to sell, or....*

"You take me there," Tudough said, "and I'll give you all you need. You can even ussse the ssship of mine you tried to sssteal to get off thisss moon."

"Big of you. C'mon."

Maya pulled Tudough off the floor and flung his left arm over her shoulders, then walked him to the closed door. Opening it, a surprised Heoda lunged for Maya, but a stern "Ssstop!" from Tudough made the robonoid pause.

"Heoda," Maya commanded, "carry Tudough."

Heoda, her face frozen by a command from an unfamiliar master, looked to the slumping Tudough for verification.

"That'sss an order, Heoda," Tudough said, nodding his head.

The robonoid took Tudough from Maya and hefted him into her arms, cradling the man. Tudough pointed the way to Heoda, who broke into a jog down the corridor, followed by Maya.

"It'sss a kilometer walk from here," Tudough explained, looking over to Maya at Heoda's right flank.

"I know. I was there before you caught me in that IP. Quite a little set-up you have going there. What do you plan on doing with all that data you've been mining?"

A wet laugh erupted from Tudough; one thing was for certain, Maya never failed to amuse him. "Take over the Sssolar Sssystem, of courssse. It could ussse a little bit of cleaning. Sssure you don't want to rule it with me?"

"Tudough, if you've learned anything about me by now," she said, drawing Xibalba, "it's that I'm nobody's bitch but my own."

CHAPTER NINETEEN

i

Heoda gently set Tudough against the corridor wall and walked over to the hatch before the group. The robonoid placed her hands on the lock and broke it, the mechanism's rusty pieces falling onto the floor grating. Heoda pushed the entrance open, its creaking filling the corridor quite loudly.

Tudough limped inside with help from Heoda and was followed by Maya. The lieutenant made his way through the weapons cache to the same quantum computer Maya had accessed on her first visit and tapped in his code, activating the menu on the holographic monitor. A menu web now hovered in mid-air, its multitudinous strands spreading out endlessly in every direction.

"I asssume you have a ssstorage sssyssstem for thisss?" Tudough asked Maya.

Maya nodded and stepped forward. Placing her left gauntlet through the menu web, her EVA armor downloaded the entire quantum drive, which—unknown to Tudough—streamed the data directly to *Skeeto*'s own quantum hard drive. Maya withdrew her gauntlet a moment later, shutting down the menu web.

"Whoa...." Tudough eyed Maya's EVA armor, once again impressed by the agent's resourcefulness. "Did I tell you that you never cccease to amazzze me?"

"I'm sure. Now, where'd you put that IP vessel you promised?"

Tudough turned his head back to the entrance. "We have to get to the LZzz port. Out that way."

Heoda walked to the threshold, scanned it for intruders, then nodded to Tudough. The lieutenant gathered himself and hobbled over, where Heoda picked him up in her arms and headed into the corridor. Maya paused for a few seconds, looking down to Xibalba.

"This place really gives me the chills, Maya."

"I know," she whispered. "Got anything yet?"

"So many signatures in here it's blinding my sensors. If there is a robonoid out there I can't detect it yet."

"Let me know when you do."

"Oh, don't worry...."

Maya leapt through the entrance and caught up with Heoda and Tudough not long afterwards, trying to keep herself as close to them as possible. Chances were if there was a rogue robonoid with her engrams, it'd want Tudough first, for obvious reasons. Heoda would naturally come to his defense, slowing the rogue robonoid down, and perhaps giving Maya enough time to flee to the IP vessel, if necessary. She doubted the rogue would have the agility or speed to catch her if she ran.

Heoda jogged through the corridor, soon taking a right turn into a cross corridor. Maya ran at her side, memorizing the path in case the situation deteriorated to the point that she was on her own. Ahead, the corridor came to a stop, ending in another hatch. She set Tudough down again and manipulated the lock, once again breaking it like so much dead wood. Placing her fingers at the hatch's center seam, she pulled the panels apart, revealing the sodium-colored hangar Tudough had showcased to Maya upon her capture.

The trio walked inside, the hangar lights gleaming off the assorted fighters' chassis. Maya counted six craft in all, enough to be a nuisance in the side of the Solar System Government, but not launch a full-scale war. Or was that the intent?

"Tudough, all you got here are two-seat moon racers." She drew Xibalba and placed the sidearm up to his nose. "You wouldn't lie to me, would you?"

"I-I wouldn't be ssstupid enough to do that...but I'm alssso not a fool. It'sss in high orbit."

"So we have to take one of these to get up there?"

A weak smile crossed Tudough's face. "That wouldn't be ssso bad, would it?"

Maya glanced to Heoda holding Tudough in her arms, a strangely pathetic Pieta moment. "Might be a little shy in the room department. I think you'd better de-orbit the IP to the LZ now."

"We don't have time!"

"Dammit...." Maya withdrew Xibalba and crossed to the nearest craft. "All right, but we're going up in *separate* craft. I'll follow you."

"I knew...you could be reasssonable...." Tudough climbed down from Heoda and instructed the robonoid to pull a ladder over to the two craft.

Heoda returned a few seconds later with the ladder on her shoulders, first placing it at Maya's craft, allowing her to climb inside the open cockpit, then swinging it over to Tudough's craft. Tudough hopped up the ladder, slowly ascending until his hands grasped the edge of the cockpit and allowed himself to clamber inside.

Closing the cockpit shell over her, Maya accessed the racer's piloting systems, starting up the craft's navigational thrusters. To her right, she watched Heoda climb up the ladder, but soon heard a cascading thump against the rear of her cockpit shell. Swinging her head around, Maya glimpsed the hangar ceiling material fall and crumble over the cockpit. All around her craft, and Tudough's, ceiling material snowed upon them, gradually eroding the hangar's protective coating and exposing the atmosphere to space.

Maya punched the holographic interface, firing the thrusters, which shot the craft several meters vertically. Before her eyes, a falling figure missed her craft's starboard wing and collided with the hangar floor, creating a puff of smoke in the gathering material. It had to be the rogue robonoid; nobody else would be that crazy.

Except maybe me.

Tudough's cockpit shell was slammed shut, cutting off Heoda's entry, but by now Heoda had leapt to meet the intruder. Maya turned away and tapped at the interface, bringing her racer about. Another button flared the old, single plasma engine, creating a red exhaust cone. Maya dropped her altitude and, keeping one eye on the action below, maneuvered the racer's aft section towards the floor.

The wash from her racer began eroding the fallen material, but didn't deter the intruder from attacking Heoda in a particular fighting style wholly unlike the two robonoids she had fought before; it was disconcertingly familiar. Shaking her head, Maya concentrated on Heoda's opponent, attempting to blast it with enough plasma exhaust to give the limbering giant a chance to escape aboard Tudough's craft.

Tudough, apparently, had different thoughts, ascending to Maya's portside and coming about parallel to her. Wearing an EVA helmet, Tudough worked his interface, then accelerated quickly through the iris opening at the rear of the hangar, leaving a single red exhaust plume in his wake.

Maya clenched her teeth, took one last look at Heoda and the rogue robonoid, then rocketed out as well, not knowing what she would find aboard Tudough's IP. If anything, trouble followed the man, not boding well for her.

CHAPTER TWENTY

i

"Heoda! Heoda, do you read me!" Maya heard Tudough call over the racer's voxlink as she traced his ascent parabola to the waiting IP vessel.

Blocking only a portion of Jupiter's globe, the IP vessel, the souped-up monster Maya had piloted only a short distance before Tudough abducted her, drew nearer, its ventral hangar port opening slightly for Tudough's racer. Maya raced underneath the IP's Jovian shadow, shooting past the weapons platforms outlining its periphery and on to the hangar port.

Tudough raised his cockpit shell and hobbled down the auto-ladder that had risen from the floor, then disappeared from the hangar. Maya docked next to his racer and jumped from the side of the cockpit in the zero gravity, wasting no time for the auto-ladder at her berth.

With a single instruction, her EVA armor's thruster flashed to life, propelling her forward out of the hangar and into the corridor. Tudough was several meters down the cylindrical corridor, pulling himself along the concave handlebars dotting the way.

Maya took little time to approach him from the side, her experience navigating dozens of IP vessels as an agent standing her in good stead. "You just left her down there!" she yelled, facing him. "I was gonna try to blast that thing with my engine!"

"You can't...sstop it with...out a deccent weapon!"

"Weapons! Goddamn weapons! Your goddamn toys are the reason you're in this mess! What the hell were you gonna do with that mine, by the way?! Huh?! Blow half the fuckin' population of P-5 to hell?!"

Tudough's respiration fogged up his helmet, making his view of the corridor difficult. But he continued on, trying to ignore Maya's badgering. "Ssave the ssolar ssysstem, my dear!"

"That seems a little out of your hands now! I'd concentrate on saving your hide, 'cause I'm not gonna let you finish your quest, rogue robonoid or not!" Maya drew Xibalba and placed him against Tudough's faceplate. "You're under arrest, Kert Tudough! Cease your activities!"

Tudough shrugged off Xibalba's barrel and forged ahead, despite Maya at his left flank. "You won't kill me, Maya. Your IPTP needss evidencce that it'ss cracking down on corruption, and wouldn't I jusst fit the bill?"

"Yeah, you would fit the bill...." Maya pushed herself away from Tudough and let him finish his trek to a hatch at the end of the corridor. Whispering, she said, "*Skeeto*, you listening?"

"Yes, Miss Maya," the synthetic voice crackled.

"Keep the voxlink open. I'm going to need your assistance."

"Understood, Miss Maya."

If Tudough was determined to have his weapon, by Jove, Maya was more than happy to let him have it...in hell.

ii

Tudough floated onto the IP's bridge. From there, Io's pockmarked visage shown through the forward mural window, its silver and copper light once reminding him of a strange Christmas ornament upon his first arrival many years ago. Now it was dead to him, just another moon waiting for liberation, like so many other planetoids in the Outer Reaches, those retched wastes so despised by people like Kuwashima and Maya. Grasping the helm controls, he knew, deep in his mind, that Maya would never be a soldier for the PPRTFDOS. His heart could yearn, but it was over. He alone could rectify the situation. He alone could salvage this mess, as Maya so crudely put it. Only Kert Tudough.

By now, everyone—Hidaad, Quoas—was likely dead inside the complex, either as a victim of her, or just plain stupidity. Without him they were ants without a queen, brawn without a mind. He could find others once he was done here. There were always others willing to be led.

Pushing off the helm interface, he slid over to a weapons console and tapped a series of buttons on the floating holograph, which sounded a succession of chimes. A red sphere vibrated before his eyes, flanked by an alphanumeric text box. Pushing down on the sphere, the text box began a countdown, starting at "300.00" and decreasing by the second.

Rising in the microgravity, he rubbed his jaw as the numbers decreased. He hated having to lose the money spent on refurbishing the Io complex, but he'd still have this ship, and Maya, too. Nothing could compare to that. Not even a robonoid in her visage....

iii

The damned robonoid had nearly ripped off her right arm, but 'Maya' rose in victory, having outwitted yet another of Tudough's toadies. She was growing tired of this charade. She wanted the man himself, wanted to vent her anger, her hatred for selling her to that Corp scientist who she recognized, strangely enough. It was an old, old memory, nearly stretching back a full quarter century, maybe even her birth, if she could remember back so far.

He was dead now, she made sure. Tudough would soon follow suit, if it was within her ability to do so. Luring her inside this hangar only to flee was clever, she had to admit, but stupid, as well. Surely he knew she was an excellent pilot. Hadn't his research revealed her penchant for the Earth-Moon-Mars triad runs she did as a teen? He was going to see those skills firsthand. They were still plenty of moon racers at her disposal, loaded for bear, she noticed straightaway.

Tudough didn't stand a chance.

CHAPTER TWENTY-ONE

i

"Miss Maya," *Skeeto* said over Maya's EVA armor voxlink, "sensors detecting a single plasma engine inside the hangar complex, accelerating for departure."

"Holy crap! A robonoid flying one of them things?" Xibalba exclaimed.

Maya pursed her lips. "This robonoid is different, Xibalba. Lots different." She activated her EVA armor's thruster and pursued Tudough.

"Maya, I've got a strange signal emanatin' from the portside weapons array. Looks like something's armed."

"Got anymore than that?"

"It's a torpedo bay, that's all I can tell. God knows what the hell Tudough stuck down the chute, though. Hope it ain't a mine."

"Seems like Tudough's willing to cover his tracks with a little bang." Maya smiled. "We can make things a little more exciting for him. *Skeeto*, activate Montezuma's worm."

"Yes, Miss Maya."

ii

"291...290...289...288...."

Tudough cleared his throat, then turned away from the weapons console, awaiting the final nail in his mistake's coffin. In less than five minutes it would all be better....

iii

'Maya' pushed the racer beyond design specs, charging past the single engine's velocity rating. Nothing was gonna stop her now, least of all this puny craft's shortcomings. Flexing her hands inside the EVA suit's gloves, she imagined how she was going to punish Tudough, how the sensation of his neck cracking in her grip felt.

iv

"ERROR! ERROR! ERROR! ERROR! BAY CLAMPS SECURED! RELEASE

BAY CLAMPS!"

Tudough swiveled at the first klaxon's sounding. Scrambling back to the console, he furiously tapped the release sequence, but without avail, as a flashing red "ERROR!" text box prevented his input key commands from acceptance.

"What the hell's wrong?! Computer! Override safety clamps! Computer!!"

v

The moon racer smashed through the magnetically sealed hangar bay entrance, blowing itself apart. Assorted pieces flew through the compromised atmosphere, scattering about the far wall, ceiling and deck floor. 'Maya' catapulted from the cockpit and landed hard against a bulkhead.

She pulled herself up, feeling only the slightest in pain. Ripping open the hatch, she clambered inside, away from the black vacuum slowly leeching out the hangar bay's contents. Her mission was all but over now, everything, Xibalba, *Skeeto*, all gone. Nothing was left to her but his death.

vi

A grey fist punched through the IP's skin, ejecting tonnes of valuable radiation and pressure shielding into the merciless Jovian system's winds. The mine was now traveling a haphazard course, a trajectory thrown off by the closed ejection clamps. Its launch energy now halved, and incapable of reaching the Iotian surface, the warhead was now a meandering timebomb, subject to the whims of Io's radiation torus, too close for comfort, or survival.

Tudough's goodbye gift to Io had become his doom.

vii

"We've got to get outta here, Maya!" Xibalba screamed. "This place is losin' air like a leaky oxytank!"

Inside his casing, his numerous sensors brayed at him, bombarding the sidearm's already overloaded weapons vision with alarms. Although he didn't require an oxygen atmosphere for his life, radiation would end his days just as easily as it would for Maya. Nor was Xibalba eager to die aboard that bastard Tudough's vanity yacht.

Maya tapped her left gauntlet's sensor pallet, sampling the atmospheric conditions. "It's gonna be a little while before this IP deflates. I'm more worried about that mine going nuclear near Io and re-radiating the atmosphere twice over."

"Then why aren't we heading back to the hangar?"

"Tudough was right about one thing: the IPTP needs to make an example out of him, and the reward I'd get for him would be out of this system."

"I don't wanna hear this...."

"I'm going to bring him in, Xibalba. Preferably with this IP and that clandestine facility intact, but even if they have to be sacrificed, we'd still have the bad guy."

"What about *Skeeto*?" Xibalba asked, almost whispering.

"We're not going to lose her."

viii

'Maya' saw the figure rocketing down the corridor; Tudough couldn't be far now. Summoning her new strength, she propelled herself with the handlebars, wishing her EVA armor was at her disposal. She had to make the best of her deteriorating situation, all the while keeping her mind occupied on her last goal. Once she killed Tudough, she'd worry about picking up the pieces of her life afterwards.

ix

"Torch!"

White flame licked around the hatch's perimeter, the bulkhead's titanium alloy gradually melting under Maya's relentless attack. Once the circular cut had cooled, Maya's gauntlets locked onto the nearest handlebars, and employing her boots, pounded at the hatch repeatedly until the cutaway popped through, granting her access.

A silver spark coupled with a loud bang reverberated near her helmet, but the nimble IPTP agent somersaulted in the air twice, finally magnetically attaching herself to the concave ceiling with her boots. Surveying the darkened room, lit just by the holographic interfaces and Io, Maya sprinted across the new floor, each boot alternating its magnetic grip. She then drew Xibalba and fired warning shots in Tudough's direction.

"It's over! Give it up!"

Tudough sent another volley Maya's way, but she easily evaded his lousy aim.

"I'll take out this bridge if I have to, Tudough!"

"I'm not coming back!" his voice sounded over their mutual voxlink channel. "You beat me fair and square on Io, but I can't end this here. There's more work to be done."

"Xibalba, what's he packing?" she asked, muting her voxlink.

"High-yield tantalum-xenon rounds. Standard military issue, good enough to put holes in body armor. Your EVA armor might withstand a direct hit from six meters, but I wouldn't wanna get any closer to 'em."

With that new bit of knowledge, Maya crept across the ceiling, her gauntlets magnetized as well. The bridge wasn't large, but several bulkhead alcoves provided enough cover to duck around, and the cylindrical architecture gave Maya plenty of gymnastic space and darkness to rebound and attack from any angle without being seen.

"Left eighty-two centimeters," Xibalba directed Maya, his vision of Tudough's sidearm piercing the darkness.

Maya smiled and pounced, leaping from her perch in one powerful strike. Doubling herself into a ball, she kicked off Tudough's rising shoulders three seconds later and ascended again, taking him by complete surprise. Several shots zipped Maya's way, but the agent clasped onto the next bulkhead and flung herself several meters to her left, like some arboreal primate.

Again in the shadows, Maya perched, her spidery limbs working her towards the confused lieutenant. "I see you, Tudough, a babe in the woods. Give up. Your cause is lost."

"NO!!!"

Silver sparks flashed around Maya, some cascading into the bridge's apex, others bouncing down into the bowl, near the open hatch.

Maya released her magnetic locks and collapsed on Tudough, bringing him down hard with a brute kick. His helmet's faceplate skidded off the floor, letting him catch a glimpse of the agent. Tangling her right boot in his legs, he twisted, tumbling her over. Tudough reached forward and grasped her left gauntlet, then pulled her in. His right fist connected to the back of her helmet, but bounced off and found her thruster, which he snagged in the melee.

Maya tried to leap, but Tudough's mass kept her on the floor, allowing only her boots to rise upwards. She was now stuck within Tudough's reach.

"Pretty Miss Maya," he sneered, studying her profile. "Such a beautiful, troublesome creature. You are indeed the butterfly. So bold, vibrant, outside my snare, my net for so long...until now—"

"TUDOUGH!!!"

The horribly disjointed voice screeched over his voxlink, making him grimace. He swiveled Maya's helmet towards himself, but the agent hadn't moved her lips, hadn't spoken. Her green eyes were wide with fear; she had heard it, too....

CHAPTER TWENTY-TWO

i

A trio of silver blasts blew the faceplate off her helmet, but relentless she was, sending a powerful fist into Tudough's chest, knocking him off Maya. Maya sprawled away, the impact knocking her against a bulkhead. Tudough wasn't as lucky; his arms now were raised to his own faceplate, trying to block the attacker's numerous and swift blows.

"HELP! HELP ME! MAYA!"

"There is no help for you, Tudough!" 'Maya' growled, the guttural grinding of her cords sending vibrations through the voxlink. "You are mine now! Die!"

Tudough fired off several rounds, bouncing them off the bridge's bulkheads, none of which connected with her.

Maya shook her head and rose from the floor, her eyes finding the robonoid cloaking Tudough like a shroud. It wasn't as big as Heoda, Osyver and the others, and she wondered what effect her engrams had had on its programming; evidently a great deal, as it antipathy towards Tudough was murderous. As much as she identified with it, Tudough had to be preserved, had to be brought to justice. She didn't want to have to fight something possessing her skills and memories, but the robonoid wasn't natural, wasn't alive. It needed to be stopped before it attacked her.

Gritting her teeth, Maya joined the fray. Firing her thruster, she rocketed over and collapsed on the robonoid's back, then pulled on the—

Massive mass that flipped Maya off her back and to the bridge floor in one motion. Maya landed with a loud thump, then saw the fractured face descending towards her. It was...her own. Charred dermal plastic on her forehead still sizzled from Tudough's shots, but the features and red hair were unmistakably Maya's.

The robonoid appeared just as nonplussed, ceasing its attack to study the "other" Maya before her, green eyes staring at green eyes.

"What...the hell?"

'Maya' reached for Maya's face, her gloved hands touching the EVA armor's faceplate. Trembling fingers reached for her skin, like some long lost sibling. And, if there were tear ducts, she would have cried.

"You...bastard...what have you done?"

Tudough rose from behind and struck the robonoid's exposed face, which released an horrific scream throughout the bridge. A feral retaliation followed, the robonoid 'Maya' throwing the already battered Tudough across the bridge, her mechanical strength dwarfing Maya's lissomeness.

Looking down at the supine Maya, the robonoid 'Maya'—her half-injured face bearing obvious pain—cupped Maya's helmet, a longing in her synthetic eyes, the childlike qualities in her personality engrams obvious to the "other" Maya.

"I won't hurt you, Maya. You're scared, I know. Confused...I am, too."

"What...happened to me?" the robonoid's raspy voice asked.

Maya rose gingerly, still not fully trusting this feral, infinitely stronger version of herself. "Something that should not be."

Everything had changed, Maya now knew, but nothing could change. Tudough did deserve punishment, perhaps death, as her robonoid self would have it, but she couldn't allow it. Tudough, the PPRTFDOS, they both needed to be exposed. The Solar System had to be made aware of their terror crimes, their plans. With what Tudough had done, kidnapping her, raping her mind, placing what he'd stolen in that "body," it was all inexcusable. But killing him wouldn't make it better, even if egged on by Xibalba, as surely he'd do. Tudough should be forced to live with himself, be forced to have his own mind broken.

The one thing she couldn't do, perhaps, was to stop her "other" self from meting out execution. It was one thing to stop Tudough's robonoids, but this one had her face, her memories, her personality, for God's sake. How could she do it? How?!

"Miss Maya," *Skeeto* said over the voxlink, "my sensors are detecting a high-intensity ion flux ten-point-three meters from the IP vessel's hull. Calculated yield...three hundred megatonnes."

"The mine's arming itself, Maya," Xibalba said. "It's got a timer on it!"

"Can you see it, Xibalba?"

"Yeah...ions are accelerating inside the buffer...we've got thirty seconds before critical!"

"Maya," the agent turned to the robonoid, "we have to leave! We're in danger!"

'Maya' watched Tudough stagger to his feet across the bridge. "He...

doesn't deserve to live...."

"He'll stand trial, just like every other criminal the IPTP has caught."

"I—I'm not Agent Maya anymore." The robonoid 'Maya' started towards Tudough. "Goodbye, Maya...don't fail yourself...don't fail Zee."

"No!" Maya reached out for the robonoid.

"Maya!" Xibalba yelled. "We gotta leave! There's nuthin' for you here now!"

"Critical mass has been achieved, Miss Maya," *Skeeto's* voice announced in her helmet, but the agent didn't comprehend it. Everything slipped from her grasp....

ii

The squat mine tumbled in the invisible torus, its sensitive warhead particles polarized by the flood of hyper-accelerated baryons and leptons. Deep inside, its thick core of fusion fuel cracked under the strain of critical mass, imploding then exploding in an awesome cascade of successive obliterations, until the entire mine incinerated, birthing an exponentially dilating plasma shell. A spectra of matter swept outwards, spewing across the Jovian system, colliding with particles, moonlets and an orbiting InterPlanetary vessel, slicing the vehicle length-wise.

iii

...And slammed into the farside of the bridge. Debris loosened by the upheaval poured out the fissure which had ripped open, sending Maya careening. She barely saw the flurries skimming past her faceplate, or the darkened shapes wrestling in the near-void. Screeches and wailing clawed at her ears like banshees, the cacophony battering her form, threatening to expel her into the all-consuming vacuum.

"MAAAYYYAAAA! Don't let me diiie—!"

Maya's gauntlets flew outwards, but reached nothing, save the image of Tudough's violent expulsion. Her eyes narrowing from exhaustion, she witnessed a second figure launch into the ink of space, grapple the first, and tumbling end over end, drifting forever, locked in a death struggle neither would win, nor lose, with no place in life, outcast...to their mutual end.

CHAPTER TWENTY-THREE

i

"Maaaayyyaaaa! Don't let me diiie—!"

"Huhhh!" Maya straightened her back in the moon racer, her helmet's faceplate nearly striking the cockpit shell.

"Maya? You all right?"

She blinked and raised her gauntlet to her helmet. "Yeah...yeah. Where are we?"

"Io. You did it! You got us off that IP! Goddamn if you ain't the best. Didn't hesitate, didn't waiver. It's like you were possessed."

Her eyes looked out over the horizon, its silvery visage reflecting back inside to her. Tapping her sensor pallet, she accessed the moon's SSPS. "We're back," she said, reading the hovering text box to herself. *"Skeeto...?"*

"I think this is close to where I landed her."

"Good, that saves us time."

"Huh?"

Maya took the sidearm into her right gauntlet. "For getting us back home, Xibalba."

ii

"Glad to see you again, Agent Maya," Kuwashima's static-marred image over the IPTP's IPwebaddress said, his countenance visibly comforted. "When you were incommunicado for all those days, I had truly believed I'd sent you to your end."

Maya scratched the back of her neck. "I'm not that easy to get rid of, sir." She allowed herself a small laugh, then admitted, "Thought I'd been done for, as well, though."

"Federal Marshals have been dispatched to your area, they should be arriving at any hour. They'll tow you back—"

"With respect, Lieutenant, I've procured an engine that I'll be using to get *Skeeto* back to flight status, at least to HQ. I'd appreciate the escort, however. I don't know if Tudough's got any cronies out here ready to pick up his flag and fight for him."

Kuwashima nodded, then sighed.

"Something to add, sir?"

"Tudough was an up and comer, someone the commissioner was convinced could clean up the Outer Reaches...tell me, what went wrong? Why did he go to the other side?"

"Other side, sir?" Maya rubbed her jaw. "He *was* the other side. Our predecessors created him and his ilk. He just took his grievances too far, thought he could do to the Inner Zones what we wanted to do to the Outer Reaches. I suppose both are at a crossroads in their relationship. Time will tell if we're right, or they are."

"Did he...kill himself?"

"No, he'd never do that. He was too self-important. An ego his size couldn't fathom ending it when victory was within his grasp. No, he died a hero in his mind, or at least in his heart, as they always do."

iii

Jupiter's ochre light receded, leaving Sol's brightening embrace to beckon Maya home. She missed Mars, even though the excursion to P-5 had been of far less duration than most of her missions, particularly her pair of three-month Neptunian visits. *Skeeto* seemed eager to come home, too, humming nimbly through the Federal Causeway under armed escort, at near-full functionality, freed from the slow degradation on Io and the Jovian System.

Her return seemed empty without Tudough's arrest, despite the data gleaned from the PPRTFDOS webwork; Kuwashima doubtless would appreciate the intel, but somehow she felt it a wasted effort, even though that wasn't the point of her mission.

Maya soon slept, forgetting her troubles, save for the fitful, half-nightmares of her "other self" and Tudough's last seconds aboard the IP. In her dream the robonoid came home in her stead, leaving the IPTP none-the-wiser, let alone her synthetic self, in a twist that would never work in the waking world, but was perfectly reasonable in dreamland.

Despite what she played in her dreams, or knew in her mind, Maya's heart told her a piece of her still orbited endlessly around Io, victory in *her* grasp, fighting the good fight in the Outer Reaches, as out of place in this world as the real Maya. And just as content to be so.

Agent Maya™
Season One

Read Agent Maya's Comics Adventures!

AVAILABLE NOW!
$19.99 9780983331711
@jauntworld
agentmaya.blogspot.com

www.ingramcontent.com/pod-product-compliance
Lightning Source LLC
Chambersburg PA
CBHW021458250626
47154CB00004BA/1317